SWEET CHAOS
SAVAGE HEARTS SYNDICATE
BOOK 1

KIMBERLY QUINN

HLB

ISBN: 978-1-963705-79-9

Cover design: KiWi Cover Design

Published in the United States of America by Harbor Lane Books, LLC.

www.harborlanebooks.com

CONTENTS

ONE YEAR AGO

Kira

"You knew there'd be a price to pay. Yet, still, you risked it." The stench of stale cigar clung to his breath, poisoning the air of the crowded car, and wafting over me like a putrid wave of death. "Did you really think you could beat me?"

Hot, fat tears streaked down my cheeks. They followed the paths of the ones before them, mimicking the leftover splashes of rain that trickled over the windows. "I-I don—" But the words wouldn't come.

How could I form words when my entire world had been shattered?

Helpless, I stared out the rain-spotted windshield at the lifeless body of my grandfather, laying in the dim light of the open warehouse door. He looked like a broken doll on the concrete. His head was turned away, *thank God*, so I didn't have to stare into his glassy eyes, but his arm was at an impossible angle, his torso riddled with bullet holes.

This was the man who'd raised me, the man who'd promised me the world, and I'd done nothing but watch as they'd shot him in the back.

His own men.

Well…they weren't his anymore, now, were they?

Ilya Markov had been a king. Iron fisted and cunning, he was a born leader who no one dared to cross. Now, he was simply dead, his blood seeping into the cracks of the pavement he once owned.

"I guess you thought you were better than me, huh? You thought your family was invincible." The man responsible relaxed in the driver's seat with an arm draped over the center console as he taunted me, his familiar, smoky voice reminding me of his treachery. My grandfather had trusted this man with his life.

And look where that got him.

I stared at the back of the traitor's head, my limbs numb and head swimming as I calculated the odds of my escape.

As though reading my mind, the bulky man beside me shifted, bringing the gun he had aimed at me closer, emphasizing the peril of the situation.

Zero.

Those were the odds. If I tried to run, there was zero fucking chance I'd make it out of this alive. Still, it might've been worth the gamble if mine was the only life at stake.

Too bad it wasn't.

Sweat trailed down the back of my neck, making me shiver despite the suffocating heat. Finally, I allowed my gaze to shift to the front passenger seat where my sister sat, frozen.

She hadn't moved or made a sound since this nightmare began. Was she even breathing?

From the backseat, I could only see her profile, but she didn't look good. Pale and thinner than I'd ever seen, it was obvious she hadn't been taking proper care of herself. And like a selfish princess, too secure in her position of power and privilege, I hadn't been paying close enough attention to notice.

Who would take care of her now?

"What about Yelena?" I asked, finding some semblance of strength, and forcing my voice to remain steady.

The traitor looked at me through the rearview mirror, his dark, seemingly empty gaze penetrating mine. Was there a shred of decency left in him? Had there ever been one to start?

"Your sister will stay with me, where she belongs. I'll keep her safe, just like I promised."

Safe. The word didn't hold much value when he was the one pledging it, but what choice did I have? There were no options here, and no way out of this hell.

No way to guarantee tomorrow unless I played his horrific, twisted game.

Unperturbed, he pulled a fresh cigar from its pack and ran it under his nose, inhaling deeply. "If you agree to my terms, you can return home to what remains of your family. Although, you probably won't want to stay long. Not after Sasha finds out you double crossed him."

Double crossed him?

That was rich when Sasha was the one who'd betrayed me. He'd gone back on his word, and by choosing this vile man in front of me, set this horrific scene in motion.

I should've never trusted him.

Fuck, I should've never trusted any of them, my grandfather included.

"But if I agree to come to your side and work for you…" My voice was barely audible over the pounding of my heart.

"What? You think everything will go back to normal?" he asked mockingly, then paused to light the cigar, casually puffing on it like it was a reward for all his hard work. "I can't tell the boys I'm giving you a second chance. Do you really think they'd want me to forgive you? With all the money you just lost them?"

"But—"

"No." His tone remained passive, but the sharp look he gave me sent another cold finger of terror down my spine. "I won't be made to look weak. I will tell them you ran. That you outsmarted Vlad—" He motioned to the burly man beside me. "—and that you got away. I'll need to punish him openly for his failure, of course, but he'll be well compensated. He'll become your contact and act as my eyes and ears, keeping tabs on you."

He sucked on the cigar before blowing a nasty cloud of it toward the ceiling. The smoke billowed up to the soft gray headliner, spreading outward before slowly tumbling back down around us, enveloping us in a toxic fog.

"Do I need to tell you what will happen if you don't cooperate?" His eyes returned to glare at me through the mirror.

I shook my head, once again unable to speak because my throat, like the rest of me, was locked by fear.

"Boss." Vlad tipped his head toward the front of the car where two battered women were being corralled. It was the two I'd hoped had gotten away for good. The only two who'd escaped.

They'd been caught and were now surrounded by thugs. Like me and Yelena, they had nowhere left to run.

At least they tried.

The headlights of the car showcased the resulting damage of their attempt to flee. Half-naked and beaten, one stood, quivering, with her arms crossed over her middle and mascara-stained tears streaming down her cheeks, while the other was a statue, her face an unreadable mask.

I'd noticed her first, the one with the poker face, because she'd been wearing such a beautiful dress. Now, the pretty pink material was a wet, torn mess. It hung from a single strap, revealing freckled skin and a simple white bra, smeared with blood.

She'd put up a fight, that much was clear, but with twelve against two, she'd never stood a chance. Fuck, none of us ever had a hope in hell.

"What will happen to them?" I whispered, afraid I already knew the answer.

"What did you think would happen?" He laughed through a puff of smoke, and it was the most heartless thing I'd ever heard. "You thought you could outsmart me. Thought your dear old grandfather would cast me aside and set them free on your whim. But I'm not wrapped around your finger like he was, and now I'm the one in charge."

Yes, I'd thought I could put a stop to the disgusting side hustle he'd been running behind my grandfather's back. I'd believed I could save these women and the others from being sold like livestock. But this was the outcome. This was the fate I'd handed them.

My pride and prominence had blinded me to the risks involved, to the point that I hadn't even considered the chance of it all blowing up in my face.

I'd been so fucking foolish.

He cracked his window, stuck his hand out, and motioned to the men outside.

My empty stomach cramped, and although I wanted to close my eyes, to block the horror from filling my vision, I forced myself to witness the women's brutal execution. Two loud gunshots rang out—a sound that would echo in my ears for eternity—and their bodies fell to the ground, one after the other like dominoes.

Just like that. As though their lives had meant nothing.

"Do you see, darling Kira? I will always win." His words slithered around my splintered soul and squeezed.

Unable to stomach the horror a moment longer, I turned my gaze back to Yelena and found her familiar doe eyes pinned on me. The expression of grief she wore was so profound, it was as tangible as the stinking cloud of cigar smoke that engulfed us.

I wanted nothing more than to reach out to her, to hold her in a warm, comforting embrace. To soothe her and tell her everything would be fine, the same way we'd consoled each other after our parents died.

But I couldn't do that. Not with all the violence and cruelty surrounding us, and not when the traitor and his thugs were the ones in control.

Especially not when it would've been a lie.

With all my remaining spirit, I channeled my love into the look I gave her, hoping like hell she could read it. Praying she understood that I wouldn't give up.

I would *never* give up.

Like the woman in the pretty pink dress, I would keep fighting. I would fight for all of us—even those I'd failed to save. Whatever it took. No matter the cost.

I wouldn't rest until my sister and everyone I loved was safe.

CHAPTER
ONE
DEX

Something's not right.

The aggravating thought stole its way into my consciousness. It was elusive, unshakable, and exacerbated by my sweating palms and the heaviness of the custom SIG P320 in my grip.

I shuffled my favorite gun from hand to hand —*unload, inspect, reload, aim*—and waited for the familiar ritual to settle my nerves. For my heart to stop beating double time, and common sense to kick in.

But it didn't.

No matter how many times I repeated the simple drill, it was still all wrong, and the uneasiness of it weighed on me like an anchor or anvil.

Or a bad goddamn omen.

Except, I didn't believe in that sort of shit.

Despite the ridiculous chill in my bones, I clutched the 9mm tighter and darted across the manicured lawn, staying out of view of the lone and seemingly useless security camera. My legs pumped strong and steady, but when I reached the back wall of the upscale home, I fell against it, panting.

What was wrong with me?

I knew my task. My purpose. Yet, I was faltering, filled with this unreasonable anxiety. It made zero goddamn sense.

The timing was right, the strategy was in motion, and it was too late for second guesses. Hell, I'd passed the point of no return long ago, headfirst with no hope of ever coming back. No desire to, either.

I couldn't let the entire job go to shit because of a *bad feeling*.

No. I fucking refused.

On a deep breath, I buried the doubts, dispelled the absurd sense of foreboding, and slipped through the unlocked window into the secluded home.

The place was a tomb. Cold, cavernous, and eerily quiet. Almost too quiet, but I held fast to my objective, surveying each room before moving to the next.

It didn't matter that I'd gone over the plan enough times I could do the job in my sleep, I was still alert, still careful. Calm and in control.

After stalking the length of the main floor, I made my way to the central staircase where the ornate oak banister loomed. It twisted endlessly up toward darkness, beckoning me into unknown danger.

Invitation accepted.

Now that my resolve was firmly back in check, I prowled up the stairs with both my gun and gaze aimed forward. No more waiting or second guesses. Only cool confidence and cunning.

It was time to kill.

"You can tell me." A woman's voice sliced the silence, shooting sparks along my spine and halting me mid-climb. "I swear."

Her words were a mere whisper, yet they called to me like an electrifying siren's song. Rhythmic and provocative, her voice dug its way under my skin, luring me closer.

But who the hell was she?

The target was alone. At least, he should be.

Was it possible, after learning every route, bad habit, and boring routine, I'd missed something? Had I lost my edge? Or had that bad feeling been on point?

Shit, maybe I was losing my grip all together because something about this job hadn't seemed right from the start, and now I was starting to believe in premonitions.

"No one else will know." The flow of her silky smooth tone washed over me, coaxing me to throw away caution.

With a voice like that, she'd be impossible to ignore, even if her presence didn't jeopardize my mission. Except, it did.

It most definitely fucking did.

My mind reeled with the sudden and unexpected variables in play. Was she a lethal threat, or an innocent witness? A minor complication, or a major liability?

Regardless of who or what she was, she put everything at risk.

I'd been in the sleepy town of Scarsdale, just north of the city, watching this house and the people who lived here for days—one woman, two young children, a mangy one-eyed cat, and my target, Nelson Moore. I knew what they all looked and sounded like. This woman wasn't one of them.

As usual, I hadn't received much intel ahead of the mission. I was told Moore was a research scientist, working for a division of BTA-Xander, a leading pharmaceutical corporation with its offices in Manhattan. He owed a significant debt to an Irish mobster, attended clandestine meetings with the Rykov Bratva, and, in general, was not a nice guy. Those were all the details I'd needed.

Once Rykov's name entered the picture, all I ever wanted was the target.

I didn't care who'd ordered him dead or how much they were willing to pay. Hell, I didn't even need an explanation. Give me a name, a target worth killing, and I'd do the rest. By the time I was ready to pull the trigger, I'd know everything there was to know about my mark.

Everything.

Was he ruthless, apathetic, or weak? Greedy, or just plain desperate? Did he sleep with the lights on? Secretly watch bondage porn? Jerk off with his right hand or his left?

Ask me anything. Whether I wanted to or not, I'd know the answer.

Including the reason he deserved to die.

My brother managed the other things. The dollars and *sense*, he called it. Finn vetted every offer and managed the relationships with our clients. He kept us out of their petty turf wars and gathered intelligence the way a magician might pull a rabbit from his hat—it seemed to materialize at his fingertips.

It was a neat trick. Except, my hands were the ones getting dirty. I was the one in the field, hiding out, spying, coming up with the action plan. The one paying the price if things went sideways.

But that's how it had always been. The way it was supposed to be.

It was my penance to carry.

Finn said this job was solid, and more than anything or anyone, I trusted him.

The only trouble? Moore hadn't left his house and was constantly surrounded by his family.

They weren't on my list.

Kids were never in my crosshairs because I was a killer, not a fucking psychopath—not yet, anyway—and I wouldn't let blameless victims get in the way.

Still, as patient as I was, I'd begun to think I might need a different approach. Some way to draw him out. Until his wife packed her bags and left with the children, leaving the scientist home on his own and making it the perfect time for me to get the job done.

Now, I was a ghost on his staircase, weighing my options, tallying my advantages, and deciding if that unexpected, alluring feminine voice was a blessing or a curse.

If my instincts were any indication, there wasn't much hope for a blessing.

Good thing I didn't believe in those, either—hopes, blessings, or even curses, for that matter. The only thing I believed in was my goddamn plan, and now I needed a new one.

I inched up the remaining stairs with my mind in a tangle, my feet carrying me soundlessly over the carpet.

"It'll be our secret," the mystery woman promised, her voice coming from the room just ahead.

Her words were a silken vow, and like everything else she'd said, could've easily translated to the bedroom. It made me wonder what kind of debauchery I was walking into. What kind of wicked, kinky game was she playing?

And why did I like the idea of finding out so damn much?

My cock perked up and took notice. Now wasn't the time, but my body didn't seem to care. Intrigue pulled me forward against my better judgment. My skin tingled, heart pounded, and balls tightened with each step.

Like a voyeur cloaked in shadows, I concealed myself outside the large master suite, where the owner of that intoxicating voice came into view.

The sight of her was even more delicious than the sound. Darkness hid her features, but streams of hazy light seeped through the tall windows, silhouetting her slender frame and allowing me the opportunity to observe her from behind.

Dressed in leather, every one of her slight curves was highlighted. Tight ass, lithe body, a gloriously long braid I wanted wrapped around my fist…

And a deadly looking knife clutched in her delicate hand.

Next to her, Moore was shirtless and simpering. Tied to a chair, he struggled uselessly to break free from his bonds, his large, hairy gut heaving with each exaggerated breath.

I might've thought this was nothing more than a bit of sexual play if it weren't for the abject terror etched on the man's sweaty face.

"C'mon," the leather-clad temptress coaxed, "I just need one tiny detail from you. You can give me that, can't you?"

"N-n-no. I don't know anything," he insisted through a wheezing stutter.

"Yes, you do. I don't want to hurt you, Nelson. But I will."

She pressed the knife flat against his stomach, and he stilled. Toying with him, she trailed the blade up and across his chest, drawing the pointed edge back and forth ever so slightly, making him shiver before freezing in place again. The action was slow, almost sensual, like a lover dragging fingers over flesh.

"You can't get out of this," she whispered, raising the hairs on the back of my neck.

Her smooth voice and cat-like prowess were mesmerizing. Enchanting. Each murmured word was a caress. Every subtle movement, a kiss. Her whispered seduction was the type of promise a man like me would kill for. An oath so delectable, I might've been tempted to get down on my knees to beg.

But only if I were a fool.

Or maybe…if I needed a Plan B.

"You're doing it wrong," I called out, kicking my spontaneously formed plan into motion.

Weapon holstered, I stalked from the shadows, leaving my bad feelings and superstitions behind—it was all bullshit, anyway. Now, it was time to implement my new strategy and take charge of this situation.

Only, the barrel of a gun was suddenly aimed at me.

Where had she hidden that weapon in her skin-tight leather? And how in the hell had I not seen this coming?

Either she was fantastically stealthy or extremely distracting. Maybe both.

Regardless, it was unnerving to have a Beretta pointed at my head, especially by an unknown adversary. But I wouldn't let those nerves show. I was a professional, after all.

And I was in control. Always.

Raising my hands in mock compliance, I forced a friendly smile. "Threats won't work. Hurt him first, then promise to make it stop. That's how you'll get answers."

Moore whimpered in response.

"Don't listen to him, Nelson." She slid the knife into a sheath strapped to her thigh, but her aim with the gun didn't waver. "No one will get hurt if you just tell me what I want to know."

"He won't tell you anything without something to gain. Or something to lose." I lowered my arms and moved into the room, one slow, easy step at a time. "He knows your threat isn't real. You'd have already followed through if it was."

"Who are you?" she demanded, her voice losing its softness. "Who sent you? What the fuck do you want?"

"Now, now, kitten. You know what they say about curiosity."

"Is that supposed to intimidate me? Just tell me why the hell you're here."

A smirk tugged at my lips because *fuck*, her hostility was adorable. "If you show me your plan, I'll show you mine."

She paused, her gaze flicking back toward the scientist, but there was no way in hell she was considering my offer. No. Something told me, despite her badass look, this woman was way out of her comfort zone, and it wasn't because I was pushing her there.

At least, it wasn't only because of that.

Unable to withstand the distance, I took another step toward her, because regardless of the gun and her hard shell, I was enthralled. "What's the matter? Don't you like that game?"

"Stay back." Her darkened gaze snapped to mine, drawing me even closer.

"Or what?"

"Or I'll shoot you, asshole."

Oh, she was a feisty one—a wildcat, not a kitten—but her aggression couldn't derail my plan. "No, you won't."

"I have a gun on you."

"Yes, kitten, it's a very impressive weapon." I eased forward another cautious step with a devilish grin playing on my lips. "I have one, too, only mine's bigger. Maybe if you behave yourself, I'll let you hold it when we fuck."

A look of shocked revulsion crossed her dimly lit features and she flinched. "You're deranged. Disgusting. Out of your fucking mind if you think I'd ever…I would never."

My smile turned downright feral because Plan B was working like a charm, and she really was fucking adorable.

The shrill ring of a phone interrupted the moment, startling all three of us.

"Please," Moore begged, deciding now was a good time to bargain. "You don't have to do this. Let me answer it and we can all get what we want."

Despite most of her face being concealed by shadows, I could feel Wildcat's eyes on me. She stared me down as the phone continued to ring, and I glared back, satisfied by the subtle quake of the gun in her hand.

"You probably t-tripped an alarm," the scientist persisted, ignorant of our silent battle, which felt a hell of a lot like foreplay. "My security company will send the police."

He was so full of shit. His security setup was a joke,

which he was likely now regretting, but I didn't need her to know that. "Sorry kitten, it looks like fun time's over. You should put the gun down and get out of here while you still can."

"Nelson." Her attention turned back to her captive, but she remained steadfast with her weapon, still pointed at my head. "I promise we won't hurt you. Just help me out and we'll leave you alone."

The phone stopped ringing.

Time was up, and I was done playing cat and mouse.

While she was distracted, making promises she couldn't keep, I ducked out of her aim and charged straight into her, tackling her around her middle.

We collided, landing on the bed in a tangled heap, and a hot gust of air rushed from her as my weight forced her down.

Despite the threat she posed, or maybe because of it, it was rewarding to have her in my grasp. To feel the curve of her back, the dip of her waist, and the exquisite press of her thighs as she struggled.

Until two armed men burst into the room and opened fire.

CHAPTER
TWO
DEX

The artistry of my Plan B was lost to the loud pops of gunfire that echoed through the room. Glass shattered, Moore screamed, and the wildcat in my arms wrestled for control of her gun.

"Asshole. Let go." Vicious, she spewed profanities and clawed at me.

"No," I grunted, dodging her attempted elbow to my head. I admired her scrappy attitude, but fuck… "You're going to get us both killed."

As though to prove my point, a hot flare of pain exploded across my shoulder as a bullet ripped through my flesh.

Getting shot hurt like a son of a bitch, every damn time. And every time, I swore it would be the last. Yet, here I was, directly in the line of fire again, too stubborn to back down.

The burning agony was a momentary distraction

from the chaos surrounding me. Still, I wasn't willing to be an open target. Or to let her go.

I rolled across the mattress, dragging her with me and leaving a trail of crimson in my wake. We dropped onto the floor on the other side of the bed just as the wall overhead was torn apart by bullets. I covered her body with mine as bits of plaster rained down, and she buried her face in the crook of my neck.

Adrenaline coursed through me. I was wounded, my mission on the brink of failure, and my life on the line. Yet, I didn't care about any of it.

The woman in my arms had stopped fighting, and even though she might be the enemy, might even try to kill me in the next second, my driving instinct was to keep her safe.

Like Emily. Only, this time, I won't fail.

The unwelcome thought was a sucker punch straight to my gut, knocking me off-kilter and leaving me breathless.

On a gasp, I filled my lungs and forced the misplaced instinct back under control where it belonged —inside the cage where I kept all my other bullshit doubts and vulnerabilities—and reminded myself why the hell I was here. How this had all started and what my goddamn purpose was.

Make it right. Kill them all.

With another sharp, deep inhale, I absorbed the reality of my surroundings. Wildcat was pinned to the plush carpet by my weight, her arms trapped tightly at her sides by my thighs and her sweet breath hitting me in short, shallow bursts.

Taking advantage of the position, I wrapped a hand around the barrel of her gun and wrenched it free from her hold.

The shooting stopped, and the room fell silent. Even Moore had shut the hell up.

"Dex," one of the men called in a thick Russian accent. "Or should I call you Bodhi Decker?"

My stomach dropped, and I froze.

"We're here for the girl," he said.

The room was cloaked in darkness, her face barely visible, but Wildcat's eyes seemed to light with fire when she brazenly yelled, "Fuck you!"

Her outburst jolted me into action. Raising my arm over the bed, I aimed her hard-won gun in their direction.

Fuck them was right.

Not only were they Bratva soldiers, but they knew my name. My real goddamn name. And they'd come in shooting. If they'd wanted something from me, they should've considered asking first. Not that I'd have given it.

Without a second thought, I squeezed the trigger.

Only, nothing happened.

"Seriously?" I gritted my teeth, dropping her useless, empty weapon to the floor and pulling my SIG from its holster.

"I don't like guns," she grumbled beneath me.

This woman was not only a maddening distraction but a hazard to my health. Whatever her game was, it was a hell of a lot more dangerous and twisted than I'd imagined. Nowhere near the risqué bit of fun I'd planned.

"Give her to us, Dex," the Russian called.

A snide bark of laughter tore from my throat. "I don't think so." There was no way I'd hand her over. Certainly not to these maniacs. Not to anyone after she'd caused so much trouble. "This pretty little pussy belongs to me now."

I didn't miss her reaction—the way her body quaked, and the sharp mewl of indignation that escaped her lips. It was a fantastic sound, and I'd have bet good money she made the same one during sex. Maybe even right before orgasm.

Too bad this wasn't the time to find out.

The man cursed under his breath and moved a fraction closer.

Armed with my tried-and-true weapon—the one I kept under my pillow most nights—I raised my arm again. I could barely make out the top of his head, but this time when I squeezed the trigger, my gun fired, and I hit my mark.

"Cyka blyat!" the other man cried as the first one crumpled to the floor.

Focused on the sound of that single Russian curse, I blindly made my next target. The shot rang out and the bullet hit, but instead of dropping to the ground, the second Russian only swore again.

I peeked from my cover and tracked him as he lurched away, wounded.

"You're a dead man, Dex." Pain laced his words as he scrambled down the hall. "Fucking dead!" His voice echoed from the first floor, followed shortly by the slam of the front door.

"Time to go." After tucking her weapon into my holster, I lifted my new hostage to her feet alongside me. I kept her close, my gun at the ready, even as she strained to break out of my grasp.

She really was a wildcat. Long, lean, strong, and agile. Built of solid muscle, she moved as gracefully as a dancer.

"Get your fucking hands off me, asshole."

She also had the mouth of a trucker. Which, for some strange reason, I found to be cute as hell.

"You can't fool me, kitten. I know you like the way I touch you. Especially when I'm saving your ass."

She snarled, bucking hard against me, and my body tensed. In another time and place, she'd be difficult to resist, but now she was just plain difficult, her moxie more trouble than it was worth.

"We're leaving." I raised my weapon, reminding us both who was in charge. "Together."

As I struggled to drag her from the shelter of the bed, a low moan caught my attention.

Moore.

The scientist had been shot in the chest and was bleeding out. He made another low sound, choking on blood that bubbled from his lips and dripped down his chin.

"No!" Wildcat broke free of my hold, running toward the dying man.

I grabbed her from behind, stopping her retreat, and forced her to watch as I shot Nelson Moore point blank in the head.

A light spray of blowback hit us, spattering our faces and chests with his blood, but she didn't react. At least, not in the way I expected.

She didn't cry out, swear, or even flinch. She simply sagged into me, like the bullet had blown away her will to fight, along with the scientist's brains.

"We have to go," I urged. "Now."

She didn't move.

Cautiously, I turned her to face me. "Did you hear me?"

Her stare was vacant, mouth slack, and when I ran my hand over the back of her head, my fingers gliding over the silky plait of her hair, she dropped her forehead to my chest.

I wrapped my hand around her braid and pulled. "Come on, kitten. Snap out of it."

Still nothing.

Easing her body forward, I engulfed her in my arms. She came willingly, her shoulders rising and falling with the hitch of her breath.

We stood that way for a moment, with my heart battering the walls of my chest and her intriguing scent flooding my senses. It was a sublime mix of leather, blood, and something indescribable. Something uniquely feminine and, like the rest of her, tempting as hell.

A foreign feeling of warmth spread through me, and *fuck*…I could've gotten lost in it. Holding her this way was somehow satisfying and right. More reassuring than my favorite gun.

Only, now wasn't the time for comfort, and I was no good with that shit, anyway.

Dropping low, I put my uninjured shoulder to her waist and lifted, expecting her protest. Yet, she hardly squirmed.

Fine by me. It'd be easier to get her clear of this place if she wasn't fighting me every step of the way. Still, her sudden calm and lack of resistance was worrisome. And worry, of any sort, was the last goddamn thing I needed.

With a final glance at the dead men, I hauled her out of the house and into the chill of the night.

A deep wooded lot ran the course of the property. For me, this was a calculated, easy escape. For her, it seemed to be a tipping point. Finally rousing out of her shock, she began struggling in earnest again.

"Put me down, you prick. I'm going to kick your ass."

I laughed, grateful to have her wild side back. Wild, I could handle. "Kick my ass later. Right now, we need to get the hell out of here. Unless you want to stay and take the blame for what I've done." My voice was rough, my words harsher than planned, but I'd had my fill of softness. I wasn't the kind of man built to be nice.

Not anymore.

Fuck, who was I kidding? I never had been. "Or did you want to wait for more Bratva soldiers to find you? Maybe you'd rather go with them?"

"Why?" she screamed, not seeming to care if we were overheard. "Tell me. Why?"

"Calm down." I squeezed her legs to my chest, forcing her kicks to stop and squashing the temptation to run my hands up the backs of her thighs.

"You killed him." Her fists pummeled my back. "You fucking killed him."

My heart stuttered and a burning ache flared to life in my chest. Another man might've mistaken the feeling for guilt, but emotions like that were useless. Hell, emotions of any kind only served to get you killed.

And death would have been far too easy for a man like me.

"I killed him because I was paid to." It wasn't a lie —not exactly. It wasn't the truth, either. But until I understood her motives, it was the best she'd get. "Besides, he was already dying. I just put the bastard out of his misery. Hell, I did that man a favor."

"I needed him."

"You're wrong. He wasn't going to give you anything. Men in this life know how to navigate it, kitten. An amateur like you doesn't stand a chance."

"I'm not an amateur."

"Right." I smirked. "Your gun wasn't even loaded. No pro's going to pull a stunt like—"

Before I knew what hit me, I was pinned flat on my back with her knees crushing my chest, one hand clutching my neck and the other cocked in a fist overhead.

She'd taken me down like a champion—swift and fluid, without breaking a sweat.

"I'm not an amateur, but I don't kill innocent people. Not like you." Her raised fist visibly trembled as she growled her revulsion in my ear. "He had information that could've saved lives. Innocent lives. And you fucked it all up. Screw you, Bodhi Decker. Take your own heat, you sick, cocky prick."

Her weight lifted, and within seconds, she was gone.

Staggering to my feet, I sprinted after her, sucking in air despite the pinch of my lungs. The little minx was going to pay for that stunt, and for messing up my entire goddamn plan.

She was barely a shadow ahead of me and next to impossible to track through the trees, but I chased after her, anyway, tripping over branches and my own feet.

Like a fucking amateur.

I broke through the treeline onto a paved roadway in time to see her pull a motorcycle from a cover of dense brush. She maneuvered it to the edge of the pavement with ease, her leather suit gleaming under the streetlight.

"Wait," I yelled, torn between demanding and begging her to stay.

She hopped on the bike with her helmet in hand and turned to me, her face fully lit for the first time.

I stumbled forward, reeling like I'd been struck again. Only this time, by her beauty.

Her heart-shaped face was framed by wisps of platinum hair. She had luscious rosy lips, magnetic amber eyes, and an adorable little cleft in her chin. She was deceptively youthful, almost angelic.

Except for her deadly glare.

It was a look of pure animosity. A look that said, *Try it, asshole, and I'll eat your fucking soul*. And somehow, that idea didn't sound half bad.

Fuck, I might've even liked it.

She was a lethal, disastrous, cataclysmic beauty. A beauty that could've ended me right there if she wanted. And I was so far gone, so deep under her spell, I wouldn't have even put up a fight.

The bike roared to life, startling me back to my senses. With her helmet secured in place, she gave me a final look over her shoulder and revved the motor before taking off like a shot.

Dazed and breathless, I stared down the empty road after her, wondering what had gone wrong. When had I lost my goddamn control?

More importantly, how in the hell would I get it back?

CHAPTER
THREE
KIRA

DAWN ARRIVED IN A PRETTY STREAK OF PASTEL PINK and purple. It was eye catching, but all I wanted was to crawl back into the night and stay there, in perpetual darkness, where this never-ending grief and bitterness belonged.

Winding my way through the city streets, I drove in circles for over an hour, making sure I wasn't followed. It might've been a bit extreme, but after the night I'd just endured and the risks I'd taken, there was no harm in being too careful.

By some miracle, I was still alive, but it seemed a small consolation after losing access to the information Nelson Moore held in his grimy little hands. Negotiating with the bastard had been bad enough, but to have him murdered right in front of me was a brutal crush of defeat.

One more bruising loss to top my skyrocketing pile.

All thanks to Dex.

Although, without him, I'd have likely ended up dead, my lifeless body left to rot at Nelson Moore's feet. Or worse, I'd have been taken as a Bratva prisoner.

My stomach plummeted at the thought of the two boyeviks, the line I'd crossed, the penalty for my actions, and the circle of hell they'd have dragged me into.

Dex helped keep me free from that torture.

I could admit it, but I still didn't like it. It burned that I needed a man to come to my rescue at all. Especially a man like Dex, who seemed both skilled and ruthless enough to kill me with his bare hands.

Those big, rough hands.

Hell, he could've probably taken me out with the flex of a bicep. Or maybe with one more hint of his grin.

That sly, sexy grin.

Not that I should've bothered noticing such things. But how could I not? The man was built to be ogled. Handsome and rugged, he had an all-American quality about him, with those exquisite, soulful blue eyes, and broody bad boy expression, his squared jaw and slightly crooked nose only adding to the effect.

And that body? *Fuck me.*

Just brushing against him I'd felt the rock-like bulk of his sculpted muscles. He was more solid than Fort Knox, and about as difficult to take down. His body was pure, dominating power, and it had not been a hardship to get up close and personal with him, despite the situation.

But his cocky attitude, not to mention his profession, ruined it all.

Or was it my impetuousness that had ruined everything?

Either way, he was off limits. An enemy. At least, that's what I'd keep telling myself, for as long as it took to get him out of my head.

Paranoid, I looked around one more time to make sure I hadn't picked up a tail and parked the bike as close to home as I dared. Even as I traipsed through seldom used back alleys, I was keenly aware of my surroundings. I wasn't looking to invite any more trouble. There'd been more than enough for one night.

For one life.

Once inside my building, a deep weariness took over. My eyes burned and limbs strained as I trudged up the chipped and stained stairs to my family's temporary third floor apartment.

Careful to avoid the loose floorboards, I crept in, easing the door closed and bolting it shut behind me.

"Finally, you're here," Babka called.

I jumped, turning to find my grandmother in her usual spot, looking out the dining nook window. She'd sit and stare at that view for hours, gazing past the cracks in the glass to keep an eye on the streets of Brooklyn below.

Always watching. Always waiting.

I let out an anxious breath. "Please tell me you didn't sit up all night again."

"Silly girl, you worry too much." She turned to me with a soft smile. The deep lines around her eyes were heavy, but her gaze was light and teasing. "I've been up only a short time. The morning sun woke me."

Her accent was thick, slipping into full-on Russian from time to time. Her mind slipped sometimes, too, but considering what she'd lived through, Babka was a lively lady.

Born in Russia at the end of WWII, she became an orphan at the age of five and was working in a garment factory before she was thirteen. At seventeen, she'd met my grandfather and swore it was love at first sight. Within months, they were married and only a few years later, immigrated to America.

He'd promised a brighter future, and she'd believed him. After all, she'd survived starvation, disease, war, and despair. She couldn't imagine life getting much worse. Yet, despite all her hardships, Babka had still been innocent at heart, and my grandfather…was not.

He'd been a strong, proud man, with big aspirations and exceedingly low morals. He'd surrounded himself with like-minded friends and dragged his entire family into a life that was filled with power, privilege, and dirty, treacherous lies.

Even after his murder, we were still living with the repercussions of his decisions, and still deep in bed with his crimes. It was our burden to carry. Our scar to bear.

Our savage, bloodstained legacy.

But Babka's spirit was still bright. No matter how

bad the situation, she always found the silver lining. Always made room for a smile.

"Did Amelia check in on you while I was gone?"

A beat of silence passed before she answered, "Is she the one with the little boy?"

"Yes, you remember Amelia. She's the nice lady who manages the building and checks in on you while I'm away. She lives on the first floor."

"Of course, I remember." She folded her arms over her chest, clearly annoyed by my implication. "She was here, and she left a note for you on the refrigerator."

A deep sigh rushed from me. At least my grandmother had someone reliable watching out for her, even if it couldn't always be me.

Amelia was a wonderful, sweet woman. A saint, really. She cared for my family like they were her own. Of course, she thought she was lending a poor single woman a hand while at work, and in a way, it was true. My job was just a little less conventional than most.

Not only was the work non-traditional, it didn't exactly pay. Not that I'd have taken the money even if it was offered. Still, if it weren't for the small trust fund my grandfather set up for me, my family would be living on the street.

Maybe Amelia would have understood if I'd told her the truth about the crime family I'd been born into and the plight of my captive sister, but that wasn't a risk I could take. I couldn't chance her running to the police, thinking she was helping.

Men of the law were the absolute last thing I needed.

Many of them were just as corrupt as the men I'd encountered tonight, and I'd have most likely been the one to end up behind bars.

"It was a restless night." Babka's voice was wistful, her gaze stuck on the view outside. "Anya was asking for you again."

A hot, tight band of worry wrapped around my chest, making it hard to speak. "Me, or Yelena?"

"Oh, I don't know anymore. So hard to tell. She calls for comfort and I think of you. You give her a home and keep her safe. Perhaps she doesn't know, either."

The tightness slid upward, constricting my throat and creating a clog of emotion that sent a tear sliding down my cheek. My grandmother wasn't watching, but I quickly swiped the evidence of my weakness away before she noticed.

"Thank you, Babka. For everything."

She turned to me again, an absent smile on her lips. "Did the universe send you any luck?"

A flash of gunfire and fear invaded my mind. There'd been so much violence, so much blood, and I'd been paralyzed by the savagery of it, unable to prevent a hitman from blowing away my last hope.

Bodhi Decker. Dex. No matter the name he used, I'd curse it for eternity.

"Kira?"

"No, I didn't find what I was after. But I'm still alive to keep looking. So, that's lucky, I guess."

"Fall down seven times, stand up eight."

I closed my eyes, avoiding the temptation to roll them.

Babka loved catch phrases, proverbs, and idioms. I had no idea where she'd learned them, they certainly weren't all from Russia, but this was one of her favorites. The more times I heard it, the more aggravating I found it.

Although, that might've only been because I understood it so intimately.

Like my grandmother, I kept picking myself up, dusting myself off, and soldiering on. But there was no way in hell I would do it with a smile on my face.

There'd be no gratitude for injustice. No acceptance of atrocity. No forgiveness of evil. What was I supposed to do; take the brutality, say thank you, and then stick my hand back out for more?

No fucking way.

I refused to simply endure. I'd continue to fight, no matter the cost, just like I'd intended. The way I'd promised myself I always would.

Besides, I didn't believe the terrible things of this world had much to do with fortune, the universe, or even God, for that matter. Every crime, act of terror, and every hurt I'd ever witnessed had all been at the hands of men.

Men like Dex.

"Fall down seven times, stand up eight," I murmured.

Babka nodded, her gaze falling back to the window,

and I stood with her a moment, looking at the view, trying to decipher its importance.

What was she watching? Who was she waiting for?

There was no magic fix for our situation. No guardian angel on the horizon. Regardless of how much I wanted to believe, I was afraid the chances were slim. The only hope for a miracle would be the one I made.

"I'm going to check on Anya and then sleep for a bit." I kissed my grandmother's wrinkled cheek. "I'll get up when she does and make us all breakfast."

"Okay, Marina. Sleep well." Her eyes were focused on the street below, but her mind had once again drifted elsewhere.

It wasn't the first time she'd called me by my dead mother's name, and it likely wouldn't be the last, but it was hard when she didn't recognize me.

Still, I couldn't blame her. Hell, I couldn't even blame dementia, because more and more, I didn't recognize myself, either.

Who was Kira Markova? Certainly not the pampered, carefree girl I might've once been. With no education or honest job, my family in pieces, and danger lurking at every turn, I was a shell of a person. Nothing more than a puppet on strings.

I'd been jerked and tossed around at the whims of others for too long. Violated, humiliated, and robbed of free will. Fueled only by anger and regret.

Without all that, who was I really? What was my purpose? Would I ever lead a normal life—one that wasn't filled with crime and terror?

Some of those questions became easier to answer when I peeked in on Anya.

Like a tiny cherub, she was curled into a ball and sleeping peacefully. Sweet and perfect, she was too young to understand the danger in our lives. Too innocent to know the truth.

I was her protector. For now, that's all I needed to be, and probably as close to average as I'd ever get.

Leaning over the small bed, I turned off the baby monitor that was linked to Amelia and kissed Anya on her forehead, sniffing the soft scent of lavender that lingered on her skin.

Yelena's favorite.

My eyes burned with fresh tears as I captured a lock of her silky, chestnut hair and marveled at her porcelain complexion. Her looks were still changing and maturing every day, but other than her soft brown eyes, she bore no resemblance to anyone in my family.

She looked just like her father.

And wasn't that just a kicker? It hardly seemed possible that a child so sweet could be born of a man so vile. Yet, here she was—living, breathing, doll-like proof.

I started to pull away, but my hand was suddenly caught between warm, chubby fingers, and wide doe eyes pinned me in place. "Mama, stay."

"It's okay, Anya. Go back to sleep, little dove."

I couldn't bring myself to correct her. How could I? She was only two, and her real mother, my sister

Yelena, had been kept from us for half those years. I was the closest thing to a parent the little girl had.

I couldn't take that comfort from her. Not when it was so rare to find any in this world. Not when this might be all I could ever give her.

Anya sighed contentedly and drifted back to sleep. I stroked her hair lightly before tucking her fluffy purple blanket back under her chin.

My tired sigh was less content, more contempt. I'd been so close to getting what I needed tonight. Nelson Moore had information, and with more time, I could've convinced him to talk.

But what if Dex was right? If I'd had the balls to follow through on my threats, would I be rescuing my sister right now?

Fuck, if I'd had any guts at all, Yelena wouldn't be captive in the first place. I'd have killed the bastard who took her before he'd had the chance, and my sister would be safe in her own home, singing her daughter to sleep each night.

With a last look at the dreaming baby, I stood, cringing at the creak of my leathers, and tiptoed out of the room.

The catsuit moaned with each step I took down the short, narrow hall. Leather was practical, it protected me while riding and helped me blend into the night, but now, it felt like nothing more than a cheap costume. It was a lie I put on to convince myself I was someone else. Someone hard and unyielding.

Someone not so broken.

In the bathroom, with the leather peeled away, I glared at my reflection in the mirror. Mottled bruising decorated my skin, highlighting all my hard edges. Even the small swells of my breasts seemed to lack softness.

After what seemed like a lifetime of fighting, I didn't feel much like a woman. Physically, I didn't feel much more than pain. Emotionally?

I was a fucking mess.

Yelena had been captive for a year, but I'd been living this dangerous life for much longer. My heart was full of the jagged scars to prove it, and tonight, Nelson Moore's death had been just another cruel and bloody cut. A vicious blow delivered by a hitman.

Dex had pulled that trigger without hesitation. Without thought. Without a single shred of fucking emotion. Had he even blinked?

For a man like him, killing was second nature, and it was disgusting.

He was disgusting.

At least, he should be, but I couldn't deny something about him also fascinated me. Maybe it was his confidence, his control, or the way he'd moved with ease through that crime scene while saying so many shameless, tantalizing things.

Or maybe it was the way he'd saved me when he could've just as easily killed me. Or the unexpected comfort of his strong embrace when I'd fallen a-fucking-part.

I wondered how much of it had been manipulation, and how much, if any, was real. Was his offer to fuck a tactic or the truth? And when he claimed I belonged to him, was that a warning or a promise?

No matter the truth or his motivation, it was sick.

Even if a perverted part of me liked it.

Liked him.

Tears pricked my eyes yet again, and I angrily rubbed at them. Violence and death had no business here. Neither did thoughts of Dex.

Regardless of my confused feelings, I had no room for a man like him in my life. Handsome savior or not, I'd had enough of criminals and killers. I belonged to no one, refused to be treated like property, and wouldn't be claimed whenever it was convenient.

There were enough men in my life who thought they ruled me. But whether or not they liked it, or even knew it, I made my own damn decisions.

And risked too fucking much for them.

On a heavy sigh, I pushed my jumbled thoughts aside and stepped into the shower, anxious for the scalding water to take away the pain. By the time my head hit my pillow, I was exhausted. But the moment I shut my eyes, images of blood and death assaulted me.

I tried to focus on something else. Anything else. But the only thing I could picture was the sexy, startled expression on Dex's face when I'd landed him on his ass.

God, that look.

It had made me feel confident, almost fearless, like the warrior I pretended to be. There'd been a moment of empowerment when he'd been pinned beneath me, with the hard press of his solid body against mine. A body that made me feel…other things, entirely.

A sleepy smile stole its way across my lips, and even though it might've been a little sick and a lot twisted, I held on to that image of him as I slid my hand between my legs.

I was so fucking aroused it hurt, and it was all his fault.

Next time I see him, I'll insist he makes it up to me. Demand he fill this aching need. First with those big, capable hands, and then with his filthy, irresistible mouth.

A jolt of electric sensation shot through me as I brushed over my clit.

Better yet, I'll pin him down again. Only this time, it'll be for fun. The shock on his face will turn to lust, and the impressive bulge in his pants will grow thick and hard. For me.

My hand moved faster, pressure building inside of me. My imagination worked overtime as I stroked the slippery heat of my throbbing core and pictured the perfect scenario to get myself off.

I'll ride him. Use him for my own pleasure. Torture and toy with him, denying him release. And he'll let me. He'll give me everything I want. Everything I need. He'll meet me thrust for thrust, angling his hips to pound into me from below. And I will—

I held back my cry as an orgasm overtook me. It was sharp and surprising. Blissful, yet loathsome. And I cursed his name all over again—both of them.

Slowly, the wave of my climax receded and my body began to relax, but I was left drowning in a strange mix of elation, apprehension, and regret.

Because there was no doubt I'd see him again, and when I did, Dex would most likely be dead. Or on his way to it.

And I'd be partly to blame.

CHAPTER
FOUR
DEX

A half-empty bottle of bourbon dangled from my fingers. My other hand was clenched in a hard fist, warding off the pain.

"How'd this happen?" My sister's brow furrowed as she inspected my wounded shoulder, her eyes straying from my injury to the bottle and back again.

"I got shot."

Her lips pressed to a thin line, and I could practically see the sassy comeback and long lecture forming in her head, but she was smart and kept her mouth shut.

"Trust me, Sunny, you don't want to know, and I'm not going to tell you, anyway."

"Why?" She straightened, her concerned glower contradicting the trace of hurt in her tone. "You've always been a risk taker. Do you think I worried any less while you were deployed?"

"It's not the same." I took a swig from my bottle, ready for this conversation to be over.

"Then explain it to me. Let me in on the truth for a change."

I pinned her with a glare, hoping she'd get the message. "You already know too much."

She grumbled incoherently and went back to prodding the sensitive flesh around my wound. Only, she wasn't as careful this time, forcing me to grind my teeth together to stop myself from cussing her out.

The truth was, I didn't want Sunshine involved in my life, yet she'd inserted herself here, anyway. Despite being younger by almost ten years, she'd always played the role of mother hen, even when our mom was still around.

Admittedly, she was good at taking care of people, and her nursing skills came in handy, especially in my line of work. I'd called her more than once to patch me up after a rough job, but it didn't mean she needed every gory detail of what I did. Not when it put her at risk.

My work was dangerous. That's all she knew. It's all I'd ever tell her.

She'd never know about my list and how I'd spent the last year hunting the men on it, killing them one by one. That the only name left on that list was the one at the top. Or that I didn't plan to stop until I'd crossed that name off.

Not until I wipe that son of a bitch out.

Hell, maybe not even then.

She'd never understand my obsession, the carnage, or why I chose to kill others who weren't on my list for money.

Or was it for fun?

Fuck, I hardly understood it myself, yet each time I took out another target, I walked a little lighter, slept a little deeper, felt a little less consumed. And a hell of a lot more dead inside.

Just the way I liked it.

Except, everything had now been upended. The construct I'd built for my life was suddenly riddled with cracks and fissures. My cage of control might not be as indestructible as I'd thought, and for the first time since starting this mission, I needed information I wasn't sure how to get.

Not just information. *Answers*.

I needed to know how two strangers, two goddamn Bratva soldiers, managed to figure me out. They knew the timing, the location, my name. It was all too well orchestrated to be a coincidence, and I didn't believe in luck. Considering they were just a couple of unknown goons, it was more than impressive. It should've been impossible.

But if they knew who I was, then they'd likely figured out what I'd done. They must've known I'd already taken out twelve of their crew. Thirteen, after last night.

Why the hell had they been so willing to fuck with me just to get to her?

Wildcat.

She was my first concrete warning that something was off. Only, I'd been too caught up in her to think straight. I'd charged in like an idiot waving a red flag. No precaution. No surveillance. Just ego and a hard dick.

Who was she? What was she after? And where in the hell had she learned to move like that?

I should've demanded answers when I'd had her in my arms. When her subtle curves were pressed up tight against me and her sassy mouth was mere inches from mine.

Why had I let her get away?

Sunny pushed a needle through my flesh with force, jarring me back to the moment and making me flinch.

"Please, hold still."

"I'd listen to her if I were you," Finn called from behind me. "She looks twitchy."

"Why don't you come closer and find out?" She flashed him a giant grin.

Their playful banter should have made me happy, but instead it only spiked my blood pressure. My life had fallen into sudden disarray—I'd been shot, for fuck's sake—and all these two wanted to do was joke around.

"What are you doing here?" I tried and failed to keep the annoyance from my tone.

Finn stalked into the room, his pronounced limp not slowing him down, and passed us both without a glance. In a single move, he claimed the chair across from me, spinning it around to straddle it backwards, and swiped the bourbon from my hand.

A dull headache bloomed to life at the back of my skull as I watched him tip the bottle to his lips, his throat bobbing as he drank.

His eyes were bloodshot and rimmed with dark circles, the lines of his face sharper than I'd ever seen. If anyone looked twitchy, it was him. And if I didn't know better, I might've thought he was strung out.

Except, the only addiction Finn ever had was to his own damn misery. Like any junkie, he tried to hide it, pretending there wasn't a problem, camouflaging his despair with jokes and sarcasm.

It was annoying, but I tolerated it. What else could I do?

"Well?" I glared at him through my pain.

"Couldn't sleep."

My head throbbed harder, going to war with my aching shoulder. "So, you thought it was a good idea to show up here?"

"Well, you are the perfect cure for insomnia." He smirked.

"Did you pick the lock to get in?"

"I would never." His hand flew to his chest in fake offense, but when I didn't play along, he dropped his act on a sardonic chuckle. "No. The door was open."

The knuckles of my clenched fist popped from the pressure. "The door was not open."

"Actually…" Sunny paused her ministrations, her hands hovering above her work. "I may not have followed all of your instructions when I let myself in."

"Dammit, Sunshine. Why can you never just do what you're told?"

"I'm sorry," she snapped, the trace of hurt still buried in her tone. My sister wasn't a pushover—hell, she was an ER nurse and could clearly handle her shit—but she had a soft spot for family and didn't deserve my temper.

"I know," I grunted. "Me, too."

Finn's head tilted at an odd angle, watching our exchange like it was an experiment in progress. "You seem upset. Should I leave?"

The stress of the night settled over me. Too much had gone wrong. There was too much I didn't know. And ever since a feisty kitten had knocked me off balance, too many unacknowledged feelings clamored to break free.

Feelings I'd never admit I had, since they were worthless, anyway.

"No," I said through a heavy sigh. "You should stay. We should talk."

"Sure." He placed my bourbon on the table and slid it across to me. "Looks like you had an eventful night."

"Yes, and he won't tell me anything about it." Sunny pulled hard on the new stitch she was making, getting even with me for my outburst.

Ignoring my sister, I kept my gaze locked on Finn. "Who gave us the invite?"

A tight line formed across his brow, finally showing a sign he might take things seriously, but I knew he understood my veiled question. I wanted to know who'd given us the scientist's name. Who'd paid to have him taken out?

Still, he hesitated before answering, "His boss."

A cold heaviness spread through my chest. "The corporate bigwig?"

It wasn't the answer I'd expected. Even though the Irish usually handled their own business, I'd assumed with the debt Moore owed, they were the ones behind the hit. Especially when two of their Russian rivals had shown up in the middle of the job.

Since Moore was in league with the Russians, I'd presumed they were there to either protect or silence him.

It didn't explain how they'd known all the details about me, or why they wanted the girl instead of the scientist, or even me, for that matter. Still, it made the most sense.

But now, Finn was telling me it was a high-powered, white-collar crook who'd paid for the work, and I was baffled. The bigwig was shady as fuck, but still…

Why would the CEO of a pharmaceutical company want to kill off one of his lead scientists? Why hire me? Better yet, how did he even know about me? And how in the hell was it all connected to Wildcat?

"Yeah. Are you okay?" Finn's features smoothed to his usual laidback expression.

He knew me too well and we'd been in the killing business together for too long. Forever, it seemed.

Before this underground life of blood, we were in the Marine Corps together. Honorable men doing honorable things. After our discharge from service, we learned the hard way there was a thin line between honor and revenge, and morality was all a matter of perspective.

But our bond was even stronger than the brotherhood. More than the killing.

We'd known each other all our lives. Hell, we'd sprouted from the same goddamn cell. He was more than just my handler or associate. Even more than my brother and best friend.

He was my twin.

And he could read my conflict like it was his own because most of the time it was.

"Job's done." I reached for the neglected booze, the bottle a comfortable replacement for the gun I was used to holding. "I'm taking some time off."

"A vacation sounds nice," Sunny suggested, ignorant of the dark nature of our conversation.

"Right. Vacation." I tipped my head to Finn. "You should take one, too. Somewhere tropical. Hot sun, surf, girls. Get lost for a while."

His bloodshot gaze was laser focused, reading between the lines. He knew what I was really telling him.

Run. Hide.

The Russian I'd wounded had vowed to kill me, and it wasn't an idle threat. The whole damn organization would be in on it by now. They'd want retribution for the man I shot down, and for keeping Wildcat under my protection.

If they found out what I was really after—that their boss, Nikolai Rykov, was the man at the top of my list—it'd be game fucking over.

I couldn't let that happen. Not if there was a chance of my brother coming into their line of fire.

Finn was older than me by twenty-one minutes. He organized the jobs and took care of my finances, but in every other way I looked after him. Always.

Until now, we'd avoided unneeded risks, kept ourselves well concealed and the criminals who thought we worked for them in the dark. Finn was the face of the business, although his face was rarely seen. He made the deals and collected the cash, but no one knew his identity. Hell, they didn't even know he existed.

Or maybe it was me who was nonexistent. From this side of our con, it was a bit confusing.

Every one of our so-called business associates thought we were one and the same. It was not only our ruse but our protection. Twins sharing a single alias, pretending to be the same person. Both living as Dex.

Both after the same thing—retribution.

Hidden identities helped keep us safe, but it was my control at all costs keeping us alive. I didn't plan for that to change, but with the Russians knowing my real name, we were in serious trouble.

"A vacation?" He rubbed his thumb back and forth across the stubble on his chin. "Haven't had one of those in a long time. But I guess, if you insist."

"I do."

We were all quiet for a moment, Sunshine busy with her stitching, and Finn and I each lost in our own thoughts.

"Bodhi?" His tone was steady when he broke the silence, yet I could *feel* his anguish. "Do you still think we're doing the right thing? That it'll all be worth it in the end?"

My heart drummed erratically, and that strange sense of unease threatened to take over again. "Yes. No question."

Maybe he thought I'd changed my mind. Or hoped I'd lie to him.

But I couldn't.

No. I fucking *wouldn't*. Not about this.

The only truth I knew for certain was that I'd lost my sense of right and wrong a year ago, when my list was made. That was the day our lives had been turned upside down. The day Nikolai Rykov killed Finn's wife, Emily.

Sweet, beautiful Emily. The girl next door who Finn and I had grown up with. The vivacious, fun-loving girl who'd been at our sides from the time we were in preschool, and who'd grown to be part of our family.

The woman I'd loved.

Her death would've been hard enough to bear if it was caused by an illness or a random accident. But it had been so much worse. Like an animal, she'd been slaughtered. Rykov had filled her last moments with terror and pain.

Finn's grief was loud, unforgiving, and endless. Mine would've been, too, but I'd needed to hide that pain from my brother. What else could I do?

My sorrow shouldn't have outweighed his. Fuck, it couldn't. I could never let him see the depth of my loss. Could never admit my feelings because it would've only been another lethal blow to his heart.

Instead, I shoved those big, overwhelming feelings down to the blackest depths of my soul and caged them for all eternity. Then, I made a plan that would give us both a new sense of purpose. Something to focus on beyond the grief.

Together, we sought retribution. *We made those fuckers pay.* Always with their lives, and with my finger on the trigger.

In the process, I became another person entirely. Now, I was an unfeeling, unmovable force of will with nothing left but the blood on my hands and a cold, dead, worthless heart.

"Go enjoy an island for me," I told him, pushing my useless melancholy aside. "I'll see you when I see you, brother."

He nodded absently, unfolded his long legs from around the chair, and left without another word.

Sunny cleared her throat like I might've forgotten about her. Like I hadn't just conducted an entire conversation in code because of her.

"Do you think it's a good idea for him to go away without you?"

"He'll be fine." I took a long swallow from my bottle. Maybe the booze could convince me it was true.

My sister stared at me with uncertainty. "I can't remember the last time he was anything close to fine. I'm afraid he's unstable, Bodhi."

Even though she could've been right, I didn't bother with a reply. Finn might've been a ticking time bomb of mental instability, but I knew him better than anyone, and he had a long way to go before he detonated.

She finished patching me up in silence, and I was thankful for it. Not that I was ungrateful for her help, but I needed to be alone.

I needed her back in her mundane little world of anonymity where her only real worry was balancing her social life with long hours at work. She was a smothering pain in my ass, but she was innocent, and I wanted her to stay that way.

Which meant she should be kept safely away from New York City, and me.

She paused before securing a strip of gauze over her handiwork. "You really won't tell me what's going on?"

"Not a chance."

"You're not going to call me back to do more of this tomorrow, are you?"

Gingerly, I shrugged into my shirt and pushed away the gnawing uneasiness. "No, smart ass, didn't you hear? I'm taking a break."

As she packed up her makeshift surgery kit, I stood, catching my reflection in the hallway mirror. The circles under my eyes were dark and heavy, the stubble on my face now closer to a beard. Truthfully, I could've used some downtime. I hadn't slept more than a few hours a night in months. Maybe years.

I was only thirty-nine, nowhere near old, but seeing my beaten appearance, suddenly I felt it.

My sister sighed when she noticed me assessing my reflection. "I think the three of us are genetically programmed to work ourselves to death, but you're the worst. I know you're not going to take a break. Same way I know Finn's not going to be okay on his own."

She reached up, running her fingers lovingly over the hint of gray at my temple. "You're always so busy taking care of him. I wish you'd take better care of yourself."

"I told you, Finn's going to be fine. And I *am* taking a break." I held her hand to my mouth, kissing the back of it. "You two will have to look after yourselves for a bit."

"I always take care of myself, thank you very much." She swiped the bottle of bourbon from me, and before I could stop her, took a healthy swig.

She cringed dramatically from the burn of the liquor, but it didn't stop her from giving me what was on her mind. "I still worry about you, though. I think the only thing that could force you to take a break is a woman, and I'm not sure you'll ever slow down long enough to find one."

Flashes of a lean, leather-clad body and deadly amber eyes tripped through my mind. "Thanks for the vote of confidence. But you don't know me as well as you think. I've already met a woman."

"Really?"

"Really." A thrill rushed through me at the thought of my wildcat. "In fact, I'm going to go chase her down right now."

My little sister gave me a knowing smirk. "You're not going to get shot again, are you?"

CHAPTER
FIVE
KIRA

IT WAS A COLD AND GLOOMY DAY FOR LATE SUMMER. But the weather matched my mood, and by the time I arrived at the corner diner, I was exhausted.

It seemed a night of dodging bullets and a well-built assassin would do that to a woman. Although, the effort of wrangling a two-year-old all day might've had something to do with it as well.

For such an angel, Anya could be hell on wheels. The only time she stopped was when she was sleeping, and if it weren't for this obligation, I'd have been facedown on my mattress, napping with her.

God, that would be nice. To have the luxury of rest when I needed it, and not worry every minute of every damn day.

The trip here hadn't helped matters. I was paranoid of being followed—more so than usual, at least—and I'd avoided my regular route, choosing a path that took nearly twice as long.

If this meeting goes wrong, no amount of caution will be enough.

With that thought lurking in the back of my mind, I took another look around, searching for the familiar faces I was desperate to avoid, before opening the door.

The musty stink of an old ashtray hit when I stepped inside the diner. It'd been more than two decades since smoking was allowed in public indoor spaces, yet the smell still somehow permeated the air. Like the thin film of grease that lined the windows, it seemed to be part of the aesthetic.

The bell over the door jingled again as it closed behind me. Some gazes turned my way, some even lingered a bit, but no one took special interest.

Still, I couldn't get my shaking limbs under control.

Sunglasses hid the dark circles under my eyes, my braid was tucked under a baseball hat, and the collar of my leather jacket was pulled high. The look may have screamed badass, but I sure as hell didn't feel it.

I scanned the narrow room with my heart beating at such an erratic tempo, it felt ready to explode from my chest.

After taking off the glasses, it took me a minute to spot him. Middle-aged, bulky, and balding, he was completely unremarkable. Despite giving off a creepy vibe, if I'd passed him on the street, I wouldn't have looked twice.

However, like me, his appearance was deceiving. Not the creepy part—he'd proven more than once he couldn't keep his hands to himself—but the rest was a natural disguise. He may have been mediocre, but he was the furthest thing from harmless.

How could he be? He was a criminal, taking orders from a madman.

Although, that was another thing we had in common, wasn't it?

After squeezing past a slow-moving group of old-timers, I slid into the vinyl booth across from him.

"You're late," Vlad complained, dragging a French fry through the ketchup splattered across his plate, not bothering to spare a glance my way.

He shoved the coated fry into his mouth, sucking the leftover sauce from his fingers before diving back to his overflowing pile for more.

I tried not to gag as I watched him repeat the motion, filling his mouth to the point of bursting. Still, he continued to shovel it in as a drop of ketchup missed his mouth and landed on his chin. It stayed there, dripping into his thick stubble, reminding me of the bloody scene from the night before.

The ghastly, brutal scene that had dashed my hopes with the squeeze of a trigger.

Had things gone differently, had my personal mission succeeded, I wouldn't be stuck waiting out the clock, enduring Vlad's awful company. I would've never needed to see him again.

Then again, maybe he'd be the one who'd get sent to take me out.

If I ever found a way to get Yelena free—no, *when* I found a way—I'd need to ensure we couldn't be tracked. Watching over my shoulder, waiting for death to strike for the rest of my life, didn't sound like fun. Especially if Vlad was the man chasing me.

But fuck, would it really be all that different from my life as it was now?

I swallowed the bile rising in my throat and forced my thoughts back to the task at hand.

"You must've been early. I'm right on time." Those words were daring, and maybe if I wasn't so damn tired, I wouldn't have been as bold. I was just so sick of taking his shit.

"It's there, under your napkin," he said through his mouthful, ignoring my contempt, and motioning with greasy fingers.

Fingers that I prayed he kept on his side of the table this time.

I landed my hand on the burner phone just as the waitress stopped beside me with a half-full pot of coffee. "What can I get you, hon?"

Hon? Fuck, I hated this place more and more each time I was here. "Just coffee."

I watched in silence as she poured black sludge into the tiny porcelain cup with a tight smile glued to her face and a trembling hand.

"Cream and sugar are on the table," she said, nodding toward the condiments lined against the wall, like they were something new.

Like we hadn't had this exact same interaction once a week for the last year. Like I gave a shit about the quality of her service, or any part of the contrived song and dance we were forced to perform.

What good were cream and sugar when she knew I wouldn't take a single sip?

"Thanks." My mouth tilted in what was meant to be a reassuring smile but felt a hell of a lot more like a grimace, and she visibly exhaled before skittering away.

"I suggest you don't waste any more time." Vlad wiped haphazardly at the corners of his mouth, somehow still missing the mess of red on his chin.

I stared at him a moment, with my knee bouncing wildly under the table and another sharp comeback on the tip of my tongue.

If only I could let those words fly. Walking this tightrope of feigned cooperation became harder the longer I was exposed. The longer I was in his presence, the higher the chance my luck or patience would fail me, revealing my true feelings. My deception.

My jaw cracked under the strain of keeping my mouth shut, but the glare I gave him said more than enough.

Thankfully, he continued to ignore me and dug back into his pile of fries.

I picked up the old-school phone again, dutifully flipped it open, and hit "dial" beside the one and only contact number. A number that was never the same, and if I were to try and trace it, would've only led to a dead end.

Not that I needed to trace it. The problem wasn't finding him. I already knew where he was. Fuck, he might as well have had a neon sign lighting the front door, it was so obvious.

No. The problem was getting past his defenses. Past his security setup and waiting assassins. Into the heart of fucking darkness, it seemed. Then, making it back out alive.

With the hard plastic of the phone pressed tightly to my ear, I listened to the hollow buzz and tried to calm my racing pulse.

After the third ring, he answered. "Kira." The sound of his cool, understated voice drove the bile further up my throat, until I was practically choking on it. "So nice to hear from you."

Like I have a choice.

I didn't respond to his greeting. It wasn't what he was looking for. In fact, a response would've been unacceptable. He didn't want a reply, he wanted me to comply. The niceties were just a game I was trapped into playing.

My obedience was a performance, one I'd never been any good at, yet I continued to act the part, anyway. Continued doing so many things I'd rather not. Whatever he asked of me.

Because, as always, he had the upper hand, and he knew it.

"Well?" The drawl of the single word didn't fool me into believing there was anything casual about the question.

My stomach pitched and rolled, but I forced the sick feeling away. I needed to get through this. To make him believe I was still on board with his deal. "Things did not go as anticipated."

Vlad still didn't bother looking up from his plate, but his hand hung suspended over his food. It was obvious he was listening to every word.

Of course he was. It'd be his job to deal with the aftermath. To deal with me, if necessary.

The sigh on the other end of the phone was heavy and dramatic, and I swore I could smell the cheap cigar on his breath, along with his hatred of me. "Very disappointing, Kira. What am I to do with you?"

Once again, no answer was allowable.

"Better yet—" he paused, no doubt to drag out my discomfort, "—what will I do with your sister?"

"Please," I gasped, my heart beating wildly. "It wasn't my fault. There were…circumstances. Your men got in the way. Sasha's men. They ended things before I got what you wanted."

"Excuses, excuses. You know how I feel about those."

"Yes." I cringed, but my eyes were glued to Vlad's hands, watching every move. Was it my imagination or was he inching toward his weapon? "I do, and I apologize. There is no excuse. But maybe if you let your men in on our deal or put a tighter leash on your dog, things would go more smoothly."

"You know I'm not willing to do that, darling Kira. The arrangement you and I have is a private one, and Sasha may be loyal to me, but he's still his own man.

The problems between the two of you are none of my concern."

Bitter rage flashed through me. "Will it be your concern if he kills me?"

"You think your death would mean anything to me?" The smoky rasp of his cruel laughter was like a knife to my gut. "Please. You're not that valuable an asset. Especially when all you do is continue to let me down."

"You're right, of course. I'm sorry." Fuck, what was I thinking? Impulsive reactions showed weakness, and I knew better than to give him that. He didn't need any more ammunition. He already had more than enough.

Even kissing his ass was a risk, but it was the best shot I had at turning this conversation around. "I promise I will do better if you could just give me another chance."

"How many chances have I given you already? I've allowed you this opportunity out of respect for your grandfather and the organization he built. Let you live freely with your niece and grandmother out of charity. Kept your sister alive out of my love for her." He paused again, and I could hear him puffing on a cigar.

His fucking endless supply of cigars. He thought having one in hand made him look so macho and sophisticated, but the awful things were just his crutch.

The same way I used my knife to camouflage my fear, he used his precious cigars to lend him importance. They were a prop to display his power, all while he cowered, hidden away in a beautiful fortress, surrounded by luxury and lackeys.

An empire erected on crime, deceit, and the blood of my family.

"I can't tolerate more of your failures, Kira. Disappoint me like this again, and you'll be begging for death."

His words were ominous and meant to strike fear. Yet, my pulse slowed, jitters subsided, and a voice in the back of my mind whispered, *"If the threat was real, he'd have already followed through."*

Fuck, it sounded a hell of a lot like Dex. It was bad enough he'd had a starring role in my dreams—those hot as sin, X-rated fantasies. Was he so stuck in my head that he was now my damn conscience, too?

It would've served me right.

Still, regardless of where those words had come from, they were true. It was all so clear to me now. Same as the threats I'd made to Nelson Moore, this one was empty.

"You'll wish it was Sasha who got to you." He was trying so hard to convince me. But why? Was it because he needed me as his secret weapon? Something else for this ruthless asshole to hide behind like the fortified mansion and the goddamn cigars?

Still, he had my sister, and even if he didn't plan to kill her now, there was nothing to stop him from changing his mind tomorrow. With Yelena as his bargaining chip, he was the one with all the power.

What was I going to do?

"Do I still get to speak with my sister?" Now, I was really pushing my luck. But this had been our deal. He'd agreed to keep my sister *safe*, and I'd do his evil fucking bidding. He needed to prove he was holding up his end of the bargain regardless of my success or failure. Especially if he expected me to continue working for him, no questions asked.

"Of course," he said, as though he was a kind and generous man, and I was an ingrate for thinking otherwise.

There was a rustling on the other end of the phone line, and then her soft voice was in my ear. "Hello."

"Yelena." The breath rushed from my lungs, and I struggled to maintain my composure. The last thing I wanted was for Vlad the creep to see me cry. At least, not ever again. "How are you?"

"I'm fine." Her dull tone gave nothing away. Was she scared? Lonely? Hurt or hungry? "How are you?"

"I'm fine, too," I answered. "Everyone here is doing good. Anya is growing like a weed, and Babka is still healthy as ever."

"That's good," she said absently, and my heart cracked wider.

Each time I spoke to her, she seemed more distant, and less and less herself. I couldn't tell if it was a protection mechanism—if she was afraid of doing or saying the wrong thing—or if she was losing hope of ever being free.

Or maybe she'd just given up on me.

"I miss you," I whispered, afraid of spilling too much emotion.

I heard something that sounded like it could've been

a sniffle, and she rasped, "I have to go." Then, there were more rustling sounds as she passed the phone back to her captor.

"What happened to the target?" he asked without precursor.

The sudden change of direction had my head spinning, and my stomach seized again. "The target?"

"Yes, Kira. The man I sent you to find. The one you're meant to tease into my trap. What happened to him?"

"I don't know. Sasha's men came after me, and I lost track of him after that." The lie slipped easily from my lips. Too easily. Just like all the other lies I'd told.

Only, this might've been the most dangerous one yet. It hid not only my personal agenda, but the truth about Dex and my unfathomable weakness toward him.

Plus, there was a witness to dispute it.

"And how is it that you lived but Nelson Moore did not?" His question was obviously a test, but even the creep sitting across from me could've passed this one.

"Is that not what you wanted? I thought..." I hesitated, glancing around the crowded diner to see who might be listening.

Vlad was now watching me intently as he chewed on another mouthful of fries. And fuck, it wasn't my imagination. His hand was resting on the hilt of the gun hidden under his cheap blazer.

He winked at me, and I recoiled as a disturbing smile spread across his face, the dollop of ketchup making him look even more deranged.

"I thought the point of involving Moore was to have him taken out." I kept my voice low to avoid being overheard.

More silence. More cigar puffing.

My pulse kicked up a fuss again, and my knee resumed its jiggling. Did he know I was lying? Was I not as slick as I thought?

Fuck. What if I was wrong and he already knew everything?

"Such a smart girl, yet, still so disappointing." His voice was as unyielding as always. "I'll give you one more chance to prove your worth."

My bouncing leg almost hit the bottom of the table, but I tried to rein it in. Sudden movements probably weren't a good idea with Vlad sitting across from me. I doubted he'd think twice about shooting me in public.

"Thank you. You won't be sorry." There was no point in prattling on when he didn't give a shit about my relief. When every word I said could be used against me. Or worse, against my sister.

Still, I couldn't seem to shut the hell up. "I won't let you down this time, I swear."

"I hope not. It would break my heart if I had to put a bullet in Yelena's pretty little head. You know how much I love her."

My stomach turned again, and this time I thought I really might be sick. "Yes, boss, I know."

"Please," he crooned. "We're like family, Kira. You should call me by my name."

"Yes, of course. Thank you, Nikolai."

CHAPTER
SIX
DEX

"Your name, sir?"

"Corbin Smith." I gave my new alias to the door attendant and straightened the gold watch on my wrist, emphasizing my boredom with his existence. "Guest of Tess Crawford."

I was in full disguise, dressed in a custom-tailored suit that fit my broad shoulders and athletic build to perfection. I'd topped off my ensemble with a black silk tie, diamond encrusted cufflinks, and the shiniest shoes a man could buy.

I'd even rented a bright yellow Lamborghini for the occasion. Although I could probably afford to buy it, what would've been the point? I had better uses for my money than drawing attention while idling in New York traffic.

Besides, I already knew I had a big dick, I didn't need to prove it.

"Thank you, Mr. Smith." The attendant marked my

fake name on the guest list. "Ms. Crawford arrived ten minutes ago. She'll be waiting for you inside, sir."

"Perfect." *Perfectly easy.*

I strolled past the two men with concealed weapons who were stationed inside the entrance. When the elevator chimed, I stepped on alone.

This game of the upper class was one I rarely played, but when I did, I played it damn well. Only this time, despite my polished, nonchalant appearance, my insides were churning.

For the first time in this journey—hell, maybe the first time in my life—I was completely solo. No partner gathering information behind the scenes. No emergency backup at the touch of a button.

I hadn't expected to hear from Finn, yet his radio silence had me on edge. I couldn't help but worry something had gone wrong. Especially when there were so many ways it could've happened.

What if Sunshine was right and he wasn't fine on his own?

What if I wasn't?

For once, I hoped my instincts were wrong and my twin was busy having the time of his life. Or at the very least, getting loaded on a beach somewhere, making regrettable choices he wouldn't remember later. If things went according to my new plan, maybe I could join him when this was over. Take a real vacation.

Or at least sleep for a fucking change.

I'd spent over a week hunting for a wildcat. Eight days of playing spy while staying off the Russians' radar, and I hadn't uncovered a single damn detail about her. I'd searched every dark corner and looked under every rock, but the only link I'd found between her, Nelson Moore, and Rykov's crew was Bowen Alexander.

To the public, Alexander was a businessman and philanthropist. His pharmaceutical company, BTA-Xander, had launched a campaign to end cancer. They were on the cutting edge of research and drug development. Each year, he gave millions to hospitals and private clinics. His generosity knew no bounds.

It was a good cover, but to the underground, he was just another corporate slime-bag with low morals and deep pockets. Easy to corrupt. Easy to use.

Alexander was the one who'd hired me to kill Moore, and with everything I'd learned about my target, I'd had no qualms. He'd been dirty, and as Wildcat had suggested, the man was a trove of information. Only, now it seemed the scientist had been nothing more than irresistible bait.

But had the lure been meant for me or her?

Either way, Alexander was the best lead I had. The only lead. Tonight, he would help me figure out this puzzle.

And help guide me to a feisty kitten.

Two more armed guards greeted me when I stepped off the elevator into the penthouse foyer. I took a mental note and sauntered into the party.

The room was decked in wall-to-wall glitz and glitter. A string quartet played softly from a raised terrace while the city's elite mingled and showed off below.

The event was a small, private fundraiser hosted by Alexander's wife. It was a bunch of ultra rich assholes squeezing money from other ultra rich assholes to try and one up each other in some strange competition of magnanimous pride. The alcohol alone cost enough to feed a small country, and the guest list boasted a handful of the wealthiest businessmen, politicians, and celebrities—all of them thieves, liars, and whores.

Of course, I hadn't been invited, but that's where Tess came in.

"You made it!" she called, her eyes lighting up at the sight of my façade.

Funny, she'd never quite looked at me with such greedy lust before. Not even when naked and on the brink of orgasm.

"I did." I offered her my arm, which she promptly latched on to with both hands.

Tess Crawford was a celebrity gossip reporter with a talent for looking pretty in front of a camera. She didn't write her own material, but her show produced fluffed up buzz pieces that made even the worst criminals look like choirboys. She had a strong arm over public opinion, which the underbelly of New York loved her for.

And she loved me. Or at least, the type of man she perceived me to be—a rogue bad boy who gave her wads of cash in exchange for her connections and occasionally showed her a good time in the sack.

She'd been an ace in my back pocket for years now.

Like so many of the other nights I'd had her at my side, she was simply an accessory. Sometimes, she was my unwitting accomplice, sometimes a simple cover, but never more than a convenience.

"I wouldn't leave you high and dry. Especially when I'm the one crashing the party."

Her laughter was a fake tinkling sound that ground its way into my skull. She batted her false lashes and gushed, "I'm happy you called."

"You mean you're happy to take more of my money."

"Not true." Her over-plump, injected lips stuck out in a dramatic pout. "I hate coming to these things without a date."

"I'm sure you wouldn't have been alone for long. You look fantastic." It was true. While Tess's personality might've grated on most of my nerves at times, she wasn't hard to look at.

Her golden hair was expertly styled, her ample curves were accentuated by her tight red dress, and her surgically enhanced cleavage—paid for by yours truly—was on full display.

"Thank you." She smiled and hugged me closer, pressing her heavy chest against my arm. "You look quite appetizing yourself."

"I know. You're eying me like I'm the buffet. But don't forget, tonight's strictly business."

"Of course." Her fingers pushed lightly against my chest, and she gave me a smile full of teasing. "Doesn't mean I can't flirt with you, though."

She laughed again, tossing her head back as though I was the funniest guy on the planet. The move sent a wave of thick hair tumbling down her back and drew the attention of every man in sight.

I couldn't help but smile along with her. My plan was right on track.

Tess composed herself and we moved a little farther into the room, accepting glasses of champagne from a passing server.

"Have you seen him?" I asked.

"Mm hmm." She sipped daintily at her drink, before confirming, "Dead center."

Quickly scanning the room, I took note of the exits and the imposing men with concealed weapons posted at each one. Besides the overdone security and a young couple who were making out like fiends in a corner, everything was as I'd expected.

Relaxing a little, I downed my drink, enjoying the way the light, bubbly liquid danced over my tongue.

Until my eyes landed on Bowen Alexander.

He was in the center of the room, exactly as Tess had described, with his billion-dollar smile poised for seduction. Only, it was obvious he was the one being charmed. The most powerful man in the room looked like a dog on a leash, wagging his tail for the woman effortlessly leading him.

Wildcat.

She was here. And she was stunning.

I'd thought of her endlessly since our run-in— consumed with finding her, learning her secrets, and teaching the little kitty a lesson. She was the key to this mess with the Russians, and one way or another, she was going to help set it straight.

Maybe even help me get my revenge.

But now that she was only feet away, my body had other ideas. The room seemed to pitch as my head spun and my cock sparked awake at the sight of her.

Her platinum hair flowed almost to her waist, her perfect lips were painted ruby, and her graceful body was showcased in the most fuck-hot dress I'd ever seen.

The midnight blue silk dipped dramatically low in front, showing off the pale, smooth valley between her pert tits, and every time she moved, I got a flash of the full length of her legs, the dress slitting indecently high up both sides.

Fucking hell. All that exposed skin. Those long, toned legs. With her sultry smile and virulent eyes added to the mix, she was a gravitational force, sucking in everyone around her.

Including me.

I was mesmerized by her magnetic beauty. It grabbed me by the balls and pulled. Hard.

My vision narrowed as my priorities reset on my new objective. My new plan. My new fucking obsession.

My wildcat.

"Dex, did you hear me?" Tess nudged my side, breaking the spell.

"Corbin," I snapped under my breath, reminding her

of my alias for the night. "Yes, I heard you. I think it's time to introduce ourselves."

Without making our destination obvious, I guided Tess through the sea of partygoers. We traded our empty glasses for full ones and stopped briefly to chat with a hungry-looking power couple who were eager for her attention.

Their conversation was banal, but I faked interest as I covertly kept watch over Wildcat and her company. When they were unexpectedly joined by Gael O'Shea, my racing heart seized.

O'Shea was part of the Irish mafia, and the man Nelson Moore had owed money to. He had a dark and bloody reputation, and no one who crossed him had lived to talk about it. At least, not pain free and not for long.

Seeing him here, casual and relaxed in this opulent crowd, and leering at Wildcat, put me even further on edge.

My carefully crafted control was already close to snapping, but when she offered her hand to the mobster with a sly grin, the champagne flute cracked in my fist.

Her sultry gaze moved back to Alexander as O'Shea slobbered over her hand, and Alexander eye-fucked her in return.

My blood pressure spiked, and dark spots momentarily took over my vision. Didn't she know who these men were? What they were capable of?

"Excuse us." I rudely interrupted Tess and her

phony-ass friends, pulling her away from their useless conversation. "It's time," I urged in her ear.

Unperturbed by my harsh tone and firm hold, she glided alongside me. She didn't know the details of my plan, especially since it had changed the minute I'd spotted Wildcat, but Tess was quick as always and played along with the deception.

"Bowen," I called, raising my hand in a friendly gesture.

It was a bold move to approach him so informally, acting like I'd known him for years. But since Finn had never met with him in person, I was banking on him not knowing my face and assuming I was just another unremarkable and easily forgettable rich asshole invited by his wife.

"How'd you get wrangled into hosting another fundraiser?" I offered him my hand, forcing myself to ignore the exquisite beauty at his side.

Accepting the handshake, he measured me with knowing eyes, his look warning he wasn't a fool. "Honestly, I'm not sure. I just write the checks."

"Maybe your wife's trying to punish you for something." I chuckled. "Did you forget her birthday?"

O'Shea's booming laugh made Tess flinch beside me. "I like this guy." He slapped Alexander on the back. "Who is he?"

Alexander's eye twitched, but he held an arrogant grin. "I have no idea."

"Corbin." I reached to shake O'Shea's clammy hand. "Corbin Smith."

Daggers were shot at me from gleaming amber eyes as I traded introductions with O'Shea. Wildcat's demure composure seemed to slip. Her hostility peeked out, but maybe I was the only one who could sense it, since it was all aimed at me.

"And who's this vision?" O'Shea turned his attention to Tess and her cleavage.

"My apologies. Let me introduce the television queen, Tess Crawford."

When Tess extended her hand, O'Shea wasted no time, pulling her forward out of my hold and bringing her hand to his lips.

"Your wife or girlfriend?" He brushed his mouth to her skin, his eyes still glued to her chest.

"No, just my date for the evening."

He grinned. "So, no objection if I borrow her for a dance or two?"

"I don't see how one or two could hurt."

If there was an objection, it should've been from Tess, but she continued playing decoy without complaint. She met O'Shea's vulgar stare with a coy smile. "I wouldn't mind."

Wildcat, on the other hand, was losing more of her poise by the minute. Her utter disgust at our show of misogyny was written all over her face.

Maybe it should've bothered me, too, but I wasn't about to blow my cover for the sake of Tess's equality. These men didn't give a shit about women's rights, plus I was paying her good money to act as a pawn.

"Perhaps we could trade. But you haven't introduced us to your date." Finally, I allowed my gaze to trail over my little kitten, and *fuck*, it was next to impossible to look away.

O'Shea barked another loud laugh, his suit jacket straining under the effort. "This one insists she's flying solo tonight." With a sarcastic jeer, he hitched his thumb at her, as though her independence was an oddity barely worth tolerating. "Although, our friend Bowen has been intent on convincing her otherwise. You might have to fight him for that dance."

I smirked, forcing my gaze to meet Alexander's. "I'd rather fight with her, I think."

O'Shea's laughter was raucous, but it didn't detract my attention from Alexander's cold expression or the deadly gaze of my wildcat, still without a name.

"Come, Tess." O'Shea tugged her by the hand. "We'll leave these three to duke it out."

"Have fun." I bent and gave her a peck on the cheek, whispering in her ear, "But not too much."

Not that she needed my veiled warning. Tess had played in these circles longer than me and was well-versed in sleaze. She knew how to keep herself safe.

I turned back to Alexander and Wildcat. His gaze was heavy with cool confidence. Hers was all feisty attitude, barely restrained.

"You'd be wise to step away." Her lips tilted to a sweet smile, but I'd have bet my rented Lamborghini she was mentally planning my torture.

Now, it was Alexander's turn to laugh. It was a

refined, almost elegant sound, and it was obnoxious as fuck.

Everything about this man offended me, from his perfectly coiffed silver hair to the toe of his shiny Oxfords. But most of all, the possessive way his arm coiled around Wildcat's trim waist.

"Funny, because you told me to stay away last time, too," I said, taunting her. "Yet, we still ended up rolling in bed together. And on the floor."

She flashed another deadly glare my way as Alexander's laughter died.

"Sorry, Bowen, but she owes me more than just a dance."

He released his hold on her and slithered toward me, not stopping until he was well within the boundaries of my personal space. Even though he strained to look up at me, neither the proximity nor our height difference deterred him.

"That's all right." His voice was low, his stare unwavering. "I prefer a dance partner who'll follow my lead. Things got a bit out of hand with the last one who tried to take over. She didn't last long, I'm afraid."

He smiled, and it was one of the most disturbing things I'd ever seen.

"Have fun with this one, *Mr. Smith*. Until next time." He strode away with his eerie grin still in place. Then, he called back over his shoulder, "I do hope it's soon."

Wildcat turned to me with a hiss. "You asshole!"

"Save it, kitten." I forced a smug smile and grabbed

her by the arm, throwing a final nod to Tess as I pulled my new, unwilling companion toward the foyer.

"Let go of me." She was seething, her muscles tense under my fingers. There was no doubt, the minute I let go, she would run.

Still, it was the best damn feeling to have her in my grasp again. For her to be under my control, right where she belonged. "Not going to happen. You've got something I want. Until I get it, you're mine."

To demonstrate my point, I stopped and tugged her close, her hands landing roughly on my chest as we collided. Our bodies lined up in all the right places, and I slid my fingers along the soft curve of her back, forcing her to sway with me in time to the music of the string quartet.

Our feet barely shuffled, and her form was stiff. Yet, with her hands clutching the lapels of my jacket, her breathing labored, and gaze full of fire, the contrived dance felt somehow erotic.

In another life, I'd have been counting down the minutes until I could take her home and fuck her. Now, though, I just wanted to get her the hell out of here. Alive.

"Or did you want to stay and find out what kind of fun that snake Alexander has in mind for you?" I whispered, my glare glued to hers.

Her mouth was a tight line of irritation, but she kept it shut.

"He wasn't fooled by either one of us, and he's not

even close to being intimidated. Now, if you don't mind, I'd like to get out of here. Preferably in one piece."

"I'm not going anywhere with—" The color drained from her face, and she cut her argument short, her gaze momentarily locked on the entrance.

I looked up in time to see Sasha Novikoff stride into the room.

This man was Nikolai Rykov's right hand, and that alone made him a dangerous son of a bitch. There was a glint of amusement in his eye, a ridiculous amount of swagger in his step, and two more brutal-looking thugs at his side, including the man I'd shot.

The target on my back might as well have been literal and fucking illuminated.

These were the men who were after her. The men who wanted me dead. The men who, knowing Wildcat's unpredictable reactions, had about a fifty-fifty shot at success.

CHAPTER
SEVEN
KIRA

No way in hell would I have gone anywhere with Dex in the lead. At least, not willingly. Not until my worst nightmare stalked through the door.

Sasha.

Despite his handsome, youthful appearance, he was a darkly foreboding presence. Maybe it was the deep scar that ran through the corner of his upper lip, the wicked tattoo that spanned his neck, or the maniacal smile he was wearing.

Or maybe it wasn't his looks at all, but my firsthand knowledge of the terror he created, and my inability to escape him no matter how hard I tried.

"Fuck." I buried my face against Dex's solid shoulder, hiding from Sasha's view.

"No shit. This way." He tugged me toward a dimly lit hall, which was clearly off limits and guarded by a large man with an unfriendly face.

I needed to get the hell out of here and far away from all these merciless men.

My mind circled itself, looking for a way out of this unexpected turn of events. A single man blocking our path wasn't an issue, but it would be a challenge to get around him without drawing attention from the room full of mobsters.

The solution presented itself when the guard gave me an obvious look of appreciation, his gaze roaming the low neckline of my dress.

With Dex still close at my side, I eased up to the leering man. "Hi there."

"What d'ya want?" His flat tone gave nothing away, but interest still flashed in his eyes.

"I was hoping to find a private place for me and my boyfriend to spend some quality time together. Do you think you could help us out?" I slid my hand up his arm and leaned in to whisper in his ear, "Maybe you'd like to tag along?"

He looked around the room, his gaze darting back to us when Dex took a menacing step forward.

Fuck, if he messed this up, I'd kick his ass. Or maybe just throw him as a sacrifice to the Bratva wolves and run like hell.

"Go," the guard grunted, moving aside.

We rounded the corner into a wide, poshly decorated hallway lined with closed doors, including one for the service elevator at the opposite end of the hall from where we stood.

Dex encircled my waist with his thick arm again, his

fingers spreading wide across my ribs, and my skin prickled from the electric sensation bouncing wildly between us. A sensation that had me strangling the shoulder chain of my small, crystal encrusted clutch as my feet moved just a little faster.

"In here," the guard called from behind us, and Dex halted, stopping me dead in my tracks.

The gilded metal of the elevator door taunted me—my escape was mere feet away. I could've run, but what would have been the point? One of them would've caught me. Maybe even killed me.

And being alone in a room with these two was still better than being anywhere near Sasha.

With a smile, I turned and prowled toward the guard. "You like to watch?" I asked, running a hand across his chest.

He tilted his head toward the open room and waited wordlessly for us to enter.

The space was lit only by the glow of the city filtering in through floor-to-ceiling windows. The office looked sterile, with a teak cabinet along one wall and a large, clean desk in the center with a computer sitting on top of it.

The door clicked shut, locking the man in behind us. "This is gonna cost ya more than just a show."

"Really? You want to fuck my boyfriend, too?"

"What?" He balked in confusion. "No, I—"

"What do you think, Dex? Should you fuck him, or should I?"

"Whatever you want, kitten." I could hear the cocksure grin in his voice, and something about knowing we were on the same side, even if only for this moment, lit me up inside.

"I don't like men." The guard crossed his arms like a child being denied the toy he wanted.

"Okay." I shimmied toward him. "You get me, then."

A salacious smile spread across his nasty face, but in a blink, my foot landed a hard blow to his head, knocking the smile away.

His deadweight hit the ground and I leaned over him, grabbing his collar and lifting his head off the floor. "Was it good for you, too?"

Out cold, he didn't answer.

"Hand me his gun," Dex urged from behind me.

I pushed the unconscious man away in disgust, his head landing with a thud against the hardwood.

One problem solved. Just one more to go.

The gun was bigger than I'd hoped, but I made sure to handle it like a pro when I turned to Dex with it aimed at his chest.

"Again?" His sigh was so damn exaggerated. Even with a loaded weapon pointed at him, he was a cocky son of a bitch. "I thought you didn't like guns?"

"I don't, but for you, I'll make an exception."

"Let's stop running in circles." He turned his open palms up, showing they were empty.

Like I was naïve enough to believe he wasn't a threat.

"You know I'm not going to hurt you. Hell, you

should be thanking me for keeping you out of Alexander's clutches. The way I see it, you owe me. And like it or not, kitten, I'm going to get what I'm owed."

"I don't owe you shit." I gritted my teeth, afraid of giving myself away. "Do you really think I'm here out of coincidence? I wanted to be in his clutches. You're just in my way of getting what I need. Again."

"You couldn't get anything from the scientist, but you think you'll get it from Bowen Alexander? What's your plan—more empty threats? Or were you going to fuck it out of him, too?" A smirk graced his annoyingly perfect lips.

"Watch it." I thrust the gun forward, using it to punctuate my words, hoping like hell it was effective. "Or you'll be next."

"Sorry, kitten, but I don't buy it. Your desperation's showing."

Adrenaline exploded inside of me, urging me to act before thinking. I rushed at him, stopping when the only thing standing between us was my temper and a loaded gun. "It's Kira!"

"What?" The deep hum of his voice pulled me closer, allowing him to capture me with his heated gaze and an arm around my waist.

Something inside of me cracked. I went willingly, shifting my aim and pressing the gun to his torso, my body brushing against his in an electrifying caress.

"My name is Kira," I whispered, unsure why I was suddenly so intent on him knowing it, but certain I couldn't resist giving in, just this bit.

"Kira." The syllables rolled softly over his tongue like he was savoring them. "I like it. A kickass Russian name for a kickass Russian girl."

My body flushed with scorching heat. "I'm a grown-ass woman."

"Fucking right you are. A wild one."

"And my family may be Russian, but I'm not one of *them*."

His arm flexed around me, pressing me tight against his rock-like body. And God, it felt so good, it was all I could do to hold myself back and not rub against him like a fucking cat. Maybe if he called me kitten one more time, I'd be tempted to do just that.

"Kira, I don't believe you. But I'm still going to kiss you."

"I dare you to try it." My words were a jagged rush of breath, lust tinting every single one.

"Are you going to shoot me if I do?"

"Maybe."

His deep chuckle was electrifying. "Then, I think I'll take my chances."

With his provocative blue gaze pinning me in place, he tilted his head toward mine.

Vengeful adrenaline coursed through me. Despite the flame he'd ignited, my dark side was out and playful. I'd left my weak will at the door. The combative, ugly side of me had taken over the moment I'd walked into this hell maze, and I wasn't sure how far I'd let it go or how much damage I was capable of.

Only, when his soft, cool lips landed possessively

over my fired-up mouth, my insides melted. Anger and aggression gave way to desire. My urge to fight was drowned by an unexpected, turbulent storm of wanton lust.

The gun at his sternum did nothing to restrain him, and my mouth became his playground as he took his time, nibbling and licking his way inside. Unhurried, he treated our kiss like the beginning—a warmup to a longer, more languorous entanglement—and it drove me fucking insane.

I turned rabid, kissing him back with lips, tongue, and teeth.

Almost involuntarily, my hand holding the gun dropped to my side, and I slid my other one to the back of his neck, grabbing hold for dear life. My leg also had a mind of its own, hiking high around his thigh, and bringing my aching center closer to the thick bulk of his powerful muscles.

And, *oh*…his stiffening cock was a long, thick promise trapped against my stomach.

I groaned into his mouth, and he grunted in return. It was a deep, rousing sound that called to all my hidden cravings. Sensation flooded my body, my nipples pebbled and skin tingled, proving I was still a warm-blooded woman after all.

It was overwhelming—the hunger, the insatiable need.

But his grip shifted and slid, kicking my brain back into gear. Because he wasn't just enjoying the moment, he was inching his way toward the gun.

Sneaky, but I should've expected the tactic from him.

My body was still raging with sensation, but I wouldn't allow him to get the upper hand. No matter what name he went by, Bodhi Decker would not win.

Not even if this was the hottest damn kiss of my life.

I lowered my leg, slowly hooking his calf, then pulled hard and fast, attempting to take him to the ground. Our mouths finally tore free from one another, but he didn't fall. He'd been prepared for my maneuver and stayed upright, with his feet solidly planted on the floor.

Fuck, he was too damn smart. Unlike me, it seemed he learned his lessons the first time around. But that was fine, I was adaptable.

Instead of trying to take him down, I climbed his torso like a tree. With my knees hugged tight to his sides, I was now the one on top, and I aimed the gun point-blank at his head.

"I tried to warn you," I sighed, sweetly.

He licked his lips, deliberately sucking the lower one into his mouth and grasping it between his teeth. His eyes sparkled as he hummed his appreciation, his mouth slowly quirking into a sly grin.

Fuck, this man knew how to get under my skin, and I hated myself even more for allowing it. I didn't care how many times he thought he'd saved me or whether it was even true. I didn't need him.

No matter how much I wanted him.

He held me in his arms like a lover, but I could

sense he was calculating his next move. I could practically see the manipulation forming on his handsome face.

"Now, let's try this again." I crushed his sides between my thighs, emphasizing my power. "I'm going to release you and you're going to move nice and slowly over to the desk and turn on the computer."

"Why?"

"No questions. Just do what I tell you. Understand?"

He gave me no answer. Not even a flinch of an eyebrow to give away his thoughts. He also didn't budge.

We stared at each other, his cool eyes intent on my narrowed gaze. I pushed the gun harder against his temple, but he remained steadfast. Completely unfazed.

"You're stunning." His eyes trailed over my face, my mouth, and further down. "And this dress is insanely hot." My bare leg broke out in gooseflesh as he ran his hand from my thigh to my knee and back again, hovering over the leather strap holding my knife in place.

"Stop."

"You sure that's what you want? Because in this position, I could just lay you over the desk, or back you against the wall, or hell, if you wanted to ride me right here like this, I'd be good."

Sexy, cocky son of a bitch.

"I've got a gun to your head, there's an unconscious man on the floor, and a gang of men who want to kill you in the other room. How can you even think about sex right now?"

"You tell me, kitten." He squeezed the back of my thigh, his fingers pressing daringly close to my ass. "You're the one who attacked my mouth like you were starved for it."

Another desperate moan tried to claw its way out of me, but I swallowed around it, holding back the show of lust as my insides quaked.

Still, I refused to let this arrogant killer get the upper hand. "I told you to stop."

"What's the matter? Afraid of a little truth?"

Air sawed through my lungs, and my chest burned with the effort to keep breathing. It was a wonder I was able to hold my aim when the gun suddenly felt so fucking heavy.

"We both know you're not going to shoot me. Same way we know I'm hard as steel right now. So, let's just stop pretending."

I dropped my aim. "Fine. I'm not going to shoot you. At least, not right now. But sex is the last thing on my mind."

"Liar."

Yes, I am. I just hoped his cock was as big a distraction for him as it was for me, and he couldn't see through the entirety of my deception. The multitude of twisted lies.

His fingers glided over my neck, making me shiver, and my reckless pulse threatened to give me away.

"Which has you more turned on, kitten—me or the danger?"

You're one and the fucking same.

I crushed my legs tighter, wedging my knee into his ribs, right where I knew it would hurt. "Quit trying to distract me. It's not going to work. The only thing I'm interested in is the information on that computer."

"Okay." He withdrew his touch from my throat, and instantly, I missed it. "But I doubt there's anything useful on there. You and I both know Alexander's not going to keep a diary of all his underworld games on the corporate hard drive. What are you hoping to find?"

A sign. A flicker of hope. A bloody fucking miracle. "A way to save my sister."

The tension between us shifted. His playful expression evaporated, replaced by a tight line between his eyebrows and a sharp edge to his jaw as he visibly clenched his teeth.

There was no turning back now. One truth was out —six words that represented my life's torment and hung in the air between us like a visceral cloud of bleak desperation.

"What makes you think you'll find that here?"

"I don't know that I will, but there's nowhere else to look without getting myself well and truly killed. I've tried everything I can think of, but she's being held by a man who's not only well protected but also paranoid. He's never in public. Never alone. And the place where he's holed up is impenetrable."

Shit. Why was I telling him this? Every detail I

disclosed only made me more vulnerable. Made the secrets and lies I was keeping harder to withhold.

I knew better, yet I couldn't seem to stop myself. "I need to find a way to get to her. To get her away from him. And then, I need to disappear."

My legs began to tremble, and my throat burned. I'd been holding on for so long, physically and mentally, but not to Dex. After a year of holding on to hope for Yelena, despair was winning.

The fight was wearing me down.

"I can get her out," he said, his stony gaze still fixed to mine.

His promise was a glimmer of light in my pit of darkness, and despite my doubtful heart and better judgment, I couldn't help but take the bait. "How? You don't even know where she is. Or how impossible the mission is."

"I have my ways. Hell, I found you, and I didn't even know your name. I can help you, Kira."

"Why would you do that? You're a fucking hitman, not a mercenary."

His eyes fell longingly to my lips. "Let's call it a professional courtesy. I'll help you, and you'll give me what I want in return."

"Forget it." Feet hitting the floor, I pushed at his chest to put distance between us, even though my body protested the move. "I'm not sleeping with you."

A low, cocky laugh rumbled through him. "If you say so, kitten."

"It's never going to happen, you arrogant prick."

His smile faded again, replaced by the sexy scowl he'd somehow perfected. "Listen, I have a feeling our goals are much more aligned than you realize. We'll find a way past Rykov's defenses together. You'll get your sister, and I'll put an end to the threat against my life. Deal?"

I swallowed hard, wondering if this could work. Could I sustain the lies long enough to get what we both wanted? Could I live with myself if I didn't at least try?

In this situation, the only sure thing was that someone would die.

"I didn't say Rykov had her."

"You didn't need to."

Fuck, if he could see through this simple ruse, what else had I given away? "How'd you figure it out?"

"I know Rykov's second in command when I see him, and I'm no genius, but it doesn't take much to put two and two together."

Shit, he thought Sasha was after me because he was following Nikolai's orders. If only that were true. If only it were that straightforward. Still, it might make my ploy a little easier to pull off.

"But if we're going to work together, we'll need some trust. That means no lies."

I closed my eyes, forcing back the truth that was trying to crawl its way up my throat. "I guess I can do that."

"Good. But let's get one thing clear…" The harsh edge of his voice had my eyes snapping open. "I don't give a shit about anyone or anything other than my mission, and if you fuck me over, I won't think twice about taking you out. I won't be made a scapegoat. Not even for a hot piece of pussy. Got it?"

God, he was an asshole, even if he unknowingly had a reason to be. Still, I didn't believe him. Not that he wouldn't end my life if it came down to it. My death was the most likely scenario, especially if he uncovered the orders I'd been issued—the deadly mandate I'd had no choice but to follow.

But not giving a shit? No. He would've simply walked away if that were true.

"Yes, I fucking get it."

"Don't worry, kitten, you can trust me. And as long as you remember I'm the one in charge, we'll be just fine. We'll make this work, I promise."

A man like him could never be trusted, no matter how pretty the promise sounded, but if there was any chance of saving Yelena, I had to take it. Even if it put my life at risk and my stupid, naïve heart full of hope in the line of fire.

"Okay." I searched his face for signs of a trap, but all I could see was calm.

"Okay then, we got ourselves a deal."

"Let's stick to calling it a professional courtesy. Anything else sounds like I'm getting in bed with the devil."

His wide, sarcastic smile taunted me, and he laughed when I rolled my eyes at the realization of what I'd said.

"Fine, kitten, we'll call it whatever you want. But I promise, you're going to change your mind about sex.

You're so keyed up right now, I could have you coming on my cock in one stroke."

My core pulsed with unfulfilled need, not minding the sound of that option one bit. Thank God my vagina wasn't in control here.

"You really are an arrogant son of a bitch," I said, attempting to cover my lustful thoughts.

"Yes, but I think you like that about me."

Lord fucking help me, but I thought I did, too.

What the hell was wrong with me? He was a killer. A man who used a code name to hide his identity. A beast of intimidating, yet sexy fucking proportions. He was supposed to be the enemy—not only my target, but possibly my biggest regret waiting to happen.

And I was ferociously turned on by him.

How the hell would I be able to save my sister without ending up dead, and keep my hands off him in the process?

CHAPTER
EIGHT
DEX

Kira snarled at me, the messy smudge of her lipstick making her look something like a rabid animal. She was adorably spectacular.

The temptation to kiss her again was fierce, and next to impossible to ignore.

I wanted more. More of her bruising lips, thrusting tongue, and biting teeth. More of her scathing words, rough touches, and unfiltered temper. I wanted it all. Her raw emotion. Fuck, I welcomed it.

Welcomed the way she made me *feel*.

But how stupidly obsessed could I be? Feelings were pointless, especially when all I really needed was some information and a good lay.

I should've run in the opposite direction from her. From anything so goddamn potent. Instead, I was drawn inexplicably to her. Just like the old saying, a moth to a flame. Only, I wasn't sure which of us would be getting burned.

I moved toward her, intent on taking what I wanted, unconcerned about the repercussions. What harm could a little fire do, anyway? So what if I lost a bit of my restraint? The cage of my control was still intact, and that's all that mattered.

A sudden noise in the hallway disrupted the moment. The sound of someone else's hushed argument moving toward us, threatening to expose us, had me wrestling my senses back in line.

I pushed away the craving, fighting hard against the distraction. With strong and practiced discipline, I took back control. *Of everything*.

I motioned for Kira to be quiet, bringing her attention to the noise in the hall.

"You know the influence in that room, and you act like this? You're such an embarrassment," a woman hissed.

"It's not her fault," a man replied. His words were tough, but his tone was yielding.

Another younger sounding woman argued, "I'm not even that drunk."

Despite only hearing parts, it was obvious the conversation wasn't about the missing guard, Russian gangsters, or finding us.

With Kira's help, I ensured the comatose guard would stay that way a while longer, then dragged him behind the desk to hide him from view.

"What's the plan?" she whispered, leaning over the unconscious man.

I beckoned her closer. "Follow my lead." Then, I kissed her hard and fast.

She didn't argue. Not even when I dragged my thumb over her bottom lip, smearing what was left of her lipstick down her chin. In fact, her dazed expression begged me to do it again.

Instead, I ran my crimson-covered thumb over my collar and loosened my tie.

With her hand in mine, I led the way to what I calculated was our best chance to escape. I paused to mess my hair a little and yanked the door open on a whimsical laugh. Together, we stumbled into the hall, taking our hostess and her companions—the young couple I'd seen making out in the main room—by surprise.

"Oh, excuse us." I faked nervousness, running a hand down the front of my suit.

"What the hell?" Madison Alexander snarled.

This woman was no slouch. She was half her husband's age, but possibly twice as savage. She played the game, knew the score, and had no qualms about proving it.

"Would you believe we were looking for the restroom?" Kira dared.

The drunk girl's expression crumpled. At first, I thought she might break down in tears, but instead, she doubled over in hysterics. The man beside her looked at me with wide, shocked eyes. It was a look of recognition, although I had no idea who he was. At that moment, I didn't have room to care.

"You have a lot of nerve, crashing my fundraiser and

entering where you're not invited. Fucking in my husband's office," Madison seethed.

"You're right," I said. "We should be ashamed. If it's any consolation, you throw a fabulous party, and we only made out a little. I couldn't talk her into sex."

The young woman snorted a laugh and fell backward onto her ass.

"Oh, for God's sake." Madison's arms flailed in exasperation. "Theo, will you please get her out of my sight?"

"Come on, Eve." He crouched in front of the hapless girl, who I now recognized as Bowen's daughter, and who was still giggling uncontrollably, despite her stepmother's glower. "Let's go get you cleaned up."

He helped her to her feet and led her away, but not before throwing another suspicious look in my direction.

"We'll just show ourselves out." I moved to leave, pulling Kira after me.

"No." Madison sidestepped in front of us, blocking our path. She stood like a sentinel with her hands on her hips and her nose in the air. "I don't know who you are. I honestly don't care. But I know my husband was interested in you." Her eyes trailed to Kira. "He was very interested in *you*."

"We were just talking. Nothing serious."

Madison's hard, heartless laugh had my hackles raising further. "Women don't just talk to Bowen. If he wants you, he'll have you. It's only a matter of time. So, you're going to do us both a favor and get it over with now."

"I don't understand," I interrupted. "You want your husband to sleep with someone else?"

"It's better that way." Her lips twisted to an ugly scowl. "He takes his curiosities out on someone else, then comes back to me when he's done. He always comes back to me, and he's always nicer when it's over."

The fingers Kira had linked with mine squeezed, her grip turning almost painful. "Sorry," she whispered, "I tried."

With a final crush of my hand, she tore away from me, hurling herself toward our hostess.

She clutched Madison's throat, turning her attempted scream into a strangled squawk. Madison's head hit the wall like a hammer, but Kira's momentum didn't stop. Their bodies crashed roughly as Kira applied more pressure, putting her weight and muscle into her vice grip around the panicked woman's neck.

It all happened quickly, but I watched it unfold as though in slow motion, enraptured by the graceful, brutal elegance of Kira's every move.

This was the wildcat. A fierce and deadly creature.

Such a beautiful fucking thing.

As Kira's threat loomed large above her, Madison's façade crumbled. Her cold bitterness gave way to agony, and terror filled her eyes. "Please." A desperate tear tumbled down her cheek as she gasped for mercy.

Kira's arm shook. It was a tiny detail that someone

else might've overlooked or explained away as fatigue or strain. But I knew better. I'd felt the same tremor right before she'd stopped fighting me. That's when guilt and reluctance had taken over her features, and she'd been unable to look me in the eye.

She was a capable fighter, but she had a terrible flaw. One that could cause her to slip at any moment. It was an unpredictable problem that might mean the difference between life or death.

Wildcat had a conscience.

Not only did she give a shit, but she allowed her feelings to rule her. Which meant her threats would always be empty, and her formidable power always cut short. On her own, she'd never make it. Not in this underground society of liars, thieves, and murderers.

Not in the world where I lived.

Her shaking arm dropped from Madison's neck, and the manicured billionaire bride gasped for air the way a porn star sucked dick—with a whole lot of drama and noise.

"Quiet." I glared, my patience and options running thin. "We're leaving, and you're coming with us."

"What?" Kira croaked.

I gave her a sharp look, warning her not to question me.

Surprisingly, she complied, backing off as I roughly grabbed Madison by her boney arm, pulling her away from the spot where she cowered.

Immediately, the rich bitch began to complain. "No. I'm not going anywhere."

"Shut up," I snarled. "One more sound from you and it'll be my hand around your neck. And I promise you, sweetheart, I won't let go."

I didn't bother waiting for her response. With my fingers gripped tightly, I led her toward the exit, hoping she'd be enough leverage to keep us alive. Kira kept pace, our hurried steps gaining speed as we made our escape.

On high alert, I was ready for a strike at any moment, but we made it to the service elevator without a problem.

"I don't like this." Kira shifted beside me as I willed the elevator to move faster, tapping the call button repeatedly.

Finally, the doors slid open, revealing an empty car.

Madison needed a nudge to get on, but at least she went in silence. I clasped Kira's hand again, and we stepped in together, blocking our hostage from leaving.

When the doors closed behind me, I took a steadying breath. Nothing had gone as expected. All my plans were once again totally fucked up. I was running on pure instinct and adrenaline, without a clue what came next.

All because of Kira.

She was a distraction. A gorgeous, hot as sin diversion I couldn't afford to get lost in. The smartest thing would've been to walk away, leave her to fend for herself, and disappear along with my brother.

Yet, I couldn't.

Not after the trouble I'd gone through to find her. Not after the thrill of that fucking kiss.

And not when both our lives, and my entire purpose for being, depended on taking down the same evil prick. Especially since Kira knew where to find him, and I didn't.

It was obvious she was lying, or at the very least, holding something back, and she was just as likely to get me killed as I was to get her naked. Still, I couldn't leave her or her sister to a fate like Emily's. Couldn't leave another woman to die on my watch. I was no hero, but there was something I could do to help them.

I could kill the man at the top of my list.

Nikolai Rykov would die, and Kira would be the one to lead me to him.

She leaned into me, bringing me back to the moment as she whispered, "Do you think Sasha will be waiting for us?"

Sasha. The name sliced through my gut.

Not because I particularly feared or loathed him. Until that moment, I hadn't cared one way or another about Rykov's second in command. He was merely a problem to solve. Another man to kill, even if he hadn't been part of my plan.

But Kira said his name in a way that sounded not only familiar, but almost intimate, and suddenly, I was filled with irrational jealousy. Fucking drowning in it.

Shit. Maybe Finn really wasn't the unstable twin, after all.

"I don't know what you want but you're not going

to get it," Madison interrupted. "You can't outrun my husband. No one can."

Kira seethed. "Lady, we don't give a shit about your husband."

She was right. Bowen Alexander was the least of our worries. He was a measured man. Predictable, with a public image to protect. Not like Rykov's gang.

Sasha Novikoff might've only been the right hand of a maniac, but it still made him dangerous. Deadly.

I pulled Kira closer, stroking my thumb over the side of hers. "We'll see who's waiting when these doors open. Better be prepared."

"Here." She snaked her free hand up, under her dress, producing the gun she'd stolen from the guard and revealing a hell of a lot of leg in the process.

My drumming heart beat harder. "You're trusting me?"

"With the gun, yes."

"Only with the gun, kitten?"

"Yes, *Corbin*." She smirked, her voice smooth and inviting. "Only with the gun."

The elevator shuddered to a stop as we reached the first underground parking level. Reluctantly, I moved my gaze from Kira and dragged Madison to the front of the car. With my new weapon trained on her, she didn't put up a fight.

"Stay behind me," I barked at Kira.

I was ready for a barrage of gunfire, but when the metal doors parted, the only thing that greeted us was silence.

With a hard shove, I sent Madison into the open. If Rykov's men were waiting to shoot, I had no qualms about making her their target. She stumbled out the door…and nothing happened.

Uncertainly, she looked around the space that was out of my view before turning back to me with a raccoon-eyed sneer. "There's no one here."

Regardless of the silence, and even with the calm ridicule in her voice, I didn't trust her.

Waving the gun, I motioned for her to get back on the elevator. She understood the threat and did as I instructed, but not without a dramatic sigh and roll of her eyes.

As soon as she was within reach, I grabbed her again, pointing the weapon in her face. "If you're lying to me, I'm going to put a bullet in your head."

"Stop." Kira boldly stepped out from behind me, into the open doorway.

My heart pumped so erratically I was afraid it might burst. "Don't you dare. I'm in charge," I reminded her as her toe inched over the metal grate.

She turned to face me with a sad shake of her head and stepped backward onto the concrete.

"No!" I pushed Madison aside, tossing her carelessly across the elevator.

Kira's amber eyes widened as I tackled her, throwing my body around hers like a shield. The momentum took us to the ground, sending hot flames of pain searing through my recently stitched-up shoulder, which took the brunt of our fall as we landed.

But still, nothing fucking happened.

No screams. No gunshots. Not even a passing threat.

Just Madison Alexander laughing and cursing at us as she disappeared behind the closing elevator doors.

"You fucking idiot." Kira slapped hard at my chest. "Get off of me!"

Slowly, I released her. With a pained grunt, I rolled to a crouch to take a hard look around the empty cavern of the parking garage.

Cold sweat trailed down the back of my neck. This had been too easy. There should've been armed guards, crazy Russian gangsters, or even a pissed off partygoer to slow us down. It made no sense for us to simply stroll out, unscathed.

But with Madison headed back to the penthouse—back to blab to her husband, no doubt—we didn't have time to sit and ponder our lucky break.

Not that I believed in shit like luck, anyway.

"Come on." I reached for Kira's hand again, but she refused, giving me a hard glare instead as she swiped her little purse off the ground.

Her rejection sat heavily on my chest, but I pushed away the sensation, choking down the last of my unwelcome softness toward her. "We need to get out of here. Now."

"Well, you wanted to be in charge. So, lead the way."

The Lambo sat in the back corner of the lot like a pretty picture of salvation. When I clicked the key fob, the car's lights flashed bright and sexy.

"Seriously?" Kira ran a finger over the hood, an impressed appreciation lighting her beautiful face. "This is a gorgeous machine."

Her hair was a tangled mess, and one long lock of it curled around her throat. Dirt was smudged down the side of her dress, and her skin was dotted with perspiration. Still, her disheveled beauty put the car to shame.

"Get in," I ordered, done with my own weakness and feeling out of control.

The Lambo roared to life, and I basked in the potent thrill of having a beast like this under my charge. Still, I drove with caution, surveying the garage in anticipation of trouble at each turn. Even when we moved into busy Manhattan traffic, I remained alert and vigilant.

"I need to go home," Kira murmured.

I glanced at her, hoping to understand where her head was at and why she thought she had any say at all.

Face pinched with concern and chest heaving with each anxious breath, she looked like a wild thing. Rebellious and unruly. Just like the material of her dress, which had bunched and fallen between her long, smooth, bare legs.

Legs that had felt exceptional wrapped snugly around my waist.

"Not going to happen." I dragged my attention back to the road, but I still caught her movements from the corner of my eye.

Body contracting like a panther ready to pounce, she inched a hand closer to the blade strapped around her upper thigh. "You don't understand. I have to."

"Too bad. Unless you want to lead the assholes tailing us straight to your front door."

Long blonde hair lashed around her as she twisted in her seat, straining to look out the rear window.

"Fuck." She slammed the seat hard with her hand. "Fucking motherfucker!"

"Whoa, kitten." I dared to run a hand over her knee as we stopped at a red light. "Take it easy on the car. It's a rental."

Eyes fixed on the traffic behind us, she urged, "You have to get us out of here."

"Don't worry. I'll lose them once we're out of Manhattan."

"Out of the city?" Her head whipped back to me, and her amber eyes were vicious. "Where the hell do you think you're taking me?"

"If you trusted me with the gun, then you can trust me in this car. Just think of it as another loaded weapon."

Her frown intensified. "The light's green." She pushed my hand off her knee and retreated to her side of the car, her eyes glued to the side mirror.

We drove at a crawl through Manhattan, and it became even more obvious the black Cadillac SUV, two cars back, really was shadowing us. Every lane change and turn I made was mimicked. Every red light I ran, it followed.

From this distance, with the darkly tinted windows, it was impossible to see who was driving, but I had zero doubt the vehicle was carrying Nikolai Rykov's thugs, and it was likely Sasha at the wheel.

Finally, we hit the expressway, but the Cadillac continued to tail us. They picked up speed, the grill of the large SUV taking over my rearview as they eliminated much of the space between us.

"Dex!" Kira's panic invaded my composure, threatening to knock me off course.

But I took another sharp breath and regained my balance. "It's all right, kitten, I've got this."

I tapped the paddle shifter and slammed my foot heavily on the accelerator. The Lambo shot forward like a rocket, jolting us back in our seats. Riding the wave of exhilaration, I white-knuckled the wheel, keeping it all under control.

Kira looked back over her shoulder again as I weaved in and out of the slower moving traffic. "We're losing them," she said through an amazed laugh. "This car is fucking awesome. How fast does it go?"

"I'm not sure." My laser focus shifted as I stole a glimpse of her luscious beauty. "Want to find out?"

CHAPTER
NINE
KIRA

"Hell, yes." The car was flying, and so was I, high on a whirlwind of conflicting emotions.

Dex let loose that gorgeous, sinister grin of his, and shifted another gear.

It'd been a night of calamity. Fuck, it had been a year of catastrophes, each one worse than the last, but in a yellow Lamborghini, traveling down the highway at death-trap speeds, and with the black SUV falling farther and farther behind us, I felt oddly free of those burdens.

Free from all the searching, lying, and fighting. The misery and misfortune. Even from Sasha and his merry band of killers. I was free to simply be alive. To enjoy riding in a fast car.

The feeling stretched and consumed me. It was a rushing, building sensation. Like an orgasm, only better.

This was liberation.

Dex shifted gears again, blowing past traffic and

breaking a handful of laws in the process. A shiver ran down my spine as I watched him, a master behind the wheel.

He drove as though possessed. No second guesses. No fear. He was one with this magnificent car. Each time I thought it impossible to go any faster, he nudged the needle just a tiny bit more.

Every maneuver was precision. Every choice, calm and calculated. Smooth and sexy, he was in total control, and it scared the ever-loving fuck out of me.

Not because with one wrong move he could cause us to crash, and not because he was dangerous—although, with a single look at his bulging arms and thick, wall-like chest, anyone could see the threat he posed. And it wasn't because he'd flat-out said he'd kill me if I went against him, either.

No. My fear had sprouted from somewhere much deeper. Because, despite his cocksure attitude, lethal capabilities, and my death warrant already signed, I was ridiculously attracted to him.

He was a manipulative, callous murderer for hire I was meant to double cross, and I wanted him more fiercely than anyone before.

It was disgusting.

This man should've repulsed me. I hated everything he stood for, everything he claimed to be. He was a killer. Cold blooded and cold fucking hearted. I'd have been smarter getting off with my own fingers, or the rumbled vibrations of the goddamn car. Yet, I was stupidly desperate for him, the hot ache at the juncture of my thighs beyond distracting.

But no matter how far off the rails my libido was running, now wasn't the time to be weak. Not with a man like him.

Not with Bodhi Decker.

I turned to stare out the window, tamping down hard on my wildly swinging emotions and out-of-control urges, and allowed my vision to relax and soften as I watched the world pass by in a blur.

Eventually, my eyes drifted closed. When I opened them, the car had slowed, and we were heading down an off-ramp.

"Where are we?" I straightened in my seat, apprehension flooding my system all over again.

"Connecticut."

"Did we lose them? Are you turning around to take me home?"

His jaw twitched and the corner of his eye was lined with tension, but he didn't look at me—not even a glance.

He also didn't answer me.

What in the hell was happening here? He'd coaxed me with a promise, teased me with a kiss, had given me little to no choice but to follow him, and now he wouldn't even speak to me. He'd basically abducted me.

Shit. I'd given him a gun. Was I his prisoner? Did he somehow know who I was and what I'd been ordered to do?

We'd crossed state lines and were headed to an undisclosed location, where he'd probably do unspeakable things to me, for God only knew how long…and *fuck me*, even that idea had my body humming with need.

Something inside me was very, very broken.

I turned back to watch out the window again as we eventually rolled into a picturesque city. There weren't any signs to welcome us to town, or perhaps I'd just missed them, but it felt inviting, regardless. Even with my future at risk and a hitman at my side.

It was peaceful. The buildings were large and pretty, set back off the street, with trees clustered in yards and on corners. And even in the dark, under the warm halo of streetlights, everything looked green and lush. It looked like the type of place where people were fruitful and happy.

Where they didn't just survive. They *thrived*.

"We need to ditch the car," he mused as we prowled through the sleepy streets. "We need to stay hidden."

"We're going into hiding?"

"Yes, Kira. If you want to rescue your sister, we need a plan. That means gathering information and resources. Everything you've got. Which also means we need to lay low for a few days while we figure it out."

His words brought reality crashing back down around me. My life was in shambles, and there was no turning back. This place, this car, this feeling of being free—it was all an illusion. A lie. And just like all the other lies I'd told, when this one broke apart, there was only bleak and bitter disappointment left in its wake.

"There's nothing to figure out. Yelena's gone, and I'll never get her back because you've fucked up my last chances." My nose stung as I forced away the tears.

"I thought you wanted my help. You still don't trust me, kitten?"

Rage flashed through me. It mixed with my never-ending sadness, swelling my throat and blurring my vision. I was weak. Helpless.

Hopeless.

I hated those feelings, and Dex even more for inciting them. "Can we be done with this charade, already?" I shifted in my seat until I was practically screaming in his face. "You're not going to save the damsel in distress. You're just going to use me to get what you want. You can't fool me into believing you're the good guy. You're a killer. A murderer. Men like you are the reason she needs saving in the first place."

The car swerved viciously, flinging me sideways and knocking my head against the window. Just as suddenly, I was jolted forward, the seatbelt pulling painfully across my chest as the car came to a dead stop at the side of the road.

"What the fuck?" I gasped, rubbing at the exposed and now tender skin between my breasts.

In silence, he gripped the wheel, knuckles white with tension. When he finally turned to me, it was with a hard, deadly glare. "Men like me? Or men like Sasha Novikoff?"

A new pain flared through my chest. It flashed and burned, leaving me breathless. Speechless. Suddenly, I wished my frivolous little clutch was big enough to hold more than just my keys, cellphone, and lip gloss, because the idea of carrying a gun didn't seem so terrible right now.

"You don't know me." His low, chilling voice raised the hairs on the back of my neck. "You think I kill randomly? No care? No selection?" His lips twisted into a threatening sneer as his hands wrung tightly over the wheel. "You don't know a goddamn thing. I'm not just a killer, Kira. I'm an exterminator. Men like me are the reason people in this country can sleep at night."

"But you get paid to do it," I whispered, holding on to my only defense.

He slammed his hand hard on the console. "Who cares if one criminal pays me to kill another? Am I supposed to feel guilty for that?"

His hard blue stare didn't falter, but for the first time, his cool disposition slipped, and I couldn't help but wonder if I'd grossly misjudged him.

Were there real feelings hidden beneath his cocky veneer, or was this simply more manipulation? Maybe he wasn't the cold, ruthless man I'd thought. Or maybe he was. Either way, it was a problem, because I clearly couldn't trust myself around him.

Still, his question hung in the air between us like a loaded weapon. *Should he feel guilty*? How in the hell was I supposed to know that, when all I felt was repentance, rage, and sadness?

The agony of those feelings was my driving force. I let them fuel and guide me, let them take right the fuck over whenever they wanted. I might not be a killer, but the mistakes I'd made and the crimes I'd committed had cost others their lives, and worse. Far, far worse.

Lost in a pool of conflicting emotions, I avoided his intense scrutiny. I went back to staring out my window, grazing my fingers over the tender spot on the side of my head.

After a long, painful silence, Dex finally gave up on getting an answer from me. Putting the car into gear, he drove another few blocks before pulling into a hospital parking garage. The overhead lights cast deep shadows, and we circled the center of the structure before stopping in a spot between concrete pillars.

"Get out," he ordered, his hands still frozen on the wheel and the engine still running.

Closing my eyes on a sigh, I unbuckled myself, grabbed my fancy clutch, and swung the door open. Defeat set in when my feet hit the ground.

Guess I'm not his captive, after all.

Fuck, why did that thought disappoint me?

I was free to keep failing, all on my own, and to face the consequences of my deception. The repercussions of failing Nikolai. Of running from Sasha.

Of being such a hot-headed, impulsive fool.

The car door echoed when I closed it behind me, the sound loud and final. I stood for a moment, waiting. Hoping. But the car continued to idle, and I realized there'd never really been any hope in this situation. It never could've ended any other way than bad.

Had fate ever been on my side?

My heels clicked over the pavement, my heart sinking further with each step, but I kept putting one foot in front of the other, my head held high.

Fall down seven times, stand up eight.

The soft purr of the engine died suddenly, followed by the slam of a door.

"This way." He cut in front of me, heading toward the exit with a backpack slung over his shoulder.

Silently, I thanked the universe and followed without question.

Once out of the garage, he stalked across the adjacent parking lot like a prowler dressed in Armani. The harsh lights cast long shadows, concealing him in plain sight. He was a mystery of the night. Part of the darkness. Enigmatic and deadly.

Despite the warmth of late summer, a chill ran through me as I strode to keep up. We moved toward the emergency entrance, and I caught my reflection in the sliding glass doors.

Fucking hell. I looked like a high-class hooker on a three-day bender…after a bar fight. Messy hair, smudged makeup, and a dirty dress that showed off all my assets. Not that I had much to show, but my neckline was exposed almost to my navel and my bare legs flashed with each long stride.

Thankfully, we kept walking past the ER entrance, and I didn't have to stare at myself for too long. Didn't have to face the person I'd become, the choices I'd made, or the next terrible decision I'd soon have to face.

We walked around the building, the lights dimming

the farther we went, until Dex stopped beside a door marked "Exit Only". He didn't try to open it, just dropped his bag to the ground and leaned against the wall, his gaze anywhere but on me.

I didn't know what we were doing here, hanging around a hospital in some unknown town in Connecticut, but I didn't have the balls to question him.

I might've been standing, but all my fight had been lost to anguish. It hounded my conscience, making me weak. The hope of saving Yelena still seemed distant, maybe next to impossible, but it was the fear for Anya's future that was breaking me down. Cracking my goddamn soul.

What if she lost me, too?

The thought was debilitating. So, instead of entertaining it, I took Dex's lead and looked for something else to occupy my attention. Anything, other than him.

After a long, drawn-out silence, and after making one too many useless wishes on one too many stars, the magnetic door lock clicked open and three women in scrubs filed out. They were chatting animatedly and didn't seem to notice Dex waiting against the wall, but they sure did notice me.

Perhaps, it was only because I was hard to miss, standing in the middle of their path. Still, I wondered what they must be thinking. What kind of woman did they see?

Hopefully not a whore, because this dress hadn't been cheap.

Two of the women cast me sideways glances as they

passed, each lighting a cigarette as they carried on their way. But the third woman paused, popping a stick of gum in her mouth as she looked at me with concerned curiosity written on her pretty face.

"Hope you weren't planning to join them," Dex grumbled from behind her. He stepped out of the shadows, motioning to the other women who'd paused to smoke a few feet away. "Your friends?"

She smiled sweetly, not shocked at all by his appearance. "I'm just out for some fresh air."

"That better be the truth. I'd hate to think you're succumbing to peer pressure. The bad girl vibe doesn't suit you, and there will be consequences."

"You said you were taking a break." Her hands landed squarely on her hips. "Yet, here you are, and you look like crap. Don't get on my back about bad habits I don't even have, especially when yours are obviously much worse."

"It's my job to look after you." He leaned toward her, menace clear in his tone and posture. "Break or no break."

"What are you doing here, Bodhi?" His real name left her lips on a frustrated sigh, shocking me and making me wonder the same.

Why were we here? Who the hell was this woman?

"I need a favor."

"Let me guess, you opened it back up, didn't you?"

His glare intensified. "Yes, smart-ass. I need access to your place. Not sure for how long. You should probably find somewhere else to stay for a little while."

She looked pensive, maybe a bit worried, but she nodded in agreement. "Okay, I can do that. You know what's mine is yours. Always."

He didn't respond to her softness, but the tight knit of his brow eased a bit as he dipped his head, his gaze landing at my feet.

"Are you any good with stitches?" She turned, addressing me like we were old friends. Like it was perfectly normal to find Dex with a disheveled woman in a cocktail dress, hanging outside a hospital in the middle of the night.

"Not really," I answered honestly.

"Yeah, I didn't think so. You look more the type to cause the injury than to fix it."

Dex barked a loud and shocking laugh. Rich and melodic, it echoed through the stillness, bringing the night to life. Suddenly, the moon glowed a little brighter, and the stars seemed to twinkle in delight.

My insides sparked as well, shrugging off the tired gloom. This wasn't a show of cocky sarcasm. He wasn't getting off on his own joke or aiming to pull anyone in with his charm. This laugh was unfiltered. Genuine.

And fuck, I liked it. A lot.

The woman's eyes widened as she stared at me in awe. "You're the one."

"The one?" I raised a single eyebrow, intrigued by her assuredness.

"Shut up, Sunshine." His voice was hard now, no trace of humor remaining.

With her focus fixed on me, she ignored Dex's

growled warning. "Yes, the one. He told me about you." She leaned closer, inviting me to do the same, and whispered, "He said he had to chase you down."

"Seriously, Sunny, shut your mouth."

"He's a bossy grump," she said, clearly not concerned for her personal safety. "But don't let that turn you off. His heart is in the right place, and I think he may have a crush on you."

"Sunshine. Last chance."

With a brilliant smile, she straightened and turned, throwing her arms around his shoulders, making him wince. "I hope she's the reason you need new stitches."

She was lovable, patient, and gutsy as hell. Whoever she was, I adored her, even though her words had my stomach twisting in knots.

"The spare key for the house is in the usual spot, and my car is in the garage if you need it." She nudged his tense shoulder before backing away. "Now, since I'm an adult, I'm going to go poison my lungs with some secondhand smoke and gossip about you with the girls. Nice to meet you…"

"Kira," Dex offered before I had the chance.

His usual sexy scowl was firmly in place, yet his tone was layered with admiration. He said my name softly, his voice stroking over the word, making it sound important. Like I was important. Like this woman, Sunshine, was right, and he might've actually fucking cared.

The knots in my stomach pulled tight all at once.

The stars blurred out of focus, and I swayed on my feet as air trapped in my lungs on a silent gasp.

Suddenly, his arm was wrapped around me, keeping me upright. "You all right?"

Nodding, I pushed out of his hold. "Just tired," I lied, still struggling to breathe.

Was it possible that Bodhi Decker—a cocksure, cold-blooded killer—was actually the good fortune I'd been wishing for?

If so, the universe had a sick sense of humor.

And I was in far too much trouble to laugh.

CHAPTER
TEN
DEX

Sticking to the shadows, I stole through the sleepy streets with Kira trailing behind me. The walk to the house was short, but with her silence stretching like a cavern between us, it felt more like I was climbing Everest.

She'd been subdued since my outburst, shrugging off my assistance, avoiding my touch, and refusing to even look me in the eye. But maybe that was a good thing.

After blowing up at her in the car, I wasn't sure I should be near her. Or how much more of our game I could withstand. She was pushing the limits of my control, rattling my fucking cage, and I didn't know how to correct course.

I sure as hell didn't know how to be nice, or if I should even bother to try. As Kira had reminded me, that wasn't the type of man I'd become. Even pretending to be the good guy in this situation would do nothing more than get me killed.

Not only me, but my whole family, and probably Kira and her sister, too.

Only, it was too late to walk away.

I was spellbound. At least, that's what I might've called it if I'd believed in things like magic, because I'd been obsessed with her from the day we met. It was unreasonable. Inexplicable. Possibly the stupidest goddamn position I'd ever allowed myself to fall into.

My only justification was that she knew the one thing I didn't. She knew where to find Nikolai Rykov.

His location was not only a well-guarded secret but one of the biggest unsolved mysteries of my life. Finn and I had been unsuccessful at getting even a hint at the information, and we'd been searching for a full damn year.

The possibility that Kira had innocently stumbled across it, or even discovered it through some sort of super sleuthing, was low. So, how had she figured it out?

I had a feeling I already knew the answer, even if I was reluctant to believe it.

We crossed into Sunshine's neighborhood, and the house came into view. Similar to the rest of the homes in this area, it was a nondescript red brick colonial with a black roof and shutters and a pillared front porch.

It was old and filled with too much of my history, but we needed somewhere safe to crash. And after a night full of the unexpected, I wanted a place I was familiar with. For now.

Coming here was a huge risk. Not only for us, but for my sister and everyone in this town. I just hoped I wouldn't regret it.

But with Rykov's men on our asses, we'd had to get off the road. We'd been too easy to spot in that ridiculously flashy car, and I'd have bet my life Sasha had called for reinforcements. Hell, I wouldn't have been surprised if every goddamn member of the Bratva was out patrolling for us. We needed to hunker down and stay out of sight for a while. At least until I could come up with a plan. Until Kira gave me the truth about how I'd wound up in this mess to begin with, and how the hell we'd get out of it.

Until I could figure out how to put an end to Nikolai Rykov.

I was fishing for the spare key from the jar of nails in the garage when she finally caught up to me. Disheveled and sporting a few new bruises, no thanks to me, she looked utterly exhausted. Yet, there was still a glint of determination in her eyes. Despite getting knocked around and knowing the odds were stacked against her, she was like a prize fighter, refusing to fall.

Beautiful, resilient, and still tempting as hell.

Silently, I unlocked the door to the house and held it open for her in invitation. She slinked past me, carefully avoiding contact, with her gaze aimed at the ground.

I hit the button to close the garage door and then followed her inside, flicking on the light.

The French country-style kitchen that greeted us was clean and spacious. I dropped my bag on the old, scratched-up table and tried to ignore the assault of memories beating at my brain.

This place was a far cry from where I'd grown up, but it was filled with things from my past, and it reminded me too much of the life I'd had before all this death and carnage.

Before my father fucked off to start another family, Mom lost her battle with cancer, and long ahead of Emily being murdered. Before everything had gone to shit.

My family had sat around this table for every meal we could. Not always all at once, and not always in harmony, but on those occasions when we were together —Finn, Sunshine, Mom, Dad, and me—we'd been happy.

We'd talked about our days, laughed at stupid jokes, had petty arguments, and just lived. We'd never thought much about the bad in this world. At least, I never did.

Hell, Finn and I had planned a life in the military, and still, all I'd ever seen was the good. The possibility of helping others and living an honest, respectable life.

Even later, after Dad had gone, after the Marine Corps had spit me out, and with my secret love for Emily festering in my veins, I only ever thought things would turn out all right. I'd figured if happily ever after wasn't in the cards for me, at least I had the love of my family.

I never could've conceived of this endless, bleak,

and bloodied spiral I existed in now. Never could've imagined I'd be able to live with such an empty, savage heart.

I'd been a blind goddamn idiot.

"So, Sunshine?" Kira's question broke through the invasion of melancholy bullshit, circling my mind.

She still refused to meet my eyes, but at least she'd started a conversation.

"What about her?"

Her arms were crossed under her breasts, drawing my attention to the neckline of her dress and the expanse of flesh it exposed. "How do you know her?"

Was that a hint of jealousy in her tone? Given her words from the car, it seemed unfathomable. Yet, it was there all the same, and it made me feel…something.

I'd intentionally pushed Kira from the moment I met her. Teased, taunted, and coerced her. Used the attraction between us, touching and kissing her, just to gain the upper hand.

And I've enjoyed every fucking minute of it all.

The idea that maybe she'd enjoyed it, too, that maybe there was more between us than deception, hostility, and her loathing…

Well, I wasn't sure I should like it so much. But I did.

"Sunny is my sister."

"Really?" Her posture remained passive, and she looked over the distressed cabinets like she was preparing to grade the workmanship, but her voice lilted upward, giving away her interest.

"You sound surprised."

"I am. I didn't picture you as much of a family man, but you two seem close."

"Why wouldn't I have a family, Kira?" My jaw tightened, and my words were roughly forced from between clenched teeth. "Because I'm a murderer?"

"No." With an adorable spark of defiance, her eyes finally snapped to mine. "Because you're so fucking full of yourself, I figured you were a spoiled only child."

There she is. My saucy little kitten.

I appreciated her bold attempt to lighten the mood, and even though I didn't feel much like laughing, I couldn't help the twitch of my lips that slowly contorted into a smile.

She smiled back. Not a wild grin or sarcastic sneer, but a soft, pretty lift of her lips. It was sweet and alluring, maybe even forgiving, and it set my frigid blood on fire.

"Definitely not an only child," I said through a light chuckle, but the sound caught in my throat as I tried to remove my jacket.

An agonizing burn engulfed my shoulder, cramping my arm and erasing my amusement. With a pained grunt, I let the most expensive piece of clothing I'd ever owned fall in a ruined heap to the floor.

"Oh, fuck." Kira's expression drew to a concerned frown.

A dark stain of blood marked the shoulder of my white dress sleeve. The crimson bloom was a stark reminder of the shitstorm of trouble we were in—the trouble that Kira had somehow helped drag me into.

"No big deal." I started to shrug but thought better of it, clenching my fist instead. "I think it's stopped bleeding. It'll be fine once I clean it up."

"That's going to be a bitch to peel off. It looks like it's stuck on good."

Her assessment was spot on. The cake of blood had almost dried, acting like an adhesive and molding the shirt to my reopened gunshot wound. Getting it off would probably hurt like hell, but it wouldn't be the first time I'd faced something like this.

Probably wouldn't be the last time, either.

"Guess it's a good thing I know where she keeps the liquor."

Kira groaned, "God, yes." And despite the excruciating ache of my arm, the rest of my body rejoiced at the seductive sound. "A drink sounds like a fabulous idea. Point me in the right direction."

I motioned to the cabinet over the fridge, and she dropped her purse on the counter before lifting her long, graceful arms to open the cupboard doors. The move opened the slits up the sides of her dress, showing off more of her fantastic legs.

I held back a growl as my dick jumped to life in my pants.

"Don't know where the glasses are, but you're resourceful, I'm sure you can figure it out. I'll be in the bathroom, down the hall. Bring the bottle." I left her to fend for herself before I was too tempted to give her a hand.

At that moment, I was willing to give her my hands, mouth, and cock, all on a silver platter. Whatever she wanted. Lady's fucking choice.

Only, she'd insisted she didn't want any of it, which meant I needed to get away from her. Far away from her messy blonde hair, tight body, and irresistible voice. I needed to rip this wound back open, so I could distract myself with the pain.

Otherwise, I'd be tempted to show her the depth and breadth of my control and prove her to be a dirty little liar.

The shirt came off easier than predicted, with only a light trickle of blood. It wasn't nearly as bad as it had been right after I'd been shot. That shit had been a disaster. This was barely a scratch.

"All I could find was a coffee mug." Kira rounded the corner with a bottle of whiskey in hand but stopped short in the doorway. She stared at the fresh drip of blood running down my arm, her mouth hanging open in shock.

I watched her shifting expression through the mirror. "All I need is the alcohol."

She didn't respond. Her eyes were fixed on my wound, her feet glued to the floor, and her hands clutched hard at the bottle of booze.

"Come on, kitten. Don't tell me an ass kicker like you is afraid of a little blood?"

"I'm not afraid. I'm tired of it." Her eyes pinched shut as though she were the one in pain, like the truth was hard for her to admit. Or maybe she was just reluctant to tell me. "I'm so fucking tired of all the violence and bloodshed, the sight of it literally makes me feel sick."

All the violence and bloodshed? How much shit had this woman seen?

"Then, you might want to turn around while I tape this back up." I pulled the first aid kit from under the sink.

One of the many perks of my sister being a nurse was that she kept herself well stocked with the best medical supplies. Sunny might've been an overbearing pain in my ass sometimes, but at least she was prepared for emergencies.

"No." Kira cracked the seal on the bottle. "I just need a shot of this, and I'll be good."

Her eyes closed again as she swallowed far more than a single shot. Or even two. She sucked the whiskey back like it was water, then wiped her mouth on the back of her hand.

"Besides," she added, seemingly unaffected, "You're going to need help."

"Don't worry, I got this. You don't need to bother."

"Yes, I do." She held the bottle out to me, her face a serious mask. "You took that bullet because of me, and I'm alive because you did."

"Well, it wasn't intentional. I wasn't trying to save your life. It was just dumb luck." I slugged back a gulp of the whiskey, but the liquor's burn couldn't compete with the sting of my words.

Although, why the truth would concern me, I hadn't a clue. Maybe it was because I still didn't believe in luck. Or maybe it was because I was starting to wish I did.

"I know." She pushed up beside me to rummage through the medical kit. "But you still did it. You saved me. Tonight, too."

"Tonight is about saving my own ass. You're just along for the ride and to give me some of the answers I need. If I can help you out along the way, then so be it."

Lips pressed in a tight line, she shook her bowed head and placed items from the kit onto the counter. With a sharp, deep breath, she turned to inspect my arm.

It seemed I'd need more time and finesse to get information out of her, but for now, it didn't matter. No matter what she was or wasn't willing to give me, we were safe for the moment, and all I really needed was to fix my injured shoulder. Regardless of how much more I might've wanted to take.

After cleaning up the excess blood, the damage didn't look as bad as I'd first thought, and the alcohol, along with some basic painkillers, was already helping to dull the pain.

Kira cut strips of medical tape, holding them out as I patched myself up. We worked in silent tandem.

But there was a weight to the unspoken words between us, and they seemed to hang like a cloud overhead. We were both morose, our banter dead. And I couldn't help feeling like I was the one who'd killed it.

"Listen, Kira—"

"I'm sorry about what I said in the car," she blurted, cutting me off. "Not for being harsh about what you do, because honestly, I still don't know if I can wrap my head around it. Killing seems so pointlessly brutal. And the money thing is just…well, it's hard for me to get past, knowing where it all comes from. Knowing the evil fucking shit these men do to get it." She paused before sliding the last piece of tape over my arm herself, her fingers gliding gently across my skin.

The touch was only to help patch my wound, but it felt like something else. Something more. It was like a token of trust or a gesture of connection, and it stirred something deep within me.

Something more than my cock.

That touch was an easing warmth against my rigid-ness. A boon to my wretched, fucked up soul. And it didn't matter that I still didn't believe in that sort of shit, there was no denying the spark was there. No denying the fucking *feelings* trying to creep up on me.

"There's a reason I don't trust you, Dex." Her voice was soft and thoughtful, just like the brush of her fingers. "But ultimately, that reason isn't your fault. It's mine. I'm sorry for judging you and for holding someone else's disgusting, vile deeds against you."

Her hand trailed down my arm before dropping away, but I caught it in mine, pulling her closer. Fingers entwined, her breath hitched as I brought our joined hands to my bare chest, resting them over the black void once known as my heart.

"Don't apologize."

She opened her mouth as though to argue, but I silenced her with a finger, placing it roughly over her succulent lips.

"You're smart not to give me your trust without some suspicion, or at least, a few questions." My rough voice strained against my growing lust. "I'm not sure I trust you much, either. But I'm willing to try. To show you I'm trustworthy. As long as you cooperate."

Her eyes moved up to mine, searching.

I stared back, allowing her assessment, hoping she could see me. All of me. Maybe she could uncover some redeeming quality I'd been unable to find in myself.

"You're right that I'm no hero. I'm not a good guy, and I know it. But I don't want to hurt you." And shit, I meant it.

Not that I ever wanted to hurt an innocent, but for the last year, I'd intentionally forgotten about the bystanders of my crimes. I was cold and heartless for a reason, and I liked it that way.

Fuck, I should've kept it that way.

My only focus should've been revenge and taking care of my family. There was no room for anything else. I certainly hadn't gone out of my way for anyone.

Kira was the first.

Her fingers tensed over my chest, driving my desire higher.

"I will help you." I trailed my finger from her lips, down her chin, to the base of her throat. "No strings attached."

"Why?"

"Because you're strong. And I understand the significance of family. Of sisters. Mine's important to me, too."

She bit the corner of her lip, and it took everything in me to hold back a groan.

"Plus, you can totally kick my ass." I smirked. "And because I want to prove you wrong. What I do may be brutal, but sometimes it's the only thing that makes sense. You need to understand that sometimes killing is necessary."

"Do you really believe that?" Her eyes bounced back and forth between mine, her pulse drumming frantically under my touch.

Eight days ago, Finn had asked a similar question, and I'd answered without hesitation, without doubt. Now, I wasn't so certain.

When she looked at me with lust alight in her expression and lips parted in a way that made me want to shove my cock between them, I started to question everything.

Most of all, my sanity.

"Yes." I explored the silk of her neck, stroking over the delicate flesh. "I think you're extraordinary. Not only an ass kicker, but the most beautiful woman I've ever met."

She swayed closer, running her free hand up to join the other, and pressed both palms seductively against my skin. She didn't reply to my compliment or call me out on my deflection. She simply stood, breathing with me in the moment.

"I'm not like him. Like Sasha," I said, wishing it were true. "I'm not like any of them."

"I believe you."

"That's a lie. But it's all right, kitten. I don't expect you to believe me. I will prove it to you, though. I promise you. We will save your sister together."

"I still don't understand why." Her gaze fell to her hands, still pressed tightly to my chest. "I'm the reason you're in this mess, and I doubt I can help get you out of it. Why would you do anything for me?"

"Kira." I pushed my fingers up under her chin, forcing her to look me in the eye again. "Rykov and his men are the reason we're both in this mess. You've been protecting yourself. That's just smart. You've outsmarted me, anyway."

She averted her gaze as an unreadable wash of emotion passed over her features.

It was such a short burst of turmoil, I didn't have time to analyze it before the furrow of her brow smoothed and she was back to being sassy. "I actually thought you were a step ahead of me, until you tackled me in the parking garage. That was pretty fucking ridiculous."

"Not my finest moment." I admitted with a chuckle. "But I was reacting to the situation. I'm a tactical thinker, and you're all impulse and attitude. You threw me off my game."

"Well, otherwise, your game's good."

I raised an eyebrow at her. "A compliment?"

"Yeah, well, don't get used to it. I'm not going to be a pushover now just because we had a heart-to-heart and I helped bandage your boo-boo." Another smile graced her luscious lips, and it was so big and wide, she practically glowed.

Fuck, she is devastating. "Good. I like it when you're feisty."

"Do you, now?" Her voice turned to a sultry seduction, beckoning me to give in. A temptation that begged me to let it all go.

But I held hard to my control. It was the only thing I had left. The only thing I still understood. "You're stunning when you're ferocious and wild, you know that? You could be deadly."

"I'm not so sure about that."

Little did she know, she was the deadliest goddamn thing—at least, for me. More lethal than Rykov's entire crew. If anyone would be the death of me, it'd be Wildcat.

And right then, I wasn't sure I cared. The pain in my shoulder took a backseat to the growing ache of my cock. Giving in just a little, I slid my hand to the back of her neck, my fingers tangling in the mess of her silky locks, and brought our mouths so close I could almost taste her.

And *fuck*, I wanted it. Wanted her. The wild, sweet, fiery, passionate intensity. All of her.

Every single delectable inch.

CHAPTER
ELEVEN
KIRA

Dex's face was serious, and his hold was hard, but when his lips finally graced mine, they were a whisper.

We lingered softly for a moment, our mouths barely brushing, our breath a warm tangle. Despite being sweet, it was electrifying. Seductive. Sensational.

This man—a man who killed others for a living— had called me wild and deadly. It seemed absurd when I was so desperate, but when he kissed me, I felt it. From the soles of my feet to the ends of my hair, I felt it.

Wild. Deadly.

It scared the shit out of me.

Because I liked that feeling—the mayhem and the madness. I craved it. Hell, I'd become it. Without it, I didn't feel like I was fighting hard enough. Didn't believe I could make it through the struggle that was my life.

He laced an arm around my upper back, holding me

in a secure embrace and trapping my arms between our bodies. "You're a fighter, Kira. A hell of a lot tougher than you believe. But by the time this is all over, you will. You won't just believe it, you'll know it. I promise."

Oh, those lovely promises, all so inviting and sweet. I was a sucker for each and every one. Especially the promise of the hard length of his growing erection pressed enticingly close to the juncture of my thighs.

I squirmed in his hold, my restless body betraying me.

"Something else bothering you, kitten?" The rumble of his deep, gruff voice was electric, and there was an edge to his tone that hinted he knew exactly what the trouble was.

How could he read me so well? Why was he always so goddamn *in charge*?

"Yes." The word escaped through a tight breath, and my body filled with untamed longing. "You were right…earlier, when we were in Alexander's office. I was thinking about sex."

"And now?" Another smirk lit his too handsome face. Clearly, he already knew the answer.

Cocky ass.

"I'm thinking about it now, too." It was a daring confession. Allowing him even a sliver of truth only made me more susceptible and moved me another step closer to giving in to him. Giving myself over to him, completely.

But the whiskey was coursing a warm and eager trail

through my system, loosening my limbs and inhibitions, and I couldn't lie to myself.

Or him, apparently.

And fuck, with the deep hunger I felt for him, I didn't want to. I was foolishly tempted to crack my secrets, my legs, and maybe even my heart, wide open.

My core clenched at the thought. "I want it."

"Yeah, you do," he murmured, his cool arrogance driving me out of my skin.

"Fuck you. I don't want to want it."

He inclined his head toward me and for a moment I thought he was going to kiss me for real—for a moment, I was ravenous for it—but his mouth moved to the shell of my ear, grazing over it.

Tingles burst over my skin as his breath ran an inescapable thrill down my neck. "You don't have to want it, kitten. You *need* it."

The whimper that sneaked past my parted lips was a sound so desperate, so out of my control, I couldn't deny he was right. As much as it pained me to concede…

I needed Bodhi Decker.

And fuck, it was such an overwhelming, potent feeling, my body vibrated with it.

Running my trembling hands down his bare, tanned torso, my fingers glided over the smooth slope of his pecs and each rigid line of his defined abdomen. His muscles twitched and flexed under my touch, and I relished the feeling of having so much power in my grasp.

Now was my chance. The moment to seize the one thing I'd dreamed of.

To make him beg for mercy.

When I reached the solid muscles carved into his hips, I didn't stop. I followed the defined ridge, sliding my hands lower, recklessly skimming the imposing bulge of his cock, and popped the button of his pants.

"No." He halted my exploration, grabbing both my wrists.

"What? Why not?" I struggled against his hold.

Effortlessly, he pulled my arms from between us, forcing them behind my back, and secured them with just one of his rough, massive hands.

"I know what you want." His voice was a teasing murmur, his restraint, unyielding. "You want dominance. You'll drop to your knees and swallow my cock. Suck and gag on me until I come down your pretty little throat. You'll try to break me."

"Yes," I panted, straining against him as his vivid description reduced me to a puddled mess. "God, yes."

His thumb gripped harder around my shifting wrists, crushing sweetly over the thrum of my racing pulse. "You forgot one thing."

"What's that?" I met his insistent gaze, then slowly and purposely licked my lips. His blue stare was molten, but he didn't lose an ounce of composure. Not even when I sucked my bottom lip between my teeth.

"I'm the one in charge here, Kira. Not you."

Fire stoked deep in my belly. I couldn't tell if it was rage or desire, or if there was even a difference between the two. This man had all my senses at war with each other—all my emotions in a tangled, stormy blur.

"Like hell you are. You think I'll bow down to you? Beg you to get me off? Fuck you. You don't tell me what to do."

His smirk turned to a devilish grin, his brilliant white teeth on full display. He was like a wolf on the hunt, and I was his prey. A meal for him to devour.

This game was far too deadly, and I should've put a stop to it, should've walked away.

But I couldn't because it was already too late. I was far too turned on, and my only thought was how much I wanted him to mark me with his tantalizing bite.

"Now she comes out to play." Awed appreciation laced his words. "My vicious little kitten."

"Screw you," I said in a last-ditch attempt to hold out. "I'm not a pet. You can't claim me."

He growled—actually fucking growled. "Kira, you're already mine."

And *God*, despite my protests, I'd never been more wet or willing.

Or so irrevocably screwed.

Because he was right. In that moment, he had me. I was unequivocally his. Both my body and my life were in the palm of his hands.

He dropped his open mouth to my collarbone, sucking provocatively at the sensitive flesh before tracing up the column of my neck with his tongue.

A riot of sparks shot to life inside me. "Never." I'd

barely squeaked out the word before his mouth took possession of mine.

His free hand moved to the back of my head, holding me in place. His other hand remained clasped in an unbreakable brace, locking my wrists almost painfully against my back.

The kiss was bruising. Punishing. Demanding.

Everything I'd wanted.

His tongue delved deep. His lips devoured. He consumed me, body and soul. With this kiss, he claimed me, just like he said he would, and it was so fucking good, all I could think was *more*.

But he abruptly pulled away, leaving me in a lust-filled daze, wilting in his arms.

"You sure about that?" His voice was composed, as always. Like kissing the life out of me had zero effect on him.

"Yes," I lied. "You can't control me."

He laughed, and the sound traveled straight to my clit. "Oh, kitten, it's going to be so much fun to prove you wrong."

I opened my mouth to protest, but before I could utter another sound, he was kissing me again. Only this time, it wasn't a rough assault.

No. This time, he was whisper soft. His lips were a gentle brush, his tongue a tantalizing tease. This kiss was affectionate. Tender. Yet, somehow, he still dominated.

His hand traveled down the back of my neck, then swept around front, following the line of my collarbone before tracing a scorching path along the exposed flesh between my breasts. Feather light, the rough pads of his fingers only grazed my skin.

I was panting now, unable to contain the rush of desire taking over. But it was so overwhelming, so unbelievably frightening, I forced myself to pull out of his debilitating kiss.

Finally, he allowed me space, releasing my trapped hands and creating some separation between our bodies. Only, instead of relief, all I felt was loss—the inescapable need to be under his possessive care.

"Giving up already?" he teased.

Boldly, I raised my arms and clung to his broad shoulders, fighting hard to swallow back the fear. "You're right about me. I'm impulsive, and always have been. I act first and deal with the consequences after. But this…" I shook my head, unable to find the right words.

"You're worried you're going to regret it. Regret me."

"No, *Bodhi*." I emphasized his real name, so he'd know I wasn't fucking around. "I'm worried that I won't."

They were the most honest words I'd said in years, and likely the most ridiculous and dangerous thing I'd ever said out loud. Especially to this man, who only hours ago, I'd swore would never win.

The man who, if he knew the truth, would rather kill me than kiss me.

Fuck, I really was a hopeless, horny bitch.

A low growl vibrated through his chest. The small space between us disappeared. His teeth grazed my ear again, and his hand wound its way back to my nape, his long fingers tangling in my hair before gently pulling.

The erotic sensation sent shivers racing down my spine and laid to waste my already soaked panties. I tipped my head back, guided by his calm, persistent force, exposing my neck to him. Making myself vulnerable to him.

My need intensified as his lips trailed over the side of my neck and under my jaw. I squirmed in his hold, my breath shallow, hot, and out of fucking control.

"What's it going to be, kitten?" His free hand cupped the side of my breast, his thumb brushing over my sensitive nipple, causing me to shiver. "A professional agreement, or fighting and fucking?"

My pulse spiked as I ran my hands over the veined and corded muscles of his arms, savoring each hard line and defined groove. "Do you really think it's wise to make a professional agreement with an amateur?"

A hint of pain pierced his low chuckle, and it was surprisingly satisfying. "Fighting and fucking it is, then."

With conviction, his mouth crushed mine. His lips devoured, tongue ravaged, and the hand in my hair pulled hard. With his injured arm wrapped firmly around my waist, he owned the kiss. Owned me.

He lifted me, sliding me onto the granite vanity, sending the medical supplies tumbling into the sink and to the floor. The whiskey went rolling as well.

I tore my mouth from his on a muttered curse and lunged sideways to catch the bottle before it hit the floor.

A lust-tinted smirk graced his lips. "Those reflexes aren't amateur," he murmured, sliding his hands up my exposed legs.

Leaning even farther, I set the bottle out of reach, keenly aware of how my dress pulled, revealing even more skin and the hilt of my knife.

He made a move toward it, but stopped short, running a single finger just below my weapon.

"Did you want to keep hold of this?" His hooded eyes studied mine, perhaps testing my limits. Or was he searching for the truth? "Since you don't like guns?"

My hand trembled with anxious need as I unbuckled the leather strap. "I really don't like guns, but that's not why I carry this. I wouldn't carry any weapon at all, but this knife is important to me."

Fuck, why was I telling him this? Why did I feel the need to make him understand?

"It's more than a way to protect myself. It was a gift from my grandfather, and it saved my life the night he died. It reminds me not to take anything for granted. Not even the things I don't like." I swallowed hard, holding back the rest of the truth threatening to spill from me.

A truth that was almost too much for me to bear.

I wanted to tell him it was Nikolai who'd murdered my grandfather. That he'd done it to seize control of the Bratva, and maybe in part, to spite me. How he'd killed innocent women all because I'd tried to stop him, then dragged my sister and me into his plans, forcing us into his sick and twisted game.

The tension building inside me felt like it might tear me apart. Because even though I wanted to tell him, I still wasn't sure if I should trust him. Especially with this.

How could I, when the last man I'd put my faith in had betrayed me so brutally? And I hardly knew Dex. If I told him the truth now, would he still help me? Would he understand the futility of my situation?

Or would he simply kill me here and now?

He'd asked for the truth and my trust. I couldn't give him the truth—not all of it—so I gave him the knife instead.

I placed it in his hands, trusting him with my most prized possession, and maybe even my life. "Save it for when we get back to the fighting."

Reaching behind me, he placed my heirloom on a shelf, out of harm's way and away from doing harm. When he returned his attention to me, it was with a look of unguarded reverence. His eyes bore into mine, his fingers grasping and digging into my hips, and he leaned forward, towering over me in a way that made me feel reckless and exposed. "Guess that just leaves the fucking."

But he hesitated, a deep crease forming across his brow.

My insides quaked, and I tried but failed to keep the need from my voice. "What's wrong?"

"I don't have a condom." He glanced at the mess of

the medical kit, now strewn along the floor. "But I'm sure there's one here somewhere."

"Do we need one?" I arched into him, hooking my heels around the backs of his legs, attempting to urge him on.

Still, he held back. "I don't know. I've never gone without one before." His eyes searched mine, and the sharp, almost tortured look on his face intensified.

"Me neither," I admitted, and the ache between my thighs grew to an impossible height. "But I was tested about a year ago, and I haven't been with anyone since."

Maybe he was right. Maybe I was turned on by danger, because something about this—about him—had me willing to throw away all caution.

I may be impulsive, but this? This was completely insane.

"You haven't had sex in a year?" The pained edge to his voice made him sound like he was ready to do violence, and part of me was anxious for that.

"Longer, actually, but I still have my IUD implanted." I wasn't just ready to jump into danger with him, I was fucking begging to do it. "I want it," I whispered, almost too afraid to say it out loud. "I want to feel every fucking inch of you, Dex. Give it to me raw. Make me feel like your dirty little whore."

"Fuck," he muttered, seeming to lose just a touch of his restraint. "That mouth is going to get you into trouble someday, kitten. But not right now. Right now, I'm going to give you what you need."

I watched with impatient hunger as he unfastened

and lowered his pants, his impossibly large, hard cock springing free. God, he looked divine. Even with bruising across his ribs, gray at his temples, and a taped-up gunshot wound on his shoulder, he was nothing short of impressive. Imposing.

With precision, he gripped my waist again, and with a sharp jerk, pulled me even closer.

I gasped, barely containing a fevered moan. "And I guess that means you're still in charge."

"Always. But you know that's what you want." His hand moved from my waist to the apex of my thighs. He stared down at me, his breath heavy against my parted lips, and slowly stroked over my lace-covered pussy.

When he pulled the scrap of material aside and slid his fingers through my wetness, I just about died, my entire body clamoring for more.

"See?" His tongue darted out to swipe a path over my bottom lip as he slowly sunk a finger deep inside of me. "You're ready to burst, kitten. Your tight, wet cunt wants me to own it."

"Prove it," I panted. "Prove that you can."

"Don't worry." His rough tone shot sparks straight to my core. "I'll make it disgustingly regrettable for you."

"Fuck, yes." All my wildness and deadliness fought to let loose, but I was under his command, and wherever he led, I'd follow. At least, for now.

His need was as palpable as my own, but he was still rock steady. Disciplined and controlled.

Until then, I hadn't recognized how badly I wanted

that. His strict rule. His need for order. His mastery of all things, including me. I wanted to feel his domination.

For him to fuck the wild right out of me.

After a couple of rough tugs on my clothing, he lined his cock up with my aching core and pushed into me on a restrained groan. It was a dazzling sound of pleasure, yet somehow, still strict and demanding.

Hands clutching hard at my ass, he pulled me farther onto him as I hugged his waist tightly between my knees, my heels hitting the counter. My legs opened wider with the drive of his hips, giving in to his silent demand. Sinking deep, he thrust hard against my spread thighs, and I gasped at the sting of his welcome intrusion.

"That's it, kitten. Take my cock like a good girl. Show me how much you like it," he urged, his mouth capturing mine in a sharp, searing kiss as he ground himself into me.

I'd known he was big, hard, and unforgiving, but the way he stretched me, filled me, and still had me aching for more...*fuck*, it was downright obscene.

My back and shoulders hit the wall, and I watched the muscles of his six-pack flex as he pulled out of me to the tip, only to surge forward again, burying himself so deep, I swore I could feel it in my throat.

Slowly, he guided my hips in a steady rocking rhythm, even as I tried to outpace him. "Look at you," he murmured as he stroked inside of me. "Fucking greedy for it."

I moaned and nodded frantically, unable to form the right words.

One of his massive hands drifted to my breast. Moving my dress aside, he plucked my hardened nipple. When he pinched the tight bud between his fingers, electric shockwaves rippled through me, from my chest straight to my pussy.

I cried out, lost in pleasure. Lost to the magnificence of this man.

His hips moved faster, hands gripped harder, and the feeling mounted, building me to a heightened peak.

I couldn't contain myself. The rush of ecstasy was too much, too soon. I writhed uncontrollably over his dick, my already drenched core fluttering wildly and the sloppy sound of our pounding flesh only adding fuel to my raging fire. "Please, please, oh, please," I chanted. "I'm going to come. Oh God, Dex, please."

"Fuck yes, you are." The muscles in his neck and shoulders strained as a wolfish look of indulgence took over his features. "That's it, you chaotic little kitten. Give it to me."

I didn't know what he wanted. My orgasm, my wild side, my soul? It didn't matter. He had me. Whatever he wanted, it was his.

"Please," I wailed. "Take it. Take me."

There was no more holding back. He reached between our bodies to where we were intimately connected, his hand taking possession of me as he strummed over my clit.

A garbled string of curses left me as my pleasure

ratcheted impossibly higher, all while he hammered into me, crushing my ass against the edge of the counter, knocking my head into the wall, and hitting my G-spot with uncanny precision.

Now, I really was wild. Free. Out of fucking control—or maybe just completely under his.

And fuck, it was perfect.

Euphoria took over as I erupted, my back arching dramatically with the strength of the orgasm, and I let out a strangled scream. My entire body shuddered and pulsed as I came, and he followed shortly after, letting out a rough groan as his cock jerked inside of me.

I collapsed in a ragged heap, not caring in the least that my neck was at an uncomfortable angle or that my ass was hanging off the counter. Along with the endorphins, he was still running the show, and for the moment, I didn't give a fuck about anything else.

How could I?

The man most likely to kill me—the man with every reason to want me dead—had just come inside me.

And I didn't feel the least bit sorry about it.

CHAPTER
TWELVE
DEX

KIRA SLEPT PEACEFULLY BESIDE ME, UNMOVING EXCEPT for the steady rise and fall of her chest. Rolled away on her side, with her fist tucked under her chin, long legs curled up to her stomach, and platinum hair spread over the pillow like a halo, she looked deceptively innocent.

But Wildcat was a hell of a lot more than she seemed.

Yes, she'd let her guard down for a moment before sex and revealed a glimpse of the softness she kept hidden under the wild. It had been just enough to show me she wasn't all dropkicks and throat punches, and her emotional outbursts were more than angry possession. All her hard looks, cruel words, and rough touches were a shield.

However, she was also a slumbering panther, ready to strike at the first sign of a threat. A deadly adversary who could turn on me at a moment's notice. A fierce fighter who'd already taken me down once, and I had no doubt she could do it again.

The only question was, would she?

Even after the electrifying, all-consuming experience of fucking her, I still didn't have the answer. I had no goddamn clue whose side of this game she was playing on.

For a moment, while I'd thrusted like a madman inside of her, I'd almost forgotten that. Hell, I'd almost forgotten everything, including myself and the deadly dynamic between us.

With her tight heat pulsing around my bare cock and my heartbeat thundering in my ears, it had been easy to ignore the uncertainties. Easy to push aside the voice in the back of my mind, telling myself it was all a mistake.

The way her body had responded to mine was breathtaking. The push and pull of our aggression, and the dare she'd set in place... *fuck*. It was a high better than any narcotic. And the sounds she'd made—the sexy as hell pleading mewls, the glorious way she'd begged, and the savage cry of ecstasy when she came— those noises were so much better than I'd imagined. Not just music to my ears, but a harmony for my goddamn soul.

At the time, the risk had seemed worth it, and I could pretend that having command of her body meant I was still in control of everything else. But now?

Now, I needed to find my fucking balance. Needed to remember how I'd wound up here with her in the first place, and the challenge that still lay ahead.

I'd been struggling to keep myself in check before sex, but now I'd have to double those efforts and stay on task because, despite this moment of reprieve, we were still in danger.

Maybe more so now than ever.

At least, I was.

The pesky crack in my armor was growing, and there was a good chance it couldn't be repaired. The feelings I'd long ago buried were itching to break free, and like the wild crashing of Kira's orgasm, if I let them loose, they were sure to take over and sweep me away.

I couldn't let that happen. Impractical emotions would not be my undoing.

Morning was only a few hours aways, but my eyes were just now willing to close. Despite the slumbering chaotic beauty beside me, the events of the previous evening had finally caught up. Maybe once I'd rested, my unhealthy preoccupation with Kira would fade.

At least, I sure as hell hoped it would. Even if hope still wasn't something I believed in.

When I finally fell asleep, it was restless and filled with my usual violent nightmares. In them, desert sand whipped my face while Finn bled out in front me, his mangled, shrapnel-filled leg slowly killing him, and I could do nothing but watch, while somewhere in the distance a woman screamed for help.

Emily. She was crying for mercy, calling for me to rescue her.

Only, this time, the dream voice was different. This time, it was Kira who yelled my name, and I was left drowning in a torrent of my own emotions as I sank deeper into the sand, unsure whose life I should save.

"Dex, Dex, Dex," she called, but instead of a scream of terror, it was a captivating cry of ecstasy. "Bodhi!"

My eyes flew open, and I was startled awake.

I was in bed, surrounded by pillows, not sand, and Kira's ass was cradling my dick. At some point in my sleep, I'd slung an arm around her middle, and she'd cuddled up against me, her legs interwoven with mine.

The only barrier between us was a sheet.

Now that I was out of the warzone of the dream and back in reality, I relaxed on a heavy sigh. Fuck, no wonder I was an insomniac with dreams like that lying in wait.

Although, if I could've woken with a gorgeous, naked Wildcat in my arms every time, it might not have been so bad.

I tried to focus on the ticking of the old-fashioned clock on the wall, hoping the white noise would drown out my overactive mind and lull me back to sleep—or at least drown out the memory of Kira's voice from my dream—but the sound only acted as a reminder that time was running out. We couldn't stay in this cozy suburban sanctuary for long.

No matter how comfortable I was, and despite the part of me that might've foolishly wanted to, I couldn't keep up this charade with Kira forever.

Untangling my limbs from hers, I removed myself from the temptation of waking her. Because even sleep deprived and wounded, my body craved more.

Outside of the darkened bedroom, the house was light and warm. I threw on a pot of coffee and stretched out in a chair by the sliding glass door to the backyard, watching the tail end of the sunrise.

Once upon a time, this had been my favorite part of the day—something I'd shared with Emily. Finn had always been a night owl, and for a few minutes each morning I could count on spending time alone with the girl next door. I'd sneak out to sit with her on her porch, we'd share some breakfast, a joke, or some gossip, and I'd try not to fall more in love with her.

That was prior to my time in the military, long before Mom got sick, and before Emily had proclaimed she was in love with my twin. Before Finn unknowingly married the girl of my dreams.

Back when the world still seemed new, and life was full of possibilities.

Now, the brilliant globe of fire in the sky was a stark reminder of the complexity of life—the fragile nature of our fucking being—and it hurt my goddamn eyes.

Or was it the shadow of my nonexistent heart that was aching?

I was on my third cup of coffee and the sun had been bright and full for hours before I heard Kira pad into the room behind me. She hovered out of sight for a moment, the electricity in the air letting me know she was close.

"Why'd you kill him?" Her sudden question was harsh, but once again, her voice was an enticing song, drawing me in, just like the first time.

"You're going to have to specify, kitten. It's a long list."

She was quiet, and I was tempted to turn so I could see her reaction, but I knew the game she was playing, the way she was testing me, and I refused to get caught in her attempt to push me away again. I waited out her silence, sipping my coffee and staring into the yard.

When she finally stepped into view, she took my breath away.

Her long, icy-blonde hair was tied in a loose braid, her face was free of makeup, and she was wearing nothing but my dress shirt. The dried blood on the sleeve made her look vicious, and her gorgeous bare legs made my cock stir.

"How many?" she whispered, her eyes narrowing in on me.

"If you're asking how many I've killed for profit, the answer is twenty-three. If you're expecting me to know a lifetime tally, I'm afraid you're out of luck."

"You said it's not random."

"It's not. At least, it was never supposed to be."

She frowned. "I don't understand."

On a heavy sigh, I set my coffee aside, feeling that same old, tired weariness creeping in. "In the Marines, we had a job to do and we did it damn well. We were highly trained because we were in dangerous fucking places, helping keep people safe. Killing wasn't something I did much of back then, and it was never random. Now, killing is all I do, and even though my targets are carefully selected, there are still times when I've had to defend myself. Like the man I killed at Moore's house —sometimes, it's unplanned."

"I still don't understand." She turned to me, leaning her back against the sliding glass door with her arms folded across her chest. "If you're a Marine, you must've had some kind of honor. Or respect for rules and the law, at least. Why the fuck would you turn to this? A paid killer."

"Someone has to do it." My teeth clenched and my jaw hardened as I stood to face her.

She didn't back down. Hell, her conviction only grew stronger. "Even if that were true, why you?"

"Because after I retired from service, I came home thinking I'd done what I could to make this world better, but when I got here, I realized shit was worse than ever. There's nothing honorable about protecting greed and corruption, and when I look around, Kira, that's all I fucking see. Criminals running the city."

My breath sawed in and out of my lungs, but she'd hit a nerve, and I wasn't willing to stop until she got it. Until she understood this wasn't just a job for me, it was a way of life.

"You have no idea how much it pisses me off that people like Bowen Alexander and Nikolai Rykov get to keep their freedom—keep their lives—while people like me risk everything to make this country safe. And no one's doing anything about it. No one cares."

With my hands fisted at my sides, my simmering anger was barely contained. Anger I'd dismissed as ancient history. A feeling I'd pretended to have dealt with, because on its own, if left unchecked, it would cripple me. Like all the other emotions I'd caged in the darkest recesses of my mind, this one would only get in my way.

"I cared." My voice wavered, but my temper held even. "Someone I knew was intent on helping victims of crime. They tried to give back to the city in a way that would make a difference, but things only ever got worse. They were trying to help someone out of a bad situation, and in the process, they were taken."

"Taken?" she whispered, and the look of indignation on her beautiful face softened just a bit.

"Yes, taken. The police weren't doing anything. Hell, they wouldn't even file a report at first. No one was doing anything. This person was important to me, and I knew they were in trouble. Knew they needed help. So, I decided to do something about it myself."

"By killing?"

"No, Kira, that's the problem. I didn't go after the first man when I should have. I trusted in the system too much, and by the time I'd decided to act, it was too late. Nikolai Rykov is still alive, and because of that, I failed."

I bit down on my sudden urge to scream, fighting hard to keep my shit together.

Her eyes grew wide, and she whispered, "What happened?"

"The person who needed my help died because I had morals," I seethed. "Because I didn't accept that I needed to fight fire with fire. Killing is the only language these men understand. So, now, that's what I do. Only, I do it from the inside, where they don't even recognize the threat. They never see me coming."

"So, what, you think you're some kind of vigilante? If you believe that, then why kill Nelson Moore? He was just a scientist. He had a family."

"You tell me, kitten." I stalked toward her, crowding her up against the glass of the sliding door. I was done with her game. Now, we'd play mine. "He was more than he seemed, and you know it. What information did he have?"

Her breath grew short and she tried to move away, but I refused to give her space. Not now. She had questions, but *goddammit*, I wanted answers.

I needed to know her plan—if she had one. What allegiance did she keep? If the mission got messy, when it came down to the wire, would she fight with me or against me?

Maybe with those answers, I'd understand my own damn motivations, and why the hell I was diving in headfirst to help her when part of me knew I was getting screwed. If I was playing hero, it had better be for the right reasons and not simply because I liked the feel of her pussy when it squeezed around my cock.

She tried to sidestep by me again, but I blocked her path, pinning her against the glass door by her shoulders. Her angered huff sounded a bit like a plea for more, but she pursed her lips, refusing to speak.

"Come on, kitten, no more lying. No more hiding," I said, turned on by her frustrated fury. "If you want me to help you get your sister to safety, I need you to tell me the truth."

She shook her head, but finally answered, "He knew." She took a stuttering breath, her chest rising and falling on a tantalizing sigh as she gave in. "Moore knew about the women."

"Women?"

"Yes. Nikolai usually has dozens of women. Some of them are really fucking young, too—girls, really. Although, most of them, he doesn't hold on to for long. The sick fucker sells them like cattle. Worse, he keeps the ones he likes." Her voice hitched, and some of her bravado melted. "My sister, Yelena, was always his favorite."

I held her arms a little tighter. "And how would a scientist know about that?"

The better question might've been how she'd found this information herself, because it had taken me almost a week of digging. But I chose to tread lightly and keep my suspicions hidden. For now.

"Because he wasn't just a scientist." Her eyes squeezed shut, her brow pinching in what looked like a hell of a lot of pain. "He was a mule, supplying Niko-lai's crew with drugs."

She peered at me through cracked lids, her face still stricken. "I wanted him to at least give up their drop schedule. At best, I hoped he'd tell me everything he knew. I thought if I had their timing, their numbers, I might be able to figure out when and where I could get past Nikolai's security. But Moore was a slimy fucker."

"Yes, he was," I agreed, already knowing some of what she'd told me, and intrigued by the parts that were new. Pieces of the puzzle were now starting to fit. "But I'm guessing he wasn't working on his own. I bet Bowen Alexander was using him to run those drugs and using Moore's debt to the Irish as leverage over him."

Her eyes flared open at my mention of Alexander. Had she already known this information? Or was it as much a revelation to her as it was for me?

"The drugs are probably being used on those women," I said, my voice full of stern conviction. "And I bet Rykov wasn't the only one Moore was selling to. He was probably supplying a lot of drugs to a lot of people." I grasped her chin, leaning a fraction closer. "Am I getting warm, kitten?"

"You're practically on fire." Her breath skated over my lips.

The temptation to kiss her was rising, but more than that, the thrill of bending her to my will was winning. "So, do you still think it was wrong for me to kill him?"

"I-I'm not sure."

"Don't play coy." I smirked. "He was in league with criminals, liked to spend time with those young as fuck women, and brought drugs to the man holding them prisoner. And now, he's not."

Her breath stuttered again. "Now, he's not. You made sure of that."

She didn't approve of my methods, that was exceedingly clear, but it didn't matter. I didn't need her fucking approval, I only needed more of the truth. Even with as much as she'd given me, I knew it was only a part of the story.

She was hiding something, and it was more than a blood-soaked history or fears for her captive sister. Wildcat was in deep. There was no doubt Rykov was pulling her strings. The only question was, how hard?

My hand smoothed down over her neck to the base of her throat, where her pulse was thrumming violently, and squeezed. "Do you trust me yet, kitten?"

"Not really." But her gaze was heated, dropping to my lips, and she made no move to stop the light compression of her airway.

Did she know I wouldn't hurt her? Could she sense my inexplicable need to be a hero?

Not just any hero—*her* goddamn hero. Or was this another test?

Either way, I couldn't afford to fail.

"I think maybe you trust me a little." My clutch on her throat softened, but only a fraction.

"I guess that all depends," she said, practically purring under my grip. "Are we fighting or fucking right now?"

She was magnetic, and despite my rock-solid composure, I could feel my will starting to crack. "Who says it can't be both?"

CHAPTER
THIRTEEN
DEX

Kira's loud and heady groan vibrated through my hand, stirring my blood. Fuck, the sound traveled straight to my cock.

There was a job to do, and I needed to keep my balance.

Sex wasn't the answer to that.

It wouldn't prove her wrong, save her sister, or get rid of Nikolai Rykov. Sex wouldn't put my life back in order, honor Emily's memory, or keep anyone safe. And it would take a hell of a lot more than mutual orgasms to win Wildcat's trust. Or to give her mine.

Still, I wanted it. Wanted her.

At that moment, sex was the best goddamn plan I'd ever had.

"Say it," I urged, getting off on the idea of hearing her beg again. "Tell me how badly you want to fuck me right now."

"I thought you didn't want me to lie." Her adorable, saucy attitude was in full effect, but although she refused to admit it, I could feel her body vibrating with need.

Her hunger was as undeniable as my own, and her arousal was so potent I could smell it.

She squirmed under my hold, her sweet, hot breath coming faster as her hands moved to open my pants.

I stopped her, grabbing hold of her wrists before she could reach my skin. If she touched me—if I allowed her to take the lead—I'd lose every ounce of my control. Then, it really would be game fucking over. In more ways than one.

"Take off the shirt, kitten."

Her eyes didn't leave mine, but her hands moved like lightning when I released them, her fingers fumbling over the buttons.

This woman truly was wild and rebellious. She withheld her trust and secrets from me, even as she revealed her body. Senseless as it was, my craving for her was stronger because of that.

I would need more from her, though. And soon. More truth, less subterfuge and distraction.

But for the moment this was enough. Hell, I'd take whatever I could get.

Both my pants and boxers were off before she'd made it past the third button on the shirt. Done with waiting, I tore it open, sending the remaining buttons flying like confetti and scattering across the floor.

She gasped, her eyes growing wide with lust and her mouth falling open on a tantalizing, "*Oh*".

I smirked, daring her to try and make a move, just so I could show her I was still the one in charge.

Fighting and fucking, indeed.

"You ruined it," she said, her voice a breathy whisper.

"Forget it." My gaze wandered down her front, taking in the large spread of bruising across her sternum. "It was already ruined."

The distorted purple and blue that dotted her skin called to me on a primitive level. This woman was more than a fighter. She was a survivor.

Tough and unyielding. Brave and beautifully brilliant.

But shit, I'd done that. She was sporting those bruises because of me. Instead of keeping her safe, I'd thrust her farther into danger. Unintentional or not, I'd been the one who'd hurt her.

Some goddamn hero I was turning out to be.

Guilt tried to push its way up from the pit where I'd banished it, but I squashed the sensation back down. I'd deal with those unwelcome feelings later, after an orgasm or two to make it up to her.

"And what now?" she purred. "Are you going to ruin me, too?"

"Is that what you want?"

"I dare you to try."

Fuck me. The things that came out of her mouth

were not only unexpectedly dirty and thrilling, but a challenge I was more than willing to accept.

I ran the rough pads of my fingers down the open front of the shirt, tracing over her taut nipples and stomach, straight to the apex of her thighs, where I hovered only a breath away from taking what I wanted, and from giving her the thing she was too stubborn to ask for.

"This is mine," I said, cupping her sex, my fingers itching to claim even more.

Her bottom lip disappeared between her teeth as she failed to hold back a throaty moan.

That sound spurred me on, and my mouth found the curve of her neck, while the hand I had between her legs ground against her pussy. "Mine," I repeated.

"You'll need to try harder than that." Her voice was full of defiance, even as she circled her hips.

I sunk two fingers deep inside her, stroking gently from within. "You love that I own your pretty little cunt. You want it to be mine. You want me to take it. To make you fucking beg."

A fierce glow of outrage lit her amber gaze. "No," she panted, unable to keep the strain of need from her voice. "Never."

Fuck, she was cute when she tried to deny me.

"Liar." I pulled my sopping fingers from her tight heat.

The whimpering sound she made nearly brought me to my knees. It was a sound so desperate, so fucking irresistible, I was tempted to give in. To let her have her way—whatever way that was.

But my will was made of iron, and my cage of control was locked up tight.

I allowed her to run her hands over my bare torso before I tugged the shirt from her shoulders, tearing it off and tossing it to the floor to join my pants.

The entire suit was now garbage, and I couldn't care less.

I took her mouth hard as I pressed her back up against the door, her skin squeaking over the glass as I lifted her, and she wrapped her legs around my waist.

She kissed me back. Her tongue dueled hotly with mine, as I selfishly swallowed her excited moans.

I was burning up, and my need for her was close to outweighing my need for control, but I still pushed her. Taunted and fucking teased. Urged her to give me the thing I wanted.

Demanded she give herself over to me.

"Say it," I ordered against her mouth. "Just admit you want to fuck me, kitten. You want your pussy to be mine."

She slipped her hand between us, finding my cock, and with a steel grip and zero hesitation, sunk herself down onto me. "No," she cried in passion.

Fuck, I almost lost it then.

"No," she repeated, her wet heat squeezing me like a goddamn vice. "I don't want to fuck you. I want *you* to fuck *me*. Own my fucking pussy, Bodhi, just like you promised."

My name on her lips broke whatever remained of my resistance. I growled, "You better hold on tight, you dirty-mouthed little minx." And took her lips in a blazing kiss.

Then, giving into the sensation, into her challenge, I held her tight and fucked her hard.

My mouth ran from her lips to her ear, and I grunted, "Is this what you wanted?"

I pulled out of her slowly, only to slam back in.

"No," she wailed, her arms hugging around my neck, fusing our bodies together.

So, I fucked her harder. I was sweating, my shoulder was burning, my legs were shaking, and my heart was racing frantically as I hammered into her. The glass door creaked from the momentum, the sound joined by her furious, mewling cries.

"Yes," she chanted. "Fuck, yes, yes, yes."

Each shout of ecstasy had my balls drawing tighter. I was panting, close to coming or collapsing, but it didn't stop me from banging her with fervor.

I was ruthless. Unrelenting. Out of my mind with the need to please her. The need to get her off.

The need to take what was mine.

Whether it was right, wrong, or some sort of fucked up shade of gray in between, Kira—the wildcat—was all goddamn mine. And despite how insane or impossible, *fuck it*…I planned on keeping her.

"That's it, kitten," I encouraged when her core started to pulse. "Give me all you've got. I want to feel you come undone."

With another strangled cry, she did.

Her body locked around me as her pussy spasmed,

sending me straight to my own climax. But I pulled out at the last minute, bathing her stomach in thick ropes of milky white as I came on a strangled groan.

Her head fell to the crook of my neck, and I held her like that as we both came down from our high—her lips on my neck, hands in my hair, and my cum decorating her body.

"I wonder if all the neighbors witnessed that," she mumbled.

"Fuck 'em," I said, even as I peered out at the quiet, fenced-in yard. "I hope they enjoyed the show."

She laughed at that, but the sound caught in her throat, reminding me neither of us were at our physical best.

"I'm sorry," I muttered into her hair. "I shouldn't have been so rough. You're hurt." Slowly, I lowered her to the floor. "You okay?" I asked, seeking the truth in her gaze.

But once again, her shields were up, and she refused to look me in the eye.

"Kitten, if you're brave enough to fuck me without a condom, twice, then you can at least acknowledge me afterward. It's a simple question. I'm not looking for a novel. Yes or no will do."

Maybe she could read my turmoil, or maybe she felt the shame that was trying to creep up on me. Whatever the reason, she listened. Her eyes flew up to meet mine. Not full of aggression the way I'd expected, but brimming with tears.

"Kira…" I cupped her jaw and kissed the corner of

her luscious lips, before meeting her gaze again. "I'm sorry."

She blinked, her chin trembling as a single tear leaked from the corner of her eye. The wet streak glistened on her luminescent skin, showcasing her pain. Her nostrils flared as she inhaled sharply, holding her breath. Holding back the tremors and the tears.

How much emotional baggage could one person carry? More importantly, how in the hell had I ever thought this made her weak?

"I'm sorry," I repeated, unsure why I was willing to expose myself to her.

I was so eager to risk my fucking life—to prove to her I was someone other than the ruthless man I'd become. But why? What the hell could I possibly gain by letting her see my humanity?

Whatever little of it I had left.

When she finally released her breath, it was a long, hot gust of air. She schooled her features as her tears dried, and a look of fire began smoldering within her.

"I don't want your fucking apology." I could practically see the fury crackle and burn as she bared her teeth at me in an animalistic snarl.

Fuck, she was fantastic.

And still, I wanted more.

Despite not knowing her intentions—whose damn side she was truly on—I wanted to pull her back into me, feel her fiery strength, and get lost in the sublime agony of it all.

I wanted to feel her wrath, punishment, and pain.

Wanted to let her devour me, body first, then whatever scraps of a soul I might have left. I invited her fury to consume me, to fill me up with something other than the compulsive order, calculated odds, and void of darkness my life had become.

But more than that, I wanted to give something back to her.

I wanted to give her consideration and comfort—if I was even capable. I wanted to hold her up when she didn't think she could continue. To be the strength she needed to carry on surviving.

"You're not used to relying on anyone else, are you?" I murmured, running a finger over the velvet of her skin. "Not used to having someone care enough to even offer a simple amends when it's due."

"Stop talking."

"Why?" I leaned in, towering over her with my arm propped against the glass door, admiring how fucking gorgeous she was with my cum on her skin. "Still afraid of the truth?"

Arching her back, she tilted her head to look straight up at me. Her eyes became hooded, and a sexy little smirk adorned her lips. Lips I was intent on kissing again.

"Who was she?" she asked, her voice a teasing treasure.

I bent even closer, my focus on her mouth. "Who?"

"You said you'd failed someone important to you— couldn't save them from Nikolai. I just wondered who she was. What was her name?"

I was frozen, my body taut with the strain of keeping myself together. Guilt, fear, love, and loathing all came crashing in.

But only for a moment.

I let those ancient feelings wash through me. Let them come and then let them fucking go. Once and for all.

"Her name was Emily. She was my sister-in-law, and I loved her." I bowed my head to hers and whispered in her ear. "I was *in* love with her."

She flinched, and I pulled back to see her mouth opening and closing in shock.

Fuck, maybe I was an asshole, but it felt good to let out this secret. To divulge the poisonous goddamn truth. And maybe even cathartic to see how many of Wildcat's buttons I could push with the name of another woman.

A woman whose memory I'd carried with me for the last year. Whose death had changed me in ways that would make me unrecognizable to her. And if she could see me now, a woman who would tell me I was acting like a goddamn fool.

Because the woman I wanted now—possibly more than I'd ever wanted anyone before—was bright and alive and standing right in front of me.

And I was manipulating her for my own self-interest.

"But that's not really what you wanted to know, was it?" I taunted, my finger stroking over her collarbone.

"I have no idea what you're talking about."

Toying with a stray lock of her hair, I murmured, "I

think what you really want to know is where you stand. If I'm *still* in love with her."

"You're such an arrogant asshole. Why the hell would I care?"

The skin at the base of her throat was flushing red, her lips pursed in an angry pout, but still, I pushed her. "Sounds like I might've hit a sore spot, kitten. You're getting a little defensive. What's the matter? Are you jealous of a dead woman?"

Instead of answering, she smirked.

With her eyes glued to mine, she ran her finger up her inner thigh, over her sex, and across her stomach, dragging the single digit through the mess I'd made.

And *goddamn*, that's all it took. I was mesmerized, my gaze falling to watch the lazy path of her finger, now sticky with my cum.

It seemed impossible, but despite my overrun of emotions, lack of sleep, and having just come all over her, my softening cock grew hard again.

The look on her face turned from playful to downright wicked.

Lust took over my body, and I was aching for her all over.

With that fierce grin still in place, she trailed her wet finger higher, circling a nipple before dragging it up to her mouth. When her tongue darted out to lick it, I thought I'd lost feeling to my limbs. But when she popped it in her mouth and sucked—her cheeks hollowing and her eyes rolling back in her head—I thought I might've died.

With a loud pop, she pulled her finger from her mouth and said, "The answer is no."

But I couldn't remember the question. I stood, mute, my growing erection refuting my all-mighty control.

"And you lied," she muttered, ducking under my arm and walking away. "I don't regret a fucking thing."

CHAPTER
FOURTEEN
KIRA

WRAPPED IN A RIDICULOUS FLUFFY PINK TOWEL WITH my hair dripping wet, I stood in the middle of Sunshine's guest bedroom, staring at the photo on the dresser and trying not to lose my shit.

My phone vibrated in my hand, jolting me from the pit of wretched misery I'd been fighting hard to stay out of.

I turned my focus to the incoming text and let out a heavy sigh. I'd been carrying what felt like a mountain of worry, but I could breathe again. Finally.

Amelia: *Everyone's good here. I packed them up this morning and moved them over to my place until you're back.*

The tension melted from my shoulders, and I smiled, thinking of how excited Anya would be to have a sleepover. She loved spending time with Amelia and her son.

Kira: *Thank you, you're a lifesaver.*

Amelia: *Stay safe.*

Stay safe? That seemed a bit odd, considering my excuse for needing her help was a last minute, out of town sales meeting for work. But I didn't have time to contemplate her meaning because another notification popped up, sending my nerves back into overdrive.

I tapped on it to view the response to the text I'd sent early this morning.

Kira: *I won't be coming to lunch, I'm busy at work.*

V: *acceptable*

To anyone scrolling through my phone, this chat history would probably seem strange, maybe even cryptic. Not that there were many messages—Vlad and I weren't exactly friends. However, despite the lack of actual words, the meaning was unmistakable.

My assignment was on track.

At least, it could be on track if I wanted to keep playing Nikolai's crooked game and continue subjecting us all to his cruel and careless whims. Or if my hidden agenda fell apart and I was left with no other choice.

But as far as he was concerned, I'd intercepted Dex at the party, just as we'd planned, and was busy wooing him straight toward his eventual demise. Which, if I thought about it, was sort of close to the truth.

Only, I was the one being seduced, and if I wasn't careful, I would also be the one to end up dead.

"Will these do?" Dex asked, striding into the room with a neatly folded pile of clothes in his hands.

Deftly, I tucked my phone back into my clutch that was sitting on top of the dresser and grabbed the brush that was there, running it haphazardly through my hair before turning to inspect his offering. "I'm sure they'll be fine. Thank you."

"It's just a shirt and leggings. No panties. I figured you wouldn't mind going without," he said with a wink. "I know I won't mind."

How the hell could he even stand the sight of me, let alone flirt with me, after the way I'd treated him? After taunting and teasing him, and then walking away?

It was a ruthless move, but I'd needed to keep the upper hand. Or, at least, keep some semblance of self-respect. Otherwise, I might've been tempted to let down all my barriers.

To give away all my secrets.

And after what we'd done—after what I'd not only allowed but encouraged—I couldn't afford to lose another layer of protection. I'd already given up enough.

He'd pushed past my defenses, first with his cock, then with his revelation. Fuck, I was still reeling from what he'd said. From his admission of love for another woman.

Those words, *"I was in love with her,"* had nearly knocked me on my ass. I'd nearly given up the fight.

I'd purposely gone digging into what he'd made clear was a painful past. I'd done it in the spirit of deflection, and maybe a touch of retribution—he'd nearly broken me wide open with his crap about owning me, after all. I'd thought it only fair to fight back.

But what he'd given me was more than I'd expected, and possibly more truth than I could handle. Because hearing him profess his love—past, present, or otherwise—was proof this man was far more than the cold-hearted killer I thought him to be. The inkling of emotions he'd let slip in the car was nothing compared to this.

The pain that crossed his face when he'd spoken of her…

God, the expression was devastating. For both of us.

It hurt to see the haunted look in his eyes, hear the tremor in his voice, and sense the rush of despair as it passed through him. I could practically feel the sorrow, the love and fucking devotion just with the mention of her name.

Was I jealous of a dead woman?

Fucking right I was.

But I didn't want to examine the feeling too closely because I meant what I'd said. I didn't feel bad about any of it.

I couldn't find a shred of regret. Not for pushing his boundaries. Not for sex. Not for spilling so much truth he'd have surely figured me out by now.

I liked it. All of it. The depravity of our encounters, the way he so easily possessed my body, how he'd wrung every ounce of rebellion from me, and the feelings I had about it. Hell, even the feelings he'd shown me—the raw passion and pain. I liked every single fucked up part of it. Way too much.

Bodhi Decker was winning, and for now, I didn't have a single objection.

"Are you sure your sister won't mind?" I said,

forcing my disastrous, jumbled thoughts aside and reaching for the clothes. "These look brand new."

"They are, but she won't care. She lives in scrubs. Hell, she probably won't even notice. But if she does, I'll buy her some new ones."

We stood in silence for a moment, both of us hanging on to the clothes, each staring into the other's eyes. Could he see the turmoil I was in? Did he know how high the odds were stacked against us?

"Are we done with the fighting?" he asked boldly, an eyebrow raised. "At least, for now—are you good?"

"I don't know," I answered honestly. "As amateur as you might've thought my plans were, it frightens me that they've totally fallen apart. We're in danger. I've got responsibilities I need to take care of, and people who are counting on me. Yet, here I am fucking around with you, and I don't know how I'm supposed to feel about that."

Maybe it was too much honesty, but after the chase last night, fearing for my life, my family's safety, and everything I'd already divulged, this little bit seemed harmless. I was too worried, tired, and raw to keep my guard up.

He used my hold on the leggings to draw me closer, guiding me gently toward him. Then, with the flick of his wrist, he took them from me and tossed them onto the bed. Before I could make sense of what was happening, he was running his hands over my bare shoulders and down my arms, massaging small circles into my sore muscles.

I began to relax and allowed my gaze to roam over him.

In only his boxers, he was hard not to ogle. His chest and shoulders were broad and strong. His abs were lean and rippling. His solid waist dropped to the all-enticing, defined edge of his adonis belt and a trail of dark hair that continued below his waistband, leading to what I knew was an incredibly impressive cock.

God, he was easy on the eyes.

When his hands smoothed over my skin, lighting a new spark of desire, it reminded me of how amazing he'd felt inside me, too. Really, really fucking amazing. Better than anything or anyone before.

We had problems to solve and lives to rebuild. This time together was nothing more than a deadly distraction. It was time I couldn't afford to waste, and a risk I shouldn't have been willing to take. Not when there could be women in Nikolai's possession who were suffering. Not when my sister's freedom was on the line.

Yelena shouldn't lose any more precious moments with her daughter. Especially not for the sake of something as frivolous as my newly awakened sex drive.

But, *fuck me*, I was helpless to stop it. Even my deception, and the imminent danger it posed, wasn't enough to turn me off. The sexual appetite stirring within me was like a new toy, only I wasn't certain I'd ever get tired of it. Not with Dex as my playmate.

He linked his fingers with mine and squeezed, bringing me back to reality. "You have the right to feel however you do, Kira. If you want me to back off, I will. At least, I'll try. I've made you a lot of promises, and I intend to keep them all, even if it means we're headed back to that professional agreement."

My eyes searched his face, still looking for the trap I felt he must be laying, yet all I saw was pained conviction and a jaw I wanted to lick. The man was irresistible. He was also consistent as hell.

And still, I didn't feel guilty. But I should. Shouldn't I?

If he knew all the lies I was telling and the truths I was keeping hidden…

"Are you bored of the fucking and fighting?" I asked, breaking the tension and my urge to come clean.

He laughed. It was a sharp sound of delight that helped dispel some of my gloom—some of the depressing fucking desperation I'd been living with for the last year.

"I don't know, kitten," he said through a gloriously wide and disarming smile. "I think I might need a break from the fighting. It's a bit tiresome, and you've worn me out. How about you?"

"Maybe a little. But the fucking was nice."

"Nice?" He laughed again, using our linked hands to pull me flush against him and setting off a streak of sparks along my skin. "Is nice the best word you can find to describe it?"

"Why?" I laughed along with him. "What would you call it?"

"Oh, I don't know…incredible, delicious, orgasmic, mind blowing—"

"Earth shattering," I said, interrupting him, my entire body beginning to hum again.

A low growl rumbled from him, and it weakened my knees. "Fucking earth shattering," he agreed, weakening every damn part of me.

God, I was in trouble. "So…not bored, then?"

"I don't think I could ever get bored with you around." He smirked. "You'd probably kick my ass if I did."

Serious, terrible trouble.

The way his cool blue gaze assessed me, seeing right through every one of my pathetic defenses, I could tell he knew it, too.

"Is it weird that we've fucked in two different rooms of your sister's house?" I blurted, pulling away from him and turning to examine the clothes on the bed.

"Nope, but that window will need to be cleaned before we leave."

I laughed again, thanking the universe I could still manage some level of deflection. If I couldn't outright lie to him, at least I could keep some things hidden. "I know your lack of shame shouldn't surprise me, but you didn't even pause to think about that answer."

"It's not only her house."

"Let me guess," I drawled, sarcasm lacing each word as I peeked at him over my shoulder. "It's yours, too."

He shrugged, his bare torso drawing my attention,

pulling my gaze back to the rest of his near nakedness. Even wounded, he was pure strength, and I couldn't deflect my way around how much I liked that.

How much he turned me on.

"She needed a place to live." His voice was cool, his words effortless. "So, I helped buy her one."

"Wow. That was awfully generous of you," I said through a tight breath, trying to keep the hunger out of my tone.

"Someone should enjoy the money I've made. I'm not spending it on myself."

"Says the man who drives a yellow Lamborghini."

"I told you, it's a rental." He scowled, but it was playful, and his blue gaze still enticed me.

"Maybe when this is all over, you can buy one for yourself." Breaking from his stare, I turned my focus back to the bed, my fingers fumbling over the leggings as I tried to unfold them. "You could put the money you're not spending to good use. A car like that seems meant for you."

"No, kitten." He stalked toward me. His bare feet were a near whisper across the hardwood, but I could feel the heat of his body as he came up behind me. "When I spend it, it'll be on something worthwhile."

My breath caught in my lungs as he moved the wet trail of my hair aside and grazed the back of my neck with his lips. "Like what?" My entire body convulsed with a shiver.

My hormones were running rampant, and my willpower was at an all-time low. In this shaky, worked-up state, in nothing but a towel, I was too vulnerable.

I tried to keep in mind that he was a killer, a fucking murderer who'd promised to end my life if I went against him, but even those thoughts didn't help. Because now, I knew he was a killer with a conscience.

The man had a moral code, for fuck's sake. One that made sense.

One I wanted to get behind.

Suddenly, I liked the idea of having a hitman on my side. The men I was up against wouldn't hesitate to cut my throat. Hell, both Nikolai and Sasha had threatened to do just that. At least with Dex on my team, my odds of survival weren't so uneven.

Maybe it was naïve to put my faith in him. The trust he sought wasn't something I should've easily given. But I did trust him. At least, I trusted his story was true. That much was obvious.

The anguished look in his eyes hadn't been fake, and even though he'd tried to hide it, his flash of rage spoke louder and truer than any of the words he'd given me. And I trusted he was a man of his word.

But that was the problem, wasn't it?

He's a man of his word.

Because of that, I was in danger. And no matter what he said next, I knew I was going to fall. Fuck, I was afraid it was already too late.

He clasped my bare shoulders, his mouth at the shell of my ear. "I'll put the money toward an agency, or a shelter. I'm not sure exactly. Something legit that can help clean the city up for good. Or at the very least, offer people a safe space. Offer them…hope." His voice hardened over the last word, like it was something difficult for him to say.

It didn't matter. Whether or not he knew it, in some small way, he'd already succeeded. Dex or Bodhi Decker, the name made no difference. He was the man I'd promised myself would never prevail. Yet, he had.

He'd already given me hope. Because of him, there was a real possibility of getting Yelena back. Of bringing down Nikolai. Maybe even of mending the fucked up, broken bits of my heart and soul.

Because I trusted him.

It shouldn't have been possible. This short window of time together shouldn't have been enough to change my mind. It shouldn't have proved a damn thing. But it had. Literally overnight, he'd changed everything.

He'd offered me hope as a lifeline, and I'd grabbed hold with both hands.

Fuck, how was he so good at this?

It was like he could sense my weakness. Like my broken edges were all sticking out and he was lifting them to get under my skin. He wasn't afraid of the darkness inside me. The wild and deadly storm wasn't enough to keep him out.

It shouldn't matter that he was a killer with a conscience. He was still a killer, and despite showing concern, showing care—moral fucking code or not— weren't they all the same?

Guilt hit me, then. Terrible, crushing guilt.

Thank God for it, even if it wasn't for the reasons I'd expected, I was happy to finally feel it. This, I recognized. It was a familiar feeling that might stop me from doing something stupid, like telling Dex what was on my mind. *Everything.*

Including the fact that I was falling for him, hard and fast.

"Most charities are grossly underfunded, you know," I said, testing his reaction and forcing my mind to stay in the moment. "You could always just donate to one of them."

With his rock-solid grip, he turned me back to face him. He stared at me, and it was clear he was thinking. But about what, exactly?

Was he working out my secrets? Did he know I was nothing more than a pawn, sent to lead him to his death? Could he sense the soul-crushing remorse I felt over it?

"You're so fucking beautiful," he murmured, pulling me closer. "I don't think you know how much."

"Is that the thing you like about me? The genetics that made up my face?"

"No." The intensity of his blue gaze was penetrating. "I'm not talking about your appearance…although, you are stunning to look at. But no, I'm talking about *you*, Kira. You're a magnificent wildcat, with a heart of goddamn steel, and that's fucking beautiful."

"A wildcat?" A smile found its way past my conscience, his words lighting me up, turning me liquid. "But you call me kitten."

A devilish smirk stole across his lips, and he linked

our fingers, tugging me even closer. Until nothing stood between us but desire and lies. "Either way, you're a saucy little minx. *My* beautiful, chaotic kitten."

I snuggled into him, practically purring under his fervent touch.

"How do you know Sasha Novikoff?" His question hit me like a stone, squashing my rampant craving for him.

Fuck, it stopped everything within me, including my heart. Stammering hard, I answered, "I-I don't really."

"You sure?" His tone was calm, but his touch was demanding. "You don't have to give me details, Kira. You don't owe me anything, but it'd be nice if you'd stop lying."

The smoldering look on his face was beyond handsome, and I wished I could enjoy it, but my insides were suddenly twisting, my stomach full of painful knots. I couldn't even smile back. I was seized by a wave of absolute terror.

All because of Sasha.

Fuck, this was wrong. All of it.

Panic took over, my body trembling from the jolt of adrenaline suddenly coursing through me. No matter which way I turned, my life was under threat. The lives of the people I loved. Even this man in front of me, the one who I should've avoided at all costs, was putting himself at risk.

Even if we saved my sister, if Nikolai was stripped of his power or if Dex fucking killed him, Sasha would never stop. He wouldn't quit. Not until he had me.

Not until I was forced to face the ugly truth.

Sasha Novikoff would never let me go.

"Come here," Dex whispered, his brow lined with concern as he pulled me against his solid frame, wrapping his arms around me.

His silence matched my own, but his heart beat a steady rhythm as he continued to hold me. It was an intimate embrace, strong and comforting. It felt like his body could protect me from the horrible truth. Like he really could be my avenging angel.

I wanted to believe in that. In him.

Surely the universe knew what it was doing when it sent me this killer? Maybe it knew me better than I knew myself. Maybe it was time I paid attention.

"He's someone I used to know," I explained, pushing past the lump of fear in my throat as I willed my body to calm the hell down. "At least, I thought I knew him, but he changed. Or maybe he was always disgustingly rotten but was good at hiding it. Either way, I don't recognize the thing he is today. He isn't the man I thought he was."

"Why are they after you? If Rykov has your sister, why does he want you?"

"I don't know." The lie slipped easily past my lips, but the knots in my stomach all pulled tighter, making me feel like I was ripping apart.

Dex pulled back to stare down at me, his face an unreadable mask of calculated thought. I held my breath, waiting, wondering. He was good at reading situations and people. Would he decipher me? Could he see how much I was keeping from him?

"We're going to figure it out," he said when I started to tremble again. "We'll figure everything out. We'll get your sister and get you both free of Rykov. I just need to know how much of a problem Sasha's going to be."

"He's a really big fucking problem." I whispered brokenly, terror winding its way around my heart.

"Yeah, that's what I thought." He tried to soothe me, running his hands over my wet hair, back, and shoulders.

Even with fear consuming me, his touch was like a live wire. Every spot his hands touched sparked and crackled. With one arm braced firmly around me, his other hand continued to roam. His fingers found their way to my neck, moving up until they were wrapped around the base of my throat, each long digit pressing lightly.

Like last time, the hold was seductive. Possessive. I leaned into it, demonstrating my trust, and loving every heedless minute.

"Don't worry, Kira. I have a plan."

A ray of light cracked through the curtain as he bent his head toward mine. The beam fell across his profile, lighting half his face, the other side still bathed in darkness.

The image captured his duality.

He was light and dark. Bodhi and Dex. Each side undeniably attractive.

All of him too good to be true.

His breath caressed my lips. "I'll deal with Sasha, and I'll make sure both you and your sister are safe. Then, I'm going to make Nikolai Rykov regret the day he ever dared to fuck with either one of us."

What had I done? This man was going to end up dead because of me. Because the truth was bigger than both of us, and no amount of violence could ever change that fact.

CHAPTER
FIFTEEN
DEX

KIRA DIDN'T SEEM SHOCKED WHEN I PULLED MY OWN clothes from the dresser in Sunshine's guest bedroom—my room, technically. Then again, after everything we'd both revealed, the fact I kept things in the house I co-owned probably wasn't all that surprising.

Despite the mix of fear and lust on her face, I'd left her alone to dress.

Once again, I needed space. If I didn't put distance between us now, this thing could easily get out of hand.

Whatever this thing was.

If it hadn't already grown wildly beyond my control.

Cleaned up and back on task, I busied myself in the kitchen while my mind ran in circles around our problem.

I needed information, and there weren't many options to get it. Without Finn to help point me in the right direction, I was at a disadvantage. That said, bringing him back in now didn't feel right. He was still in too much danger, and even though he knew the risks, he shouldn't be the one to pay the price.

He'd paid enough, and I owed him more than the threat of imminent death.

So, no. He needed to stay out of the picture until I knew how to get to Rykov. Until Kira gave up everything she knew and led me to our goddamn victory.

On instinct, I grabbed my laptop from my bag and logged on to the secure remote server Finn had set up, sending a coded message to the best hacker I knew.

Okay, yes, Robin was the only hacker I knew, and technically I'd never met the person. Hell, for all I knew it could be a group of hackers, but Finn trusted them, so it made them the best in my books.

Dex: *Need some info on an old friend. Can you help?*

The response came within minutes, and although it would've normally been Finn doing this part of the work, the familiarity of their tone helped set me at ease.

Robin: *Happily. Just let me know what you need.*

My fingers were poised to type out my request. The demand for a solution was drumming at the back of my mind. Yet, I hesitated.

What I needed was a way into Rykov's compound. Even though Kira hadn't disclosed its location, I trusted she would. The drive to save her sister had to be bigger than the desire to protect her secrets. Right?

The only trouble would be getting past the Bratva

boss's security. We needed a way inside. Robin could help us come up with that.

Except, the thing I asked for—the thing that came flying from my brain, through my fingers, and had me hitting *send* faster than I could think—was not the thing I needed at all.

No. What I asked for was a thing of calamitous, covetous desire, mixed with a fuck ton of uncertainty. All feelings I didn't want to acknowledge but somehow seemed unable to keep locked away.

Dex: *Sasha Novikoff. I need everything you can find.*

Robin: *You got it. That'll be 3 and 48.*

Three thousand dollars and forty-eight hours before I had the information I wanted. Two entire days before I knew the truth about Sasha, and maybe more importantly, Kira's connection to him. The truth she didn't seem willing to tell me herself.

Yes, she'd let some of her walls down and given me hints of her vulnerability, but she still hadn't given me everything. Not even close. Sasha was just one of the clues. Her utter terror at the mere mention of his name didn't line up with the rest of her spotty as hell story.

He was someone she used to know. What the fuck did that mean? And how long ago were we talking? Because based on her reaction, it all seemed rather fresh, and extreme. Far more severe than rational.

Hell, she was more fearful of Sasha than she was of Rykov, which made no sense at all. Unless my suspicions were right.

Unless Kira was working for Nikolai Rykov, and this whole fucking thing was a setup.

As much as I didn't want to believe it, I had to face the facts. Had to keep my goddamn head in the game and not lose myself to her seduction. Because whatever her secret, it was a deadly one. And I wasn't ready to die just yet.

But what, then? What the hell would I do if my instincts were correct?

Killing her didn't feel right. Not when I knew she was likely a pawn, and especially not after toying with her in our little game of Truth or Dare. And not after fucking her. Twice.

I might have been a cold and calculated killer, but I wasn't that big of an asshole.

Could I use her as a bargaining chip? Or should I stick with the plan, take out Rykov, and set both her and her sister free?

Or maybe…just fucking maybe…I'd keep her, make her mine the way I truly craved, and throw away the key.

"So, what's the next move?" she called from the bedroom, practically reading my mind and jarring me out of my reckless thoughts.

With my common sense returning, I clicked back to my message thread with Robin and added to my request.

Dex: *I also need some intel on our usual suspect.*

As though they'd been waiting for it, Robin's reply popped up on the screen almost immediately.

Robin: *Anything specific?*

This was the part of the game I was good at—taking charge, following instinct, not allowing annoying emotions to get in the way, and keeping myself and mine the fuck alive. Planning, plotting, scheming, strategizing. The part where I moved one step closer to the thing I wanted most.

Payback.

Kira wandered into the room just as I was hitting send on the new message.

"Did you hear me?" She was fussing with the hem of the borrowed T-shirt, which was too big on her and made her look a bit too average. Like she was naïve and boring, instead of the smart, bold renegade I knew her to be.

But, honestly, it didn't matter what she wore when I was constantly imagining her out of it.

"I heard you," I replied, dragging my attention away from the fact that she wasn't wearing a bra, and motioned to the eggs and bacon cooking on the stove. "Working on that now."

Fuck, I was starving. Not only for the food, but for her. Other than whiskey and coffee, I was running on fumes. Still, if she offered to fuck me again, it would be no contest; I'd be balls deep within seconds.

"Okay. What else?" She glared at me, seemingly unimpressed with my plan to feed her.

"That's up to you." I slapped the laptop shut and turned to plate our meals, taking my time and waiting her out.

What solution would she offer? Would she give up

Rykov's location without my prompting? Would she help lead me to triumph over the evil fucker or only push us further into chaos?

After a moment of silence, she answered. "Aren't you the one in charge of this operation? All I know is that I need to get back home as soon as I can."

Shit, maybe I was wrong. Maybe she wasn't a rival agent, after all. Maybe she was just another ordinary woman, in way over her head.

But what kind of girl next door knew how to drop-kick an enemy unconscious?

"Well, we can't just go storming the gates without a solid plan. Not if we want to live." I scowled and set a plate in front of her at the breakfast bar. "And you can't go home until we've won. Hell, maybe not even then. They'll be watching for you there."

Her pulse was an erratic, visible staccato at her neck. "No, they won't."

"Kira, I know you're smarter than that. You think they can't find you? They know who you are. They found you at Moore's house, and I'm sure they were at Alexander's party looking for you. They're obviously tracking you. Trust me, as die hard ignorant as these men seem, they're not all idiots. Sasha and Nikolai, at the very least, will have figured it out by now."

She glared at me, her fingers encircling the fork I'd set out like she was considering using it as a weapon. It would've been a bold move, and I was almost disappointed she didn't try it.

Still, as much as her adorably feisty side turned me on, right now wasn't the time. We didn't need to fight each other when there was a much deadlier foe to track down.

"Listen," I said, keeping my voice low, like I was calming a feral animal. "Home isn't going anywhere. Let's focus on finding a way into Nikolai's compound. A way to save your sister. If we do this thing right, we can be in and out before they even know it. Then, you can go back home for whatever's so damn important before disappearing for good."

Instead of soothing her, my words seemed to hit a nerve, causing her rage to boil over. "I don't need you to explain the situation to me, Dex. I've been living this reality for too long not to get it. I don't need to be fucking managed. If Sasha could somehow find my very well-hidden home, then I'd already be dead."

"Hidden? Do you live in a cave? How the hell do you believe any place is concealed? Even here, we're not completely safe. And trust me, I've gone to a lot of trouble to ensure this house can't be traced back to me."

"I don't need to explain all my shit to you. I need to get my ass in gear and save my sister." She was seething now and was truly a force to be reckoned with.

But her choice of words hadn't slipped past me. If *Sasha* had found her home, she'd already be dead. No mention of Rykov in that statement at all. It was the brigadier she feared above the boss—the weapon, but not the man wielding it.

"Will you at least tell me why you're in such a hurry? I'd like to know why you're so eager to risk our lives."

She mashed her lips together as her eyes flitted around the room, as though looking for an easy escape. Her white-knuckle grip on the fork began to shake.

"Come on, kitten," I coaxed. "This is how you build trust. I give a little, or in this case, a lot, then you give a little. Anything at all would be nice at this point."

"What exactly have you given?" She huffed. "A sob story about unrequited love and a couple of orgasms? Do you think that's impressive? If you don't want to help me, that's fine. I don't need a fucking sidekick, anyway."

Her words sliced a deep and ragged path across my heart—what was left of it, at least. And fuck, it hurt. Not because my memories of Emily were fresh and exposed, but because Kira still didn't trust me.

And despite the common sense that screamed at me to walk away now, I couldn't. Because I cared.

Goddammit, I actually fucking cared.

Enemy or not, she'd somehow dug her wild claws into me, ripped past the cage of my control, and made me feel again. Her forced admission had triggered something deep within me, something that rivaled all the emotions I'd banished.

These weren't the same old tired feelings. It wasn't the weak and faded memory of the affection I'd felt toward Emily. Not even the anger I'd held over the injustices of the world.

No, this wash of emotion was something altogether new. Something undefinable. Something I didn't want to acknowledge because feelings of any sort were futile.

Especially when they put our lives on the line.

I took a deep, steadying breath, and placed my palms on the counter. I might've been close to a breaking point. But so was she. I could feel it. I needed to tread lightly. "Don't do that."

"Do what?" She pursed her lips as though she were trying to prevent herself from saying more.

"Don't use spiteful cruelty to push me away. It's cheap and vindictive, and it doesn't suit you at all. You're better than that. Plus, I've got to say…as a deflection technique, it's unbelievably obvious."

A light flush crawled up her neck. "Fuck, you're such a frustrating, cocky ass."

The tension between us shifted to something a little less murderous, and I smiled. "I think you like my cocky ass."

I didn't miss the heated look that passed over her features. "I think you're full of yourself."

"That technique won't work, either," I said through a light laugh. "Just cough up the info. It's not like I'm going to tell anyone. I've got no one but you to tell right now, anyway."

And shit, just the thought—the realization that I had no one on my side at the moment but her—rang loud and true.

I still didn't fully trust her. I couldn't when I knew she was still lying to me, and when she was still too afraid of the fucking truth. But goddamn, I wanted her there. It was foolish, but I wanted her to be the one I could turn to, and I wanted to be that for her as well. I just needed to convince her I wasn't her enemy.

Even if she was working for mine.

She stared at the food in front of her, her expression unreadable but gorgeous. "What are you getting out of this, Dex?"

"There's not all that much I need, kitten. I've got family, some money, and I'm hanging out with a hot as hell ass kicker. If I get to kill a few Russian mobsters soon, I'll be set."

"Don't get cute," she grumbled.

"I'm not cute. I'm cocky, remember?"

She ignored my teasing and the pressure to come clean, continuing to push the food around her plate. It reminded me of how hungry I was. Putting aside my need for answers, I made quick work of my meal.

I was chasing the few remaining scraps, wondering if I should just lick the plate clean or start in on the food she wasn't touching, when she broke the silence.

"It's my fault." Her eyes stayed glued to the counter as she toyed with the fork. "All of it."

The uncertainty written on her beautiful face was enough to bring me to my knees. Kira was a pendulum of emotion, constantly swinging from one extreme to the next. Each swing was a brutal upheaval, but she wasn't simply hanging on to that wrecking ball, she was riding it.

She was the most beautiful, destructive force I'd ever seen.

I waited her out, moving to the opposite end of the short counter, trying to stay out of her fray, because this looked a lot like the eye of the storm.

"She's so young," she whispered. "And she's counting on me. I'm all she has."

"Your sister?" I prompted when she didn't elaborate.

She inhaled sharply, squeezing her eyes shut before she finally replied, "Yes, Yelena. She's trapped with a despicable madman because of me, and I don't know how I'll ever make amends for that."

Her words were clipped, her voice matter of fact. There was no doubt it was the truth. At least, the truth as she believed it. Yet, somehow, it seemed like she was lying. Or using this bit of anguished truth as a cover for something else.

What the hell was she hiding? Still, I played along. "How is it your fault?"

Finally, she stopped fidgeting, stopped avoiding me, and met my gaze. "Because she went to him willingly, and I did nothing to stop it. I was so busy with my own life—with my aspirations and plans—I did nothing to prevent what was happening right in front of me. I should have seen it coming. I should have fucking known…"

Her words cut short, and once again she was breathing through what looked like a hell of a lot of turmoil. It was tempting to go to her, to wrap her in my arms and whisper reassurances in her ear. But what would've been the point?

I had nothing to offer other than the promise of vengeance, and we both knew that wasn't what she wanted.

"I'm in a hurry because every minute I waste is another minute my sister is suffering. Another minute I have to live with the guilt. I know rescuing her won't solve everything, but maybe I'll be able to look in the mirror again if I do."

Fuck, her words hit too close to home.

It was all too reminiscent of the burden I carried for Finn. "Rushing isn't going to fix anything, and I think you know that. It's only going to wind up getting you hurt. Or worse, your sister."

Her expression shifted to something softer, yet more resolute. "You're right."

I cocked a brow at her, the beginnings of a smile tugging at the corner of my lips. "I'm going to need you to put that in writing, kitten. I can't believe you're not arguing with me."

"Like you said before—I'm getting a little tired of fighting with you." I could see her strength rebuilding in the gleam of her amber eyes. "We can save that part for later."

A bark of laughter bubbled up and out of me. It was a short burst of uncontrolled happiness that helped loosen the tight band of strain around my chest. It probably should've made me feel weak, or uncomfortable at the very least, but it didn't.

Fuck, I almost liked it. "It would be my absolute pleasure."

"So, for real, what's the plan?" she asked, leaning forward over the counter.

"Right now, let's focus on building our strength. Eat. Rest. Sleep. I've got a few irons to throw in the fire, but we'll make a solid plan once we're back on top of our game. We might be outnumbered, but we've got one advantage they don't."

Her head tilted to the side in an inquisitive, adorable pose. "What's that?"

"They have no idea we're coming."

She shot upright in her chair, her head snapping straight and her eyes darting away from mine, down to her plate of food. "Oh, right. Of course."

Shit. Maybe I should've known Kira had already given us away, but I'd honestly hoped she hadn't. That was the problem with relying on worthless drivel like hope, though, wasn't it? It could never be counted on.

No worries. There were other ways to gain the element of surprise. More than one way to win.

But I didn't say that part out loud, because Kira didn't need to know the inner workings of my plan. Not if I wanted to keep us both alive and eliminate the sons of bitches we were up against.

People were going to die. I just needed to make sure it was the right ones. Even if Kira didn't approve of the bloodshed, I'd bet her untouched breakfast she knew it was inevitable. As she'd pointed out, she'd been living this life for too long.

Yet, that only raised more questions, didn't it? The biggest one—how the hell would I get us both out?

She continued avoiding eye contact while she pushed her now cold food across the plate.

"If you're not going to eat that, I'd be happy to," I offered, half joking. I was hungry. Insatiably so. But even with all the food in the world, I knew I wouldn't be satisfied until I'd tasted revenge.

"I'm vegan." She shrugged.

"You don't like guns or killing, blood makes you uncomfortable, and you're vegan." I shook my head, grabbing the food out from under her. No point in wasting it. "How've you managed to keep yourself alive without me? What does a vegan-wildcat-warrior-princess eat?"

She smirked, a spark of wicked humor lighting her face as she popped her finger in and out of her mouth. "There are other sources of protein."

I paused, mouth open, the fork full of egg hovering in mid air. Good thing it hadn't hit my mouth yet, I might've choked.

"Quinoa, soy, tofu, beans—it's a long list," she said in a mocking tone.

The smile that stretched my lips was wide and full of hungry greed. "That's a dangerous fucking game you're playing, kitten."

Her amber eyes flashed deadly, her tantalizing voice calling to all my basic instincts. "It's your game, Dex, I'm just following your lead. You're the one in control, remember?"

Those words should've lit me up and made me feel invincible, but somehow, they only made me feel unsteady. "Such a saucy little kitty," I said, pushing hard against my discomfort.

"Nope. I'm a wildcat."

"Fucking right you are." Wild and chaotic, like fire and goddamn brimstone.

And fuck me, I was ready to burn.

CHAPTER
SIXTEEN
KIRA

Eat. Rest. Sleep.

What kind of fucking plan was that? It had sounded so ridiculous when he'd said it, I'd almost laughed out loud. Except, nothing about it was funny.

How did he expect me to relax when everything was so messed up? My sister was still in the hands of a monster, the man whose betrayal had upended my life was still stalking me, and every minute I spent playing house with Dex put me at greater risk of falling for him.

Or falling harder for him, at least. At this rate, I'd be in love with the cocky ass by tomorrow.

Which made his plan the worst one I'd ever heard.

But I went along with it, anyway, because what other choice did I have? If I wanted his help to rescue Yelena—and I did—then I needed to do things his way. It didn't matter how anxious or furious it made me.

Or that my stupid, reckless heart soared each time he glanced my way.

Not that he spent much time looking at me. He'd buried his face in his laptop and didn't come up for air, other than for food and to take a couple of phone calls. Which, I noticed, he left the room for each time.

Clearly, eating, sleeping, and resting weren't the only things he had in mind. There was something much bigger percolating in that gorgeous, hard head of his, and I could tell from the flash of his cool blue gaze that he was on to me. He might not have figured it all out, but he was analyzing every reaction, tracking my every move, and cataloging each and every word I said.

If he hadn't already woven together the fraying strings of my lies, it wouldn't take him much longer. Fuck, with my luck, he'd probably unraveled all my secrets on day one and been simply toying with me ever since.

Although, that didn't seem to fit his mode of operation. Despite the fun we'd been having, this wasn't all a game for him. And now that I understood the truth about Emily—the ghastly, unmerciful, soul eroding truth—Dex's true motivation was unmistakable.

He didn't just want to save the damsel in distress, he wanted to put an end to the villain who'd endangered her. He was going to kill the nefarious man who'd murdered the woman he loved. It seemed so obvious now, but he'd likely been plotting his revenge against Nikolai since the day Emily was taken from him.

And here I was, like the golden fucking goose on his doorstep—the person who could hand him what he'd been after the whole time.

Or get him killed.

That was it. There was no third option. As much as I'd wished for a miracle, I had to be realistic about our chances. The pressure of it was getting to me.

Hell, I'd almost let my worries for Anya slip and told him all about her. And what then? Once that bit of information was out in the open, there'd be no way to put the genie back in the bottle. Her existence—the mere mention of her name—could bring this entire charade crumbling down on top of me.

Despite the stress and my guilty conscience, I'd fallen asleep on the couch while Dex was still chasing whatever information about Nikolai's operation he could find. At least, that's what I assumed he'd been doing. It was hard to tell when he'd barely spoken a word to me all afternoon.

But when I woke the next morning, I found myself tucked into the guest bed.

Alone.

I wandered out, confused and disheveled, to find Dex in the exact same spot, hunched over the computer with a deep scowl on his face and a cup of coffee in hand.

"Did you even sleep?" I asked through a yawn.

His eyes popped up from their intense study of the screen in front of him, and for a moment he seemed shaken by my presence. Like being in the same room as me was a test of his will.

"I got what I needed." His shoulders rolled, and simultaneously he slapped his laptop closed.

He sure did keep a tight lid on that thing…and everything else. He'd yet to share a single detail about his stellar plan to get past Nikolai's security, and he was treating me more like an enemy combatant than an ally.

Not that I could blame him. I hadn't given him much of a reason to trust me yet, either.

Impossible as it seemed, I'd have to try harder.

"Hungry?" His tone was still gruff, but he'd at least stopped giving me the side-eye.

"You don't need to worry about me. I'll just make myself some toast."

"No worry." He swept around the counter, retrieved a grocery bag that looked ready to burst at the seams, and began to unpack it. "I've got everything you could possibly want right here. Fresh fruit, stuff to make vegan pancakes, and even vegan bacon…whatever the hell that is."

My stomach did a happy little somersault, but it wasn't from the thought of eating a proper meal. "You went out and bought me food?"

"No, I just had it delivered from Sunny's usual place. I got her some stuff to replace what I've eaten, too."

He could shrug it off all he wanted, but this might've been the most thoughtful thing any man had ever done for me.

On tiptoe, I scurried toward him, pretending it was the groceries that had me excited instead of his thoughtfulness. Still, I couldn't contain the giddy feeling. "You bought me food," I murmured, winding my arms around his thick middle. "Thank you."

"No big deal," he grunted. "Figured I better feed you properly if you're backing me up. You're a liability if you're running on empty."

"You know, it's funny because a couple days ago you told me I should be thanking you. Yet, every time I've tried, you've downplayed it. For a guy who's so high on himself, you surprisingly don't like to take credit for the good stuff you do. Why is that?"

For a moment, his body stiffened like I'd caught him off guard with my assessment, and I was prepared for him to dismiss me again. But he shifted toward me, sliding an arm around my upper back, and allowed me to mold myself even closer to him.

"Because I don't think I've done much to earn it," he said, his low tone sending tingles through me. "I'm good at what I do, and I don't mind the odd compliment, but just because I'm not an asshole all the time doesn't mean you should thank me for it."

Now, it was my heart doing the stupid fucking somersaults.

I stood, basking in the warmth of his cynical stare, and surrendered to the feeling. There was no denying how much I liked this man. Even the parts I should've found despicable, I now somehow found appealing.

And that was a big fucking problem.

Food or not, Dex was right—I was a liability. Most of all, to myself.

"Okay, then, you just let me know when you think

you've earned it. I'll be ready to thank you properly."
With a light slap to his six-pack, I untangled myself
from him and turned my attention to breakfast.

Was I a tease? Maybe. If the look on his face was
any indication, definitely.

But fuck him, he deserved it.

And I needed to keep some level of self-protection
in place.

I went to work preparing banana pancakes and tried
to ignore the gnawing ache building in my gut. Because
there was a part of me that, despite my best efforts to
remain unattached, wanted only him. All of him.

That part of me wanted to push aside all the lies,
impossible odds, and even common sense and be with
him. It was an unfathomable fantasy that kept playing
out in my head. Me and Dex, together for real. No more
running and hiding. No more hurt and heartache.

Just the two of us against the fucking world.

Too bad we'd been sworn enemies before we'd ever
met. Maybe if I hadn't forced the hand of destiny and
allowed Nikolai to take over, things could be different
between us. We could live a different kind of life.

Together.

Except, if I hadn't tried to intervene in Nikolai's
business—if the paths of our lives had gone any other
way—Dex and I would've never encountered each other
in the first place.

But maybe that would've been better. For him, at
least.

Pouring batter in a pan on the stove, I watched

from the corner of my eye as he set out plates and silverware for us. The knives and forks, I noticed, were set far out of my reach. Still, the whole thing felt downright domestic—like the fairytale I wished could be true.

Until he turned his big body to face me head on and asked, "So, Wildcat, where is Rykov hiding?"

Now, the ache in my stomach was a sharp, angry stabbing. The kind of pain reserved only for those moments when the guilt to confess and the necessity of avoidance were at war with one another.

After too long a pause, during which I weighed my options about how much truth to give him, all while his intense scrutiny made me squirm, I finally muttered, "Long Island."

"Long Island?" The scowl he shot my way was one for the record books. His eyes narrowed, lips twisted, teeth gnashed together, and brows furrowed intensely.

And despite the mortal peril I was in, the look had me shifting on the spot for a whole new reason. How was it possible for me to be even the slightest bit turned on right now?

Shoving hard against the desire building in my system, I met his glower with a wall of defiance. "Yes, you heard me. Long Island," I said, drawing out the words in a mocking tone that was sure to piss him off. At least, I hoped to push some kind of button to distract from my uncertainty.

"I thought you wanted to save your sister. Isn't that the point to all of this?"

My breath caught in my throat, making me stumble over my words. "I-I…yes. Of course, it is."

"Then stop stalling and tell me where the hell we can find Rykov." Despite not raising his voice, the menace was clear in his tone. "I want details, Kira. Every single one you've got. We're not going to be able to come up with a worthwhile plan without them."

An image of the storybook-like home with its winding drives and ornate, manicured gardens infiltrated my mind. With its stone turrets, stained glass skylights, pristine marble floors, and decadent indoor pool—lazy river included—the luxury of the place was over the top.

And once upon a time, it was meant to be mine.

My grandfather had purchased the property and planned to give it to me on my thirtieth birthday, along with so much more.

But that milestone birthday had come and gone, with zero recognition of its passing. The place I would have called home was now the lair of a madman. A fucking torture palace. A wasted dream gone to rot.

And I had to give it all to Dex.

Every last, intimate bit of knowledge I had about the property that had once held such beauty and promise. A home I wouldn't have wanted now even if it was the last standing structure on earth.

"He's on an eight-acre estate on the north shore, in a village called King's Point," I said, with my heart banging double time. I felt sick from the injustice of it all. "There are a few buildings on the property—guest cottages and whatnot—but he'll be in the main house. The one with the gold front door."

His expression shifted to something of disbelief. "Real gold?"

"Yes. It's gold plated."

He shook his head, as though he still couldn't quite believe it. "He's been right under our noses this entire goddamn time."

"What do you mean?" So, my theory was right. He had been looking for Nikolai—trying to take him down —and his offer to help me wasn't quite so magnanimous.

I couldn't fault him for this either, though. If I believed killing would solve any of my problems, I'd be out to do the same. Whatever it took, and whoever I needed to use along the way.

"Nothing," he muttered, turning to the fridge to put away the remaining groceries. "I just can't believe he stuck so close to the city. I figured, as paranoid as he is, he'd be somewhere less accessible."

"Well, the place is a gated fortress, so I wouldn't exactly consider it easy access."

The pancakes were done, but I was too busy watching him to eat. Too busy worrying over his reaction to what I'd just disclosed. It was hard to gauge with his back to me, but it wasn't a hardship to keep my eye on him. Even in his T-shirt and jeans, his body was a masterpiece.

"And tell me, kitten…" he murmured, the velvet

stroke of his voice causing my insides to heat, "How did you come across all this information?"

CHAPTER
SEVENTEEN

KIRA

Fuck. I should've seen his question coming. Should've been prepared for Dex to want all the layers beneath the peak of surfaced truth. Because this was who he was, how he fucking operated. He waited for me to get comfortable, watched for my guard to lower, then struck mercilessly and without warning.

My mind spun as I pieced together a believable lie. There was no way I could give him the truth.

I couldn't let him know Nikolai was living in a home I legally owned. Not now. Not when there was a real shot at getting Yelena free from her abuser and making all my missteps of the past worth a damn.

His arms braced against the countertop, like he was prepared for bad news. Like he already knew everything and was waiting for my admission.

And shit, maybe if I gave it to him—told him all about my impossible life—he'd take pity on me. Maybe he wouldn't reach for the gun he had hidden somewhere, probably close by. Perhaps, he wouldn't put a bullet in me.

Or maybe he would.

I trusted him to protect me from Nikolai, and even Sasha and his men, but I still couldn't take the risk he wouldn't be the one to kill me.

"Nelson Moore." I practically shouted the man's name, feeling brilliant when it came to me.

"Moore…the scientist…" Slowly, he turned to face me, his arms crossing over his chest as he leaned back against the counter.

"Yes, Moore. I told you I was after any bit of information I could get from him. He didn't give much, but he did tell me a basic location. I did some digging and figured it out from there."

"You figured it out from there." His tone remained passive and so did his posture, but the sexy scowl on his face was vicious. "How, exactly?"

"I don't know," I stammered, thanking God I hadn't eaten anything yet, otherwise I might've thrown it up. "I looked at online maps and narrowed it down with property records."

"And you did that all on your own, in less than eight days?"

It felt like all the oxygen had been sucked out of the room. Each breath I took was tight and shallow, and my head started to spin.

Fuck me. Why had I believed I could keep up this farce?

Dex was nothing like the other men I was used to

dealing with. He was smarter, more systematic, and despite being cocky, wasn't actually a narcissist. I should've known he wouldn't fall for my pathetic attempts to protect myself.

Still, I had to try, even if lying to him made me feel terrible. "What? Is it supposed to be difficult?"

Like lightning, he came at me. I barely had time to react before he had me trapped up against the kitchen counter. A jolt of fear shot through me, followed closely by a molten flow of desire.

His thick arms locked to the granite on either side of me, his powerful thighs forced my legs apart, and the solid wall of his chest brushed mine. He was so far up in my space we were practically connected. With a little less clothing and a slight adjustment to our hips, we could be.

And *God*, the way he looked at me…like he wasn't sure if he wanted to strangle me or fuck me senseless, but goddammit, he was going to teach me a lesson either way.

It was sensory overload. And I was too turned on to stop him.

Unlike the other times we'd wound up in similar positions, this time, I didn't want to fight. This time, I wanted to allow him to control me. To give him whatever he wanted.

How the hell could I resist him?

"You're not as hard as you pretend to be, kitten," he murmured, the tenderness in his tone contradicting his aggressive demeanor.

I opened my mouth to argue, because how the fuck would he know anything about how tough I could be? Hell, after everything I'd already lived through, I was practically made of steel. But he seized my jaw with his enormous hand, covering my mouth and half my nose along with it, making it difficult to breathe.

Yet still, regardless of how easy it would've been for him to suffocate the life from me, a shock of desire coursed through me. It was a hot buzz of electric sensation that shot out from my skittering heart and raced through my body, causing me to shudder from its intensity.

He licked his lips like it turned him on, too, and I quivered some more. God, this man really would be the death of me.

"I know what you're going to say, but I didn't call you weak." His voice was a smooth rumble, and he searched my eyes—fuck, his magnetic blue gaze pierced my damn soul. "I know you're a powerhouse. You're physically, mentally, and even emotionally resilient. But I also know how much that costs you. How much you suffer for the sake of holding all your shit together for others."

My hands, that up to this point had felt like useless weights at the ends of my trembling arms, rushed up to meet his encroaching torso. And despite the layer of his T-shirt and my utter helplessness, the feel of his sturdy frame and his steadfast temperament lent me a strength I'd somehow been missing.

His breath fanned over me, and he leaned impossibly closer. "When I say you're not hard, what I mean is, you're not callous. You give a shit. You care about everyone and everything around you too damn much. Probably to your own detriment."

I squeaked out a muffled protest, which sounded a hell of a lot more like a surrendering moan, but his hand didn't budge.

"You can't push me away, and I won't let you tear yourself down, either. No matter what happens with Rykov. No matter what happens between us. You need to know I've got your back, Kira."

A well of emotion rose up inside of me, too big to hold back. My throat swelled as tears formed in my eyes and I struggled to breathe under its crushing weight.

Dex's tight hold of my face loosened, and he moved his hand to the back of my head, tangling his fist in my sleep-mussed hair. "Okay? Are you with me?"

Unable to force words past the tears that threatened to choke me, I nodded. Even if I could speak, what was there to say that could've conveyed the fucked up mix of emotions I was feeling? Because no matter how twisted it was, even the bold-faced liar in me wanted to be with him.

Wanted to be owned by him.

As though he could read my mind, he pulled me into him, and whispered against the shell of my ear, "You're mine, kitten. And Lord fucking help me, but I'm not letting you go."

My insides were already liquid with desire—the need between my thighs building to a demanding ache

—but it was my willpower that was giving way fastest. There wasn't much resolve left in me, and if he pushed even a fraction harder, whatever was left would likely dissolve.

Or maybe it'd just ignite like the rest of me, and all that would be left of my self-protection would be a dusty pile of ash.

"Fuck, I want you," he groaned, grazing my earlobe and sending another jolt of blazing, greedy lust coursing through me. But it was more than the physical craving making me feel weak. It was his admission.

He wanted me. Wanted to keep me?

He kissed a hot trail from my ear, along the edge of my jaw, until he was hovering just a whisper away from my lips. "What do you say?"

Dex had never come close to admitting his desire for me. At least, not like this. He'd always been too busy breaking me into submission. And even though I knew he was a master manipulator, something about his words, about the untamed look in his eyes…he wasn't lying.

And I couldn't keep up the fight. Not against him.

The surge of misaligned emotions was still stuck in my chest, and I didn't trust myself to speak. What the fuck would I even say? I want you, too? Please don't kill me?

Instead of words, my arms found their way to curl around him, my fingers digging into the hard line of his back, urging him to shift even closer.

The fingers he had woven through my hair pulled

gently, and he forced my still watery gaze up to meet his. "Answer me, Kira."

"Yes." The word rushed from me without hesitation. Hell, I wasn't even sure what I was agreeing to, but if Dex was offering something, I wanted it. Death by orgasm, maybe?

Bring it the fuck on.

But before either of us could explore the meaning of our exchange, his phone pinged and vibrated in his pocket, and fuck, it was so close to the juncture of my thighs I was ready to crawl out of my skin.

"Shit," he growled, landing a solid kiss on my lips before pulling away to retrieve the device.

A dark look passed over his features as he scanned the screen, and although my breath was still short and shallow, my body began to cool.

"What is it?" I asked when the knot of emotion in my throat had finally loosened.

His sharp blue gaze darted up, but he avoided making eye contact before his focus was back on the phone. "A lead."

A lead? That was all he had to give me? After sharing such a profound fucking moment?

"Good," I said, attempting in vain to hide the sudden pain in my sternum. Why did it feel like I'd had a sword shoved through my heart? "Maybe now we can get on track and form a real plan of attack."

"Don't worry." The phone disappeared back into his pocket, and his demanding stare was back on me.

"You're going to get exactly what you wanted. The window of opportunity on this one is tight. We should get moving."

The tenderness in the center of my chest spread, and my heart beat frantically to keep up. No matter how I felt—wounded, uncertain, and perhaps in the biggest predicament of my life—now, it was time to fight.

Fall down seven times, stand up eight.

While I forced myself to eat cold banana pancakes, he began packing up provisions. Some of the food he'd bought went into a bag, along with more medical supplies than most people needed in a year.

The more he packed, the more my anxiety rose.

Once I was done eating, I cleaned up the kitchen and went to work on the rest of the house. Dex disappeared at some point during my scrubbing, but I didn't mind. Hell, the more elbow grease I used, the less space I had to question what was coming. What we were going up against.

I was just putting the finishing touches on the sliding glass door—the squeak of the window cleaner reminding me a bit too much of the sound of my skin sliding over the smooth surface as Dex worked me to that mind-bending orgasm—when he strode into the room, behind me.

"Sunny's shoes are the wrong size. The best I can do is a pair of flip-flops."

"Better than my heels, I guess." Let's just hope I didn't need to run in them.

As we headed out the door, my body hummed with anticipation, and even though I knew we had a long way to go, I couldn't help but feel like things were finally coming together.

Finally, I'd find a way to get Yelena away from Nikolai's torment. She'd be reunited with Anya and Babka, and we'd all be able to live free from the atrocities my grandfather's precious organization had created for us.

But when Dex passed through the garage, walking toward the driveway, my stomach sank.

"Aren't we going to take this car?" I stopped beside the most average looking sedan on the planet.

He raised an eyebrow and shot me a look like I was out of my mind. "It's my sister's."

"Yes, but didn't she say we could use it? Wouldn't it be easier to blend in?"

He stalked back toward me, taking my hand in his, and pulled me toward him as he walked backward out of the garage. "I can't leave her without a car. If shit goes wrong for me, she may need it."

Everything about this town had seemed so calm and wholesome. The thought that the danger we were in could somehow impact it and hurt someone as vivacious and giving as Sunshine…fuck, I couldn't let my mind go there.

He punched the code into the automatic door, and I watched as it shut on this sweet home and all my naïve fantasies about staying here with Dex.

"Does that mean we're taking the Lambo?" I asked, steadying my mind and gathering my courage as we walked down the driveway, hand in hand.

He smirked. "Don't get too excited, kitten. I'm still the one in the driver's seat."

CHAPTER
EIGHTEEN
DEX

"THE MEETING IS SET FOR NINE TOMORROW MORNING, but I want to be there ahead of time to scope it out and make sure we're not walking into an ambush." I continued watching the road as I spoke, easing the car into the left lane. "I'm also going to need a few things from my place. We'll head there first and get some rest, since we've got time."

Kira didn't argue. In fact, she hadn't said anything since we'd left Sunny's house. Hell, she didn't even raise an eyebrow when, instead of driving toward Manhattan, I headed for Throgs Neck Bridge, leading into Queens.

And that worried me.

Because when she'd said she was with me, I believed her. Sure, she might've only agreed with a single word, but she'd volunteered her "yes" with such eagerness and conviction, I could feel its truth in my gut. And goddamn, when I'd kissed her, I could taste her compliance on her lips.

Kira was all in.

Or at least, she wanted to be.

But something was off, and just like the last time I'd had this feeling, it was an unavoidable, annoying sensation that kept burrowing deeper and deeper under my skin. I didn't believe in curses or luck—good or bad—but I trusted my instincts. Right now, everything inside me was screaming that this situation was all fucking wrong.

Yes, we were intentionally headed toward danger, but that wasn't the problem.

The trouble was that she was still hiding parts of herself from me—the most crucial ones. The parts that could put an end to Rykov's reign of terror. The integral fucking pieces I'd have to somehow lure out of her before one or both of us ended up in the ground.

"This lead is shaky at best." I said, watching her reaction in my peripheral vision. "An offer of information right after my contact went looking? Even they thought it was a bit too convenient. It could be legit. Could be worth the chance. But it could backfire on us, too."

She continued to stare out the window, wrapping and unwrapping the chain of her little purse around her clenched hands. Still, she didn't speak.

"Maybe you should sit this one out, and I should go in alone."

Her entire body seemed to jerk as she swiveled her

head to shoot daggers at me. Still, despite her mouth falling open in a sexy show of disbelief, and even though she choked out an alluring sound of dissent, she didn't say a goddamn word.

Neither did I after that.

Kira resumed her fidgeting, getting her legs in on the action this time. Knees jiggling and fingers twisting, her agitation continued to escalate until the East River came into view.

The minute the first bit of gray-blue water was revealed from between the oncoming vehicles, she was transfixed. With her breath held and movements stilled, she stared out across the water, her eyes glued to the hazy strip of land on the horizon.

King's Point.

I followed the line of her gaze, sneaking glances of my own as I drove. From this distance, the yacht-sized piers and celebrity-worthy mansions looked like little more than colorful dots decorating the shoreline.

Was one of those specks the place Nikolai called home? If I looked hard enough, could I see the glint of the gold goddamn door?

It was impossible to know. Still, it was nice to imagine it—the soon-to-be crime scene after I'd finally done away with the evil son of a bitch.

Once we'd crossed into Queens, I followed the flow of traffic to the edge of Brooklyn, and the neighborhood where I kept an apartment. The evening rush hour had long since passed, but I continued to drive below the speed limit, on the lookout for anything or anyone suspicious.

Everything seemed normal, but I wasn't willing to take chances, not when the potential for answers was so close at hand. I continued driving, circling back around three times before finally finding a spot to park more than four blocks away.

"This is where you live?" she asked, finally breaking her silence.

After everything I'd said in my attempts to get her to talk to me, this was the thing that drew her out of her shell? The fucking borough where I paid rent?

"Sometimes." It wasn't much of an answer, and I could tell from the way she pursed her lips it irritated her, but with so many variables still at play—the biggest one being Kira herself—saving her feelings was the last thing on my mind.

But she didn't push for more.

It was a good thing, too, because the lull between us allowed me to keep my senses homed in on our surroundings. I studied every car that drove by, scanned each person we passed, checked for the lights that were normally on and the ones that weren't, and plotted what to do about the man who'd been following us for the last two blocks.

Not wanting to alert our tail that I was on to him, I took Kira's hand in mine, grumbling as I tugged her roughly to my side. "Get your ass over here, you're too far away."

Fuck, I sounded like an overbearing prick.

Although, the way she shivered at my touch led me to think she liked it.

Still, her gaze whipped up to meet mine as our shoulders bumped, and she shot me an adorable look of defiance. "The distance was intentional."

"Why's that?" I held her stare, trying to convey with my best hard look that we had company.

Seemingly oblivious, she kept rolling with her sassy attitude. "Because whenever I get too close to you, I end up making terrible decisions. Decisions I still don't regret, by the way. Even though I should."

Despite it being the absolute worst timing, her brazen tone and bold admission sparked a flame in the center of my chest. It was hardly a flicker, but the burn was enough of a distraction that I almost forgot about our shadow.

Almost.

I leaned into her. "It's hard to regret something so fucking good, isn't it, kitten? But those bad decisions will have to wait. Don't look, but we have a visitor. Behind us, about twenty paces."

Her shoulders stiffened. "Shit. Do you recognize him?"

"No, but that doesn't mean anything." I gave her hand a squeeze. "Don't worry, I'll come up with a plan to get us out of this."

I expected her to respond with urgency, maybe even a bit of fear. Instead, she flexed her fingers around mine and looked me dead in the eye. "How about, just this once, we ditch your plan and I take the lead?"

Fuck, I wanted to kiss the petulance right off her luscious lips.

I took a deep breath, and for the first time in a year, I let someone else take control of my destiny. "You'd better have a solid scheme in that pretty head of yours."

She pulled me to a dead stop by our joined hands, stretched the chain of her purse over her head so it slung across her body, then lifted to her toes and kissed me.

The breath seized in my lungs and a surge of adrenaline coursed through me as her tongue swiped deftly over mine. It was short-lived, ending with my bottom lip captured enticingly between her teeth before she released it on a sweet smile.

With a wink, she turned and started walking us straight toward our pursuer.

His hands were in his pockets, head bent low, and he studied the ground at his shuffling feet as we passed him. The guy was so conspicuous I would've laughed out loud if the situation wasn't so damn vexing.

They'd found me. Despite all my rules and precautions, they'd learned my name and found the place where I laid my head at night. I'd warned Kira of the dangers of going home, of the possibility of being caught.

Why hadn't I thought the same would apply to me?

I'd called her an amateur, but right now I was the one acting like I was new to this game. And the only explanation I could come up with—the only goddamn line of defense I had—was that my mind was too stuck on Kira to think straight. I was so preoccupied with unraveling her secrets and trying to be her hero, I'd forgotten myself.

She'd made me weak.

But, hell, I'd known she would all along, hadn't I? And still, I was obsessed, unable to walk away.

As soon as we'd moved past our tail, she peeked at him over her shoulder, and after only a few more steps, pulled me into an alley.

"Move," she hissed as she dropped my hand and broke into a run, the sound of her borrowed flip-flops echoing off the surrounding buildings.

She darted past a couple of rusting dumpsters, then seemed to disappear. Fuck, this woman wasn't just an ass kicker, she was a damn ninja.

When I reached the spot where I'd lost sight of her, I discovered another narrower side alley—and Kira, climbing a fire escape. I took the sharp right, stealing a glance behind us, and discovered the man was headed our way.

"Keep that sweet ass moving, kitten," I called to her as I scaled the rickety ladder, pulling it up behind me.

By the time we hit the top, our stalker had figured out where we'd gone and was beginning his climb. I didn't stick around to watch, but he seemed to be losing speed.

Kira, on the other hand, didn't miss a beat. She sprinted across the adjoined rooftops like it was an Olympic sport, not even slowing when she reached the ledge on the other side. She dropped to a crouch, grabbed hold of the curved handle of the next ladder, and vaulted out of sight.

I stopped short, peering down at her as she hustled toward the ground. She looked up at me with a wide smile, and I nearly fell over the damn edge.

She was in her element, and she was beyond stunning.

Wild and fucking deadly.

And I was seriously cracked, because as I joined her on the descent, I found myself smiling, too.

When my feet finally hit solid ground, Kira was waiting for me with a motorcycle beside her. A fucking motorcycle.

"Is this your bike? The same one from the night we met?" Was it a coincidence it was here? Something as ridiculous as fate? Or something else entirely—something a hell of a lot more deceitful than I wanted to wrap my head around at that moment.

With a huff, her hands landed on her hips and she narrowed her eyes at me. "You mean the night you killed the one man who could've helped us walk straight through Nikolai's front door?"

She was right. But goddammit, I didn't want to admit that out loud, either, and we sure as hell didn't have time to stand around and argue about it. She glanced up, drawing my attention to the rooftop. But there was nothing—no sign of the man who'd been shadowing us.

"Let's get out of here," she said as she threw her leg over the bike. "But this time, I'm driving."

We traveled in more of a straight line than I'd have liked, but Kira handled the bike with incredible ease, despite having nothing on her feet but a thin strip of foam. She wound us through traffic while sticking to the speed limit and kept us moving without drawing unneeded attention.

We didn't go far, though. After only a few minutes, she pulled into another narrow lane and stopped at a gated chain link fence.

"Where are we?" I asked, dismounting behind her.

"No time to explain." She popped the padlock on the gate and opened it, motioning for me to bring the bike. Once the gate was locked again, with us behind it, she covered the bike with a tarp that had been hanging nearby.

"Tell me—" I grabbed her roughly by the shoulders, forcing her to look me in the eye, "—what the fuck is going on."

She stared up at me with the most open look of longing and sincerity I'd ever seen from her. "Bodhi, you've asked me to trust you. And I do. But right now, you need to trust me. Okay?"

When she used my name like that, I wanted to trust her—to be able to set my need for command aside and put my faith in her. She was right, it's what I'd been asking of her this whole time, after all. So, maybe it was time I give her a little.

Even if faith felt a bit too much like hope, and even if I still wasn't sure I was buying that shit.

Her fingers laced around mine and she urged me to follow her to a scarred and dented steel door. Without hesitation, she yanked it open and walked right in.

A small but bustling industrial-looking kitchen greeted us, the smell of lemongrass, garlic, and spices infiltrating my senses. I peered at the people working, wondering if anyone would object to our presence, but they all seemed too busy with their tasks to notice.

"This way." Kira tugged on my hand, leading me away from the kitchen and down a long narrow hallway to another door. She knocked three times.

We waited in silence until an elderly woman opened the door. Without a word, she bowed her head to Kira in a way that made her seem like royalty and motioned for us to enter.

Fuck, I had so many questions, but with Kira in charge, and the threat of being caught at the forefront of my mind, there simply wasn't time.

The woman closed the door behind us as we entered the apartment, but Kira didn't stop. She dragged me through the small living space, past an old man whose rapt attention was fixed on a loud and ancient television screen, to a door on the other side.

She paused momentarily to look up at me, as though she wanted to ensure I was still with her, then tugged open the door and walked outside.

We were in a basic, nondescript neighborhood. Cars were parked up and down the street, and brownstones pressed close on both sides.

Kira led the way down the block, across the street, and up the stairs to the front entrance of one of the homes. She stepped in ahead of me but turned as I entered to ensure the door closed silently behind me. Then, she raised her finger to her lips, indicating I should stay quiet.

I followed her up more stairs to the third and final floor, and she led me down the short hallway to one of the two doors that were across from one another. With the key from her tiny purse, she unlocked it and whispered, "No one else is up here, but we still need to be quiet."

Allowing the door to swing wide, Kira stood back and waited for me to enter. With my heart pounding like a jackhammer in my chest and my mind struggling to keep up, I accepted her invitation.

The walls were a warm but boring beige, the floor creaked under my weight, and the sparse furniture was old and worn. Still, the place was clean and well cared for. And even if there were cracks in one window and a few chips in the ceiling, it was a home.

Kira's home.

She didn't need to say it. Instinctively, I knew it was true.

With the door closed and locked behind us, she kicked off the dirty flip-flops, limped into the room to stand beside me, and looked around as though seeing it all for the first time. "It isn't much." She folded her arms around herself and sighed. "But it really is off the radar. We'll be safe here for the night."

Her words were meant to be reassuring, but my blood still pumped hard through my system. When my eyes landed on a small bin of children's toys, even more questions popped into my brain.

But fuck, where should I even start? The chase, the handy motorcycle, the fact that her apartment was so goddamn close to mine…and there was a child in the mix? Was it her child? How much more was she hiding from me?

When she caught on to my line of sight, her eyes pinched shut with a pained expression.

"I think you have some fucking explaining to do, kitten."

On a heavy breath, she nodded. "Okay, but I think I need a drink first. How about you?"

I didn't argue—a drink sounded like a brilliant damn idea. I simply grunted my agreement and watched her pad away into the kitchen as the hole where my heart should've been expanded.

She returned a moment later with full glasses in hand and motioned for me to join her on the couch, downing half her drink before we were even seated. She passed me the other drink as I did my best to calm my jangling nerves, turning to me with her eyes cast down to the swirling amber liquid in her glass.

My gut was uneasy and my chest was too tight, but I slugged back the alcohol, anyway, continuing to wait her out in stony silence.

Finally, she peeked up at me through the fan of her dark lashes. "I know what you must be thinking…" Her words trailed off and she cleared her throat. But she didn't say any more. Her eyes dropped away from mine as her fingers toyed with the lip of her glass, brows drawing into a worried frown.

Fuck this. Letting her lead might've worked out fine for our getaway, but I didn't have the patience for more. I took the glass from her and set it on the table beside me, along with my own.

She watched my slow, purposeful movements with her breath held and color rising in her cheeks. And goddamn, despite the bite of frustration fueling me, the look on her face—the heated look of anticipation—made my balls start to ache.

Without warning, I lunged toward her, grabbing a fistful of her hair and locking her close to me with my arm braced around her back.

She came to me willingly, her body turning pliant as she stifled an anguished moan and bit down on her bottom lip.

"You want to know what I'm thinking?" My breath was jagged, my voice raw. I should've demanded answers. Instead, I teased, "I'm thinking how easy it would be to work you to the brink of orgasm…to get you to the point where you're so wet, so fucking needy, it hurts. To the point where it feels like you might die if you don't come. And then, just when you think you can't handle another second, I'd stop and withhold that pleasure until you've spilled every single one of your secrets."

"God, you're an asshole sometimes," she rasped, the hungry look in her eyes tinged with something that resembled fear.

"Yes, I am. But believe it or not, as much as I like to hear you beg, I'd prefer not to use sex as a torture technique." I leaned in, brushing my lips against the velvet of her cheek. "I'd rather we left that for later, and just for fun."

Her body quaked, and I wasn't sure if it was lust or panic making her tremble, but I didn't want to push her any farther. I had a feeling I wouldn't need to.

I let her go, reclining back against the couch until only our knees were touching and she was breathing normally again. "Now, tell me the truth."

With her spine straight and her gaze hardened on mine, she said, "She's my sister's little girl. My niece. I live here with her and my grandmother."

It was her sister's child, not Kira's. I didn't know why that made any difference, but the tension in my chest loosened and the turning of my gut eased. "Where are they now?"

"Downstairs, with a neighbor. She doesn't know the truth about my life, but she's good at keeping them safe, regardless."

I hummed my understanding and made a mental note to find out more about the neighbor.

"My niece calls me Mama," Kira continued, her eyes turning glassy. "She's only two. She doesn't remember her parents. Not really."

More of the puzzle was coming together, and along with it, my resolve to do the right fucking thing. To help her, no matter the cost. "What's her name?"

Her lips pursed momentarily before seeming to come to a decision. "Anya."

"Anya," I confirmed as my fingers met the bare skin of her arm, stroking a light path down to her hand.

She nodded, full of solemn determination. "Anya Rykova," she choked. "She's Nikolai's daughter."

"Fuck." There were only a few pieces that remained out of place, but even without them, I was able to see the outline of the bigger picture. The deadly path that lay before me.

"If something happens to me…" She shook her head as her voice broke over the words. "Right now, I'm all she's got. I can't let her down."

Now, my need to be a hero truly was reborn. Any hesitance or doubt I'd entertained dissolved as I allowed the feeling to take hold. It was a good one—one I recognized, but bigger and stronger than ever before.

It was the need for vengeance.

Sasha's blood, Nikolai's blood, and the blood of every member of their sick fucking gang might be enough to quench it.

"That's not going to happen," I promised, visions of their deaths making me smile. "Not as long as I'm around."

She looked ready to tell me more, like there was something important she'd left out. I wasn't going to push when we were finally getting somewhere. Not when I could see the amount of trust it had taken for her to bring me here—for her to give me what might've been the biggest and possibly most damning secret in her arsenal.

But soon. Yes, soon, Kira the wildcat would give me everything, and I was going to take it all.

CHAPTER
NINETEEN
KIRA

THE LOOK IN HIS EYES TOLD ME HE WAS READY TO DO some serious damage. Only, I wasn't sure what kind.

My entire body had been wracked with nervous tremors from the moment he'd stepped over my threshold, and since then, the feeling had only doubled.

I'd wanted to come home—to check on the well-being of my family—but I hadn't imagined doing it with a hitman at my side. Especially not when we were on the run, and my family couldn't know I was here.

And not when having him in my personal space felt so fucking *right*.

But now, with the truth about Anya out in the open and all my other secrets at risk of being exposed, I didn't know what came next.

I knew what I wanted. It was the same thing I always seemed to want when he was nearby, no matter how inopportune the timing or how much danger we were in. I always wanted more with him.

More *of* him.

"I get it now." His fingers danced over the back of my hand, making my skin tingle and allowing the body tremors to take an even stronger hold. "This whole time, I thought you were protecting yourself, but you were only protecting her."

"Oh no, I'm protecting myself, too." The words were out of my mouth faster than I'd had time to think, and I mashed my lips together to prevent more from pouring out.

After everything we'd been through, and after all the fucking truth and trust I'd given him, the last thing I wanted was to make him doubt me. Or to give anything more incriminating away.

The severity of his expression didn't change, but there was a glint of levity in his gaze when he said, "I guess self-preservation comes naturally to an ass kicking ninja-wildcat-warrior like you. But it only makes sense when you're responsible for so much."

"What about you?" I turned my hand over so his fingers traced over my palm. "Who are you protecting?"

His hard blue gaze was like a knife to my throat. "You."

And *God*, every bit of my soul spilled out around me. The choke of tears I'd felt only moments ago returned, making my nose sting as I struggled to hold them in. "What about *her*?" I asked, my heart joining the lump of anguish in my throat.

The crease in his brow deepened. "Who?"

"Emily." Her name was barely a whisper, yet it still hurt to say.

His fingers that had been drawing circles over mine didn't move away. They simply stopped, falling stock still, like the rest of him. "If you're implying that I'll let you down or that I can't keep you safe because of what happened…"

The agony in his voice nearly broke me. How had he misunderstood? Shaking my head, I grabbed hold of his hand. "No. No, that's not what I meant—"

"Because I'm a different man now, and I know what we're up against."

"I know—"

"I promise you, Kira," he interrupted, "I won't fucking fail you." And I fell just a little bit harder.

This man had no idea, and I was too much of a mess to figure out how to tell him. How could I explain that what I was really asking—what the stupid, fantasy believing part of me needed to know—was if he was still doing this all for her. When he killed Nikolai, would it be with her name on his lips?

Or was there room in his broken heart for me?

Tears were still threatening to let loose, but I was also more turned on than ever. Pushing hard against the swell of emotion, I rose up on a knee, placed a hand over his rock-like chest, and straddled him. With my legs hugging his bulky thighs, I rested my weight against him, hoping I could show him how I felt.

I needed him to know that, despite my better judgment and the ridiculously short time I'd known him, he was important to me. That, as much as he'd claimed to own me, I wanted to own him, too.

"I believe you." I nudged as close to him as I could get, still holding his tortured gaze. "I believe *in* you."

His fingers flexed, biting into the curve of my hips in the most delicious sort of way, and his chest expanded on a heavy breath that stole a bit of my own.

It was impossible for me to resist him. I ran my hands from his pecs to his broad shoulders, across the hardened line of his jaw and into his thick, dark hair. Every inch of him was power and control, and I wanted all of him to be mine.

I didn't want to share him—not even with a ghost.

"I only meant that she had or has a special place in your heart, and I just wondered…" My voice faltered and my pulse skipped violently.

One of his hands moved up to cup my face, his thumb swiping through the wet trail of tears that suddenly dripped down my chin.

"Emily was a pipedream," he said with conviction. "She was my brother's wife, for fuck's sake. It's not like I was ever going to get in the way of that. She was just the girl next door. The girl we grew up with. The first girl who ever held my hand. All loving her ever did was make me miserable."

He licked his lips and his thumb pushed back through the streaks of tears on my face. "But that's not what you're asking, is it? You want to know how I feel about you."

"Yes," I said. My body shuddered, unable to hold back the rush of emotion that went with it.

"Until I met you, I thought I knew exactly what I wanted. And I do. I still want that. But I also want you, and those things are in stark fucking contradiction to each other."

He swallowed hard, his throat bobbing in a way that made me want to lick it.

It took him forever to continue his thought, but when he finally did, he said it with fervor. "I won't lie to you, Kira. I'm not sure what this is between us, but it *is* something. You've made me feel things, even when I haven't wanted to." His eyes that had been holding mine with such intensity dropped to my lips. "And that's pretty fucking substantial for a guy like me."

It was a pretty fucking substantial answer, too. The kind of response that made my insides heat and my mind wander to devious places. "Bodhi?"

"Yeah, kitten?" His long fingers raked through my hair, pulling just enough to cause the bite of pain I'd come to love.

"I want to make you feel even more." I licked my lips, anticipation getting the better of me. My hands drifted to his belt buckle, my fingers slowly working the leather through the clasp. "Will you let me?"

I waited for him to stop me—for his hands to encircle mine and for him to take back control. But he didn't. He kept his vivid blue gaze on my face, and I wondered if he could see how much I wanted this. If he could tell that by allowing me this bit of power, he would give me what I needed.

By the time I'd opened his pants to reveal the black band of his boxer briefs, I was practically panting.

When my fingers skimmed the head of his covered shaft, he grunted, "Come here," and pulled me in for a heated kiss. Our mouths clashed in a hungry dance, and I moaned as he flexed his hips, allowing my hand to slide further over his cock.

God, he was already hard, thick, and imposing. I couldn't wait to get my mouth on him. As I struggled to free him from the confines of his pants, his mouth trailed down my chin and over my neck, making me feel like I might come apart.

He lifted his hips and effortlessly pushed both his jeans and briefs down to his knees, then gripped me tightly around the waist again.

My breath caught when he growled at my ear, "Do your worst, Wildcat."

I sat back to look him in the eyes—a lust-filled smile taking hold of me—and wrapped the fingers of both hands around his hard length. The expression on his face was unyielding, and his jaw looked ready to crack under the pressure. But still, he didn't stop me.

My hands pumped in a slow, steady rhythm, relishing the smooth glide of velvet over steel. I watched him watching me, and the ache between my thighs grew more demanding. When I skimmed over his balls, his breath caught and held, and when I leaned in to place a kiss on his lips, he let it out on a low groan.

I kissed down his neck, savoring the salt on his skin, until he shifted to pull his shirt over his head.

With his wide chest, defined abs, and proudly jutting cock on display, he was a masterpiece. A fucking prize waiting for me to claim him. But when he raised his hands, as though in surrender, and rested his arms along the back of the couch to give me free rein, I almost faltered.

A voice in the back of my mind whispered this wasn't right—that a woman like me could never truly deserve a man like Bodhi Decker. He was too fucking good to be true, and I was nothing but a liar.

But I shoved the condescending voice of conscience aside and dragged my lying lips over his chest and down his stomach as I slid over his lap and positioned myself between his knees.

Salt, sex, and pure male potency invaded my senses at the first swipe of my tongue over his crown. The taste of a man had never made me wet before. Then again, no man had ever made me want to come just from the look of lust in his gaze, either.

Not until Dex.

I took my time, running my lips over his entire length, savoring the dip and ridge of every vein, and kissing the spongy bulge of his mushroomed tip. With each swirl of my tongue, I expected him to take over, but he only continued to watch me with something akin to worship on his handsome, rugged face.

When I finally took him in my mouth, he sucked in

a sharp breath, making my nipples pebble and my pussy quiver.

God, I was so fucking turned on. With my hands grasped around his base and my knees digging into the carpet, my lips stretched around his impossible girth, and I angled my head to take more of him. I couldn't fit much —he was too fucking big—but when he hit the back of my throat, making my eyes water, I let out a heady moan.

"Fuck, yes," he grunted, reaching out to tangle his fingers back through my hair.

That was it, I was done for. I'd wanted to be in the position to make him come undone, but with one rough touch I was the one ready to unravel. More than the desire for power—more than anything—I craved his command.

Not because I wanted to be bossed around or because I liked the stern sound of his orders. No, it was because when he took over, he was actually taking care of me. And I needed that.

After a year of being depended on by everyone else, I needed to be the one who was looked after.

My mouth continued to lavish him, but I moved my hand to cover his at the back of my head and pleaded through our connected gaze for him to take control.

"That's right, kitten," he murmured, wrapping his fist with my hair. "You like when I'm the one in charge, don't you?"

I did my best to nod and uttered a muffled sound of agreement around his cock.

Before I knew what was happening, he'd pulled me off him and was shifting positions. His hand remained locked to my head, but he was suddenly standing before me, with one knee on the couch and his other hand clutching around my neck.

He bent close to me so that our mouths were brushing and whispered, "You're going to open like a good girl and I'm gonna fuck your pretty mouth. Okay?"

"God, yes," I cried, too desperate to pretend I wasn't aching for it.

"Hands on your thighs," he ordered, and I obeyed. "Eyes up here and don't look away." His breath coasted over my lips as our gazes clashed and my body hummed. He kissed me hard and fast. "Open."

Then, still leaning over me as far as he could, and with his hands like iron around my head and neck, he slid his cock down my throat and did as he'd promised. He fucked my mouth like he meant it—exactly the way that I wanted—making me gag and gasp as the fire licking at my center grew to an impossible roar.

But not for long.

After only a dozen or so punishing strokes, he stopped, looped his hands around my arms and pulled me to my feet. "Enough. Take me to your bed, Kira, I need something more."

Confused about what I'd done wrong, new tears formed in my eyes, and I swiped angrily at them as he toed off his shoes and stepped out of his pants.

Out of habit, I picked up his discarded clothes, then

led him to my room. I didn't bother looking behind me to see if he followed. Not that I needed to—he was like a giant in a dollhouse, and I was all too aware of his every move.

The tears continued to fall as I placed his clothes on the chair in the corner of my room.

But why the fuck was I crying? It shouldn't matter if I hadn't pleased him, if he'd had better, or he wanted something else. Making Dex happy, making him feel anything at all, shouldn't have been on my list of priorities.

Yet here I was, falling apart because the killer didn't like my blow job.

"Did I hurt you?" he asked, his deep voice laced with concern.

"No," I gasped, and immediately regretted even trying to answer.

I could feel the imposing force of his massive frame as he came up behind me. "What's going on in that beautiful brain of yours, kitten?"

With his big hands clasped to my shoulders, he tried to turn me to face him, but I shook my head violently and stayed stubbornly rooted in place.

Yes, he'd already seen me cry. But this? This was far more than a few little tears. This was a fucking breakdown, and I couldn't let him see it. Hell, I could hardly face it myself.

I was fully clothed, and he was naked, yet I was the vulnerable one. I was the one who'd lose everything when he decided to walk away. When he inevitably chose to honor a dead woman over me. Because who the hell was I, other than the woman who'd planned to stab him in the back?

"Kira." His arms banded around me, and before I knew what was happening, the ground disappeared from beneath my feet and he was carrying me the short distance to the bed.

He maneuvered me like I was weightless, laying with me on the center of the mattress and pulling me into a sturdy embrace, cocooning me in the shelter of his arms. His hands, which I'd seen do unbelievably terrible things, latched on to me with conviction. Like by sheer force of will, he could stop me from falling apart.

As he landed soft kisses at the top of my head, he murmured, "You can tell me. Whatever it is, I promise you can tell me. It won't change a damn thing."

My chest ached as my already shattered heart crumbled to dust, but I forced myself to meet his persistent gaze. Forced the words from between the fragments of my broken identity. "I want to be enough for you—to be good enough for you—but I don't think I ever can."

"Fucking hell, Kira." His voice cracked around the words. "Don't you get it? You're the best fucking thing…the first person to get through to me in more than a goddamn year. The only person who's not family who I'd risk my life for. The only woman who's ever made me so stupidly delirious, I'd be willing to do just about anything for you. To keep you."

"But I thought—"

"You thought fucking wrong," he growled, his arms

crushing me to him and his words knocking the wind from me. "You think I'm the one in control because I tell you what to do. Because I like to hear you beg. But you're the one with all the power."

"Show me," I whispered, the insatiable crawl of need clawing at my insides. Only this need was for more than something physical. This need was for something downright divine—a communion of our fucked-up souls.

He rolled, pinning me on the mattress beneath him. "Gladly."

When his mouth took mine, I expected a bruising assault. Instead, I got passionate affection. His arms released me, allowing his hands to roam, and he took his time, exploring my body. Finally, my clothes came off, and he dropped his head between my legs, licking and sucking in a languorous pattern that nearly drove me out of my skin.

"Bodhi, please," I begged when I'd finally had enough of the teasing. "I need you. I need more."

"I know, kitten." He climbed back over me, his wicked grin slick with my juices. "Same way I wanted and needed more of you."

Oh fuck, I was such an idiot.

But he was sliding into me with such gradual, pained precision, there was no time or desire to further reflect on the assumption I'd made. On the lie I'd told myself and had nearly allowed to tear me down.

Especially not when he braced his weight on his elbows, molding his body to mine, and locked me to him in the most intimate of ways. It was a way that made me believe he'd never let me go.

I returned the sentiment, hugging his waist with my legs and framing his head in my hands.

He fucked me slow and sweet, with the kind of tenderness reserved for long-term lovers. There was no mad frenzy. No challenge or aggression. Just the give and take of sublime pleasure that built to a heightened peak.

And damn…it built, and it built.

From the first few deep strokes of his magnificent cock, I was coming. It was an orgasm without limits. My body clenched and released, and he worked me through it. Until another wave hit, pulling me into ecstasy. Over and over.

"You feel so fucking good," he murmured as he pumped his hips just a little harder, hitting a spot so deep inside of me, I thought I might break.

"You do, too," I said on a sharp moan, another climax impending. "You make me feel…" But all words were lost to passion.

"Fuck, Kira, you make me feel alive."

I cried out, unable to hold back the surge of emotion. The sensation was too overwhelming.

"That's it." His voice strained with need. "Give me one more."

He angled his hips so there was just the right pressure against my clit, moving in me like a man possessed.

Bliss crashed over me, and I spasmed around him,

my body coiling tightly despite being completely wrung out. The feeling of euphoria was so fucking profound, I broke into tears all over again.

His mouth fell open as I shuddered and sobbed his name, and on a strangled shout, he came inside me.

If I'd had the energy for regrets, it might've been that this moment—like every other good thing I'd ever had in my life—would have to end.

No matter how much I wanted it, Dex and I couldn't last.

And I knew I'd be the one to ruin it.

CHAPTER
TWENTY
KIRA

THE NEXT MORNING, I WOKE BEFORE THE SUN, WITH Dex sleeping peacefully under me. I was draped over his chest with my body curled around him and the soft puff of his breath tickling across my shoulder.

It felt superb.

In the hazy, blossoming light of pre-dawn, with my brain sleep sluggish and body still worn the hell out from the night before, I could almost trick myself into believing this was real. That I wasn't leading him straight into the viper's den, where one or both of us was likely to lose everything. I could pretend we were an ordinary couple, making a life together.

That we were happy.

After hours of the most intimate and all-consuming sex of my life, I should've felt that kind of joy. Should've been at peace. Instead, I was consumed with the soul-crushing realization this was all about to end.

Last night, I'd been too exhausted to move, and

perhaps too blissed out to put thought to my feelings. Too wrung out to worry and too satiated to extricate myself from his magnetic hold.

Dex hadn't seemed eager to let me go, either. He'd pulled me over top of him, wrapped his arms around me, and mumbled something that sounded like it could've been "the best" before falling asleep with a smile on his face.

It was ridiculous, but despite the exhaustion that had been trying to pull me under, I'd forced myself to stay awake just so I could trace the defined edge of his jaw and marvel at how handsome and peaceful he looked in his sleep. It was the first time I'd seen him rest, and I luxuriated in the feeling of his solid frame in my bed while I let my imagination run wild, dreaming up scenarios where this thing between us became permanent.

Still, I'd expected to wake up alone. To find him puttering around my kitchen or hear him in the shower. I'd anticipated waking to discover the connection I'd felt between us had all been a dream. Or at the very least, extremely one-sided.

But he was still here.

And I was still so completely fucked.

Because although I'd decided long ago there was no way I could stab him in the back and live with myself, I had to keep up the act.

Nikolai would be waiting. Maybe even watching if the tail at Dex's apartment was any indication.

He would expect to hear from me soon, and it didn't

matter that I wanted to avoid the vile man forever. If I didn't give him something, I'd be putting us in even greater danger. But I'd have to be extra cautious now. I couldn't let him know I was off script because if he had any inkling I wasn't still following his orders, it would be the end of the line for both me and Dex.

Yet, if I continued playing along with Nikolai and Dex found out…

Fuck. What choice did I have? Either way, my life was at risk.

The frayed edges of all my secrets were slowly unraveling, but if I could hold them together for a little longer—keep pretending to be a badass who could handle her shit—maybe I wouldn't end up with my heart crushed in the process.

"Good morning, kitten." The rough pads of his fingers ran over my back, sending sparks rippling across my skin.

My lips trailed hungrily over his chest, and I hummed, "Good morning to you, too."

He encircled me in his sturdy arms, gripping me like I was his lifeline.

And *God*, I wanted to be that for him. To be the one he could count on. The person he turned to when the feelings he tried so desperately to deny finally got the better of him. When he lost faith in himself and realized killing others had only been a way to punish himself.

But even the thought of that was overwhelming. How could I be anything other than what I was? I was a liar and a thief—taking a man who didn't belong to me.

A man who deserved so much more than what I could offer.

Because what could I give him, other than chaos?

"Time to go to work," he said, kissing the top of my head. "Let's get in the shower and get moving."

I scowled. "That might just be the worst idea I've ever heard."

"What are you talking about?" Confusion lined his brow.

Despite the overwhelming sense of dread trying to creep up on me, I wanted nothing more than to show him all the deliciously lust-tinted thoughts his suggestion had brought to mind. "I can be in and out of the shower in under five minutes. But only if I do it alone," I murmured, unable to stop myself from flicking my tongue over his nipple.

I really was an insatiable vamp.

His deep laugh was loud and genuine, and lit me up from the inside out. "Fair point. Guess you better get your sweet ass moving, then. Timer starts now." He gave me a swat on my behind as I jumped out of bed.

We hustled to get out the door as the sun was rising, neither of us saying much more until we were certain we hadn't been followed.

"I know I keep asking, but what's the plan?" I linked my fingers with his as we walked the long way around to retrieve my bike. It was five blocks out of the way, but at least we didn't have to traipse through anyone's home this time.

"This was smart," he said, motioning to the alley

where we'd parked and seeming to ignore my question. "It's the kind of precaution I'd take. In fact, it's the exact type of measure I thought I had been taking."

He helped me move the gate aside and watched as I took care of the tarp, his stern gaze taking in every little detail. "It brings up a question that's been lingering in the back of my mind, though. How was I made in the first place? How the hell does Rykov know everything about me?"

The insinuation was clear in his tone, and my stomach sank. Did he think I'd given him away, even though it made zero fucking sense? How the hell would I have known a damn thing about him?

"What are you implying?" I dared, resolved to face my destruction head on.

His head tilted and his brow crinkled, like he was doing his best to puzzle me out. Then, suddenly, he was in my space with his cool blue gaze locked on mine. "The plan is for us to do a thorough inspection of the meeting place and its surroundings. We'll look for any sign this might be a trap. Then, assuming the coast is clear, I'll go in and talk to the informant."

My heart stuttered a beat and I let out a breath, but my mind was still reeling as I got my bearings again. "What about me?"

"I need you to keep a lookout. You brought your phone, right?"

I nodded, and he held out his hand until I placed my unlocked phone in his palm. I waited with my stomach rolling over itself while he typed his number into my contacts.

Fuck, I hoped like hell he hadn't analyzed that list too hard. The last thing I needed was him questioning why there were only three names in there, and why one of them was only an initial.

"There." He expertly flipped the phone through his fingers, passing it back to me, and I took another shaky breath. "You can text me an SOS if you see anything suspicious."

He wanted to go in alone. To leave me behind while he got the information. Information that could potentially lead us into Nikolai's stronghold and get me to my sister.

And then what? Would he take it and run?

If this informant turned out to be the real deal, Dex would have everything he needed. He could finally get his revenge. And he wouldn't need me to do it.

Could I trust him? I wanted to believe I could, and everything in my soul told me he was more than the cold-hearted hitman I'd first imagined him to be. Hell, I'd just told him last night that I believed in him, and it had been the truth.

Still, there was a little voice in the back of my head whispering how it was a huge mistake to give any man my trust.

Just look at what had happened the last time I did.

But this was different. This was Bodhi Decker, and although he might've seemed too good to be true, he hadn't let me down yet.

With some lingering reluctance, I agreed. "Sounds like a plan."

"Trust me, kitten." He planted a quick kiss on my cheek. "If we show our faces together, we become an even bigger target. This guy could be on the up and up, or he could be one of Rykov's men. Hell, it could be twenty men waiting to take us down."

My stomach seized. "But if it is—"

"If it is, I'll take care of it myself. And if I can't…" He pulled back to look me in the eye. "Well, I'd rather rest easy knowing I'm not taking you down with me."

"You really are the most annoying man on the planet sometimes. you know that?" I laughed, despite being filled with almost too much dread to function.

I squeezed my eyes shut and tried in vain to find some of the lightness I'd been bathed in earlier—the place of contentment that had felt a little too close to happiness.

He pulled me in close, wrapping his arms around me, and nuzzled the shell of my ear. "If this all goes smoothly, I'll make it up to you later. I promise."

The gruff edge to his voice and the memory of his body moving in and over mine sent a wave of desire coursing through me. I pushed it aside, praying the universe didn't let me down.

This was a promise I really hoped he could keep.

We arrived at the meeting location well ahead of schedule, giving us the advantage of being able to case it out. But nothing seemed out of place. It was a busy little laundromat in the heart of Queens with apartments above, shops on both sides, and a cafe on the opposite corner.

The rooftop from a block over gave us an excellent vantage point. We were able to scan the entire area, and we watched the comings and goings for over an hour. Not a damn thing looked out of the ordinary.

If this was a trap, it was a brilliant one.

"Looks good over there, too." Dex returned from the other side of the rooftop. "Time to decide, kitten. Are we doing this?"

Although my gaze would normally be drawn to him —his imposing form took up a lot of space—I couldn't tear my eyes away from the spot below. I was too afraid of missing something. "I don't think we have a choice," I whispered.

"Agreed."

A sense of urgency hit me, then. It might've been doubt, a desire to do my part, or maybe it was just plain old fear. Whatever the reason, I felt the inexplicable need to stay with him. Not to be left alone.

My eyes snapped to his, imploring for his under-standing. "I want to go with you."

"No." His face gave nothing away, but his no-nonsense tone was exacting. "There's no way in hell I'm risking your safety."

"Fine." A frown pulled at my lips, but as I tried to keep it under wraps, it turned into something that felt a hell of a lot more like a snarl. God, I was angry. And I wasn't even sure I understood why. "But I'm not staying up here. If something does go wrong, I should be close by to help you."

"The only other place that makes sense is the coffee shop. It's filled with people, and you can have a decent view of the laundromat without having to sit at the window."

Reluctantly, I agreed to his revised plan. Not that he was giving me much, but considering how stubborn the cocky jerk could be at times, I would take whatever I could get. At least, this way, I wouldn't be stuck on a roof a block over if things got out of hand.

He left me at a high table in the cafe, with a warning to be careful and a soft kiss on the lips.

I wanted the kiss to linger, to feel the intensity of his energy and the comfort of his control, but all too soon the moment was over. Before I could even wish him good luck, Dex was out the door.

A cup of coffee warmed my clammy hands, and I did my best to take strength from that. Only, it was next to impossible when the rich aroma, which would've normally made my mouth water, made me want to wretch.

Or maybe that was just the giant ball of anxiety that had taken over my system. Because my real strength—the only one I believed I could truly rely on—was stalking across the street into what might very well be a trap. And all I could do was watch.

At first, nothing happened. Dex wandered into the laundromat, looking like he was just an ordinary guy without a care in the world. He did a slow loop of the machines, pausing every now and then as though he were deciding which one looked best. Then, after seeming to come to a decision, he leaned against one with his arms crossed.

It was strange to see him from this perspective—as though I were a casual observer and the tall, attractive man across the street had simply caught my eye. Even from a distance, he dominated my field of vision and captivated every ounce of my attention.

Maybe that's why I didn't notice the dark shadow that had passed over me until it was too late.

The sickening smell of almonds and vodka invaded my airway, drowning me in a wave of nauseating memories. Two things that for the last year, I'd done my best to keep away from. That I'd have sooner faced immeasurable pain than be forced to remember.

But here they were, accompanied by the muzzle of a gun jammed against my ribs and an arm slung around the back of my tall stool.

I sucked in an uneven breath and swallowed back the vomit threatening to surge up my throat. My gaze remained glued to Dex, currently glancing at his phone, completely unaware of my predicament.

But maybe that was better. At least, he was safer over there.

The owner of the arm and the gun leaned into me, his breath fanning across my cheek in a way that had once meant something special but now only served as a reminder of all his betrayal and treachery. And all my devastating regret.

"Lyubov moya," he murmured, an endearment that once upon a time might've melted me like butter.

Not now. Not ever again. I refused to acknowledge the fiend at my door.

But that didn't eliminate the threat. It didn't stop him from poking me harder with the gun, to the point I almost lost my nerve.

"Look at me," he demanded.

I committed my view of Dex to memory, and turned to face my biggest nightmare.

"I've been looking for you," Sasha said with a wicked smile. "You shouldn't have run."

THE INFORMANT WASN'T GOING TO SHOW.

After waiting ten minutes longer than I should have, with my eyes covertly scanning the street for trouble, I was ready to walk away. I'd need to chalk it up to bad intel, a nervous informant who'd changed their mind, or worse—a fucking hoax.

At least, I hoped. Even if hope still wasn't on my list of things to believe in.

I scrolled through my phone, reading and then re-reading the latest messages from Robin as the minutes ticked by and my stomach grew heavier, wondering what had gone wrong.

There was a lot of information in our conversation thread—Robin really was the best hacker around, and they seemed to have their fingers on the pulse of the major crime syndicates in this city—but there was nothing more about this meeting or the person who claimed to have insider access to Rykov.

Not that it surprised me. In my experience, informants were generally unreliable if they were spooked, and most of them had serious trust issues and a whole lot to lose. Having one back out at the last minute wasn't unheard of.

Except, this didn't feel like someone simply changing their mind. It felt a hell of a lot more like a setup.

Someone was playing a game of cat and mouse, and I'd walked right into it like a fool. It was the kind of manipulative ploy I'd engaged in many times, but never on this end of the equation, and never with so little information or strategy to back me up.

This side of things felt a little too much like losing control, and I didn't fucking like it.

Yet, if this was some kind of mousetrap, where the hell was the danger? Why was I still standing here, unscathed?

Something's not right.

The thought was like a sucker punch, nearly knocking me out of commission. The unsettled feeling expanded until it was deep, unyielding, and made my goddamn skin crawl. Only this time, instead of shrugging it off as superstition or delusion, I paid attention.

Something was most definitely wrong, and I had a feeling it had something to do with Kira.

But it wasn't just that she'd been hiding bits of herself from me. Or that she'd fallen apart in my arms last night, only to seem wary again this morning. And even though I knew she'd been working for the enemy, I also knew she hated him as much as I did. That she'd do anything to get her sister back.

Did that include double crossing me? Was this setup somehow part of her plan?

No. I shrugged the thought off almost as soon as it entered my brain. She might've been keeping secrets, but she wasn't malicious. And although our time together had been short, I trusted my intuition. Everything I knew about Kira told me she was innocent. Like me, she was caught in a dark and disturbing game, and her only option this entire time had been to play along.

And now? Fuck, now, I had the innate sense that she was in danger. Because there was only one other option for what was happening here, and I was a fucking idiot for not seeing it sooner.

If this situation was a trap and the snare wasn't here…

It could only mean it was with her.

In my misguided attempt to shield her from danger, I'd left her alone like a sitting duck. I'd allowed my burgeoning feelings to not only weaken me, but to impair my judgement. Except, it wasn't my own life I'd put at risk.

It was hers.

A band of pain constricted my chest, and it felt like my racing heart might burst from the pressure.

I glanced out the laundromat window to the people on the street. No one seemed bothered or out of place, and no one looked familiar. The coffee shop across the street where I'd left her was still bustling with regular business.

On the outside, it all seemed normal. Yet, everything inside of me screamed that it wasn't.

Without making my interest obvious, I scanned as far into the interior of the coffee place as I could manage, hoping to catch sight of her beautiful, contemptuous face. But from this distance, and with the mid-morning sun reflecting off the window, it was impossible.

Just as I was about to give up waiting and go to her, the door to the shop opened, and Kira stepped out, as gorgeous and wild-looking as the day I'd met her.

Only, she wasn't alone. Sasha Novikoff was at her side, with an arm draped possessively over her shoulders and wearing a smug look of satisfaction.

He swaggered alongside her like he was king of the world, with his cavalier attitude on full display. His head tilted in my direction, and he said something to her with a wide and malevolent smile spreading his lips.

The look on Kira's face was solemn, yet she didn't put up a fight, and I just about lost my goddamn mind.

With my body at war with my brain and no fucking clue what to do, I stood rooted in place, watching as Sasha strongarmed the most kick-ass woman I'd ever met away from me. But not before shooting an audacious look my way.

The nervy prick wanted me to know. He'd planned it this way so I could witness the power he had over her, and to make me feel weak.

The ugly fucker clearly didn't know me because, even without a plan, I was the farthest thing from helpless. My first instinct was to confront him and demand he take his vile, filthy hands off my kitten. Or, better yet, I'd break every one of his fucking fingers as I did it for him.

But as they moved toward the opposite corner of the street, two more of Rykov's men stepped out to join them. It was the same two from Bowen Alexander's party—the one I'd shot and injured, and the dead man's replacement.

I didn't want to jeopardize her safety by following them too closely, but I couldn't just hang back and let them take her, either. My mind sprinted over the various possibilities and outcomes, trying in vain to come up with a makeshift solution.

Fuck, if I had my rifle, I'd snipe the assholes here and now.

But I had nothing. Not a goddamn inkling of how to get her back without getting one or both of us killed in the process. What the fuck was I going to do?

Never in my life had I felt so alone.

Yet, as I hustled outside to watch them make their way down the street, I realized that was the answer. I needed backup. Someone in my corner. Someone I could trust with my life, and even more importantly, *hers*.

I needed my brother.

Another notification from Robin was waiting on my phone when I opened it to call Finn. The subject line was one word—the one I'd subconsciously been waiting for.

Sasha.

But it was too little, too fucking late when the maniac already had his hands on her.

I swiped past the message and opened my contact list, all while following Kira from as far a distance as I dared. I couldn't lose sight of them, but I couldn't let them know I was here, either. Although, they'd likely expected me to track them.

What was their plan?

Shit. What was mine?

Finn's line rang twice before he answered. "What's happening?" His normally chipper tone was absent. In its place, there was concern laced with violence.

"Nothing good," I confirmed, knowing he'd read the anxiety in my tone. "Where are you?"

"I'm here."

I was too preoccupied to make sense of his meaning, and too close to the edge to be nice. "What the fuck are you talking about? Are you in the city?"

"No, you stupid fucker," he said through a cheeky laugh. "I'm here. Well, sort of. Look up."

My eyes darted up to the adjacent rooftops, but there was nothing. No sign of anyone skulking around.

But then, something appeared above the buildings, silently hovering on the horizon.

"A drone?" I could see it, yet I still didn't quite believe it.

"Yeah, brother. Military grade. I can see and hear almost anything."

"But where are you?" I asked, my gaze returning to the street up ahead and the three odious men who'd recently landed themselves on my kill list. Rykov might've still been at the top for the moment, but Sasha had definitely entered the running.

"I'm at your place." Finn cleared his throat. "You're getting low on toaster waffles and whiskey."

How the hell had he gotten into my home when I hadn't even made it up the fucking block? There were too many questions. Too much overflowing emotion. I didn't know which damn way was up.

Something inside me split open, and all my worst fears began to tumble out. The sense of worry—of unbelievable wrongness—hit me so hard, my long stride faltered, and I practically stumbled down the street.

"What the hell are you doing here? I told you to get out—that it wasn't safe."

"I know, but when did I start taking orders from you? You should've known I wouldn't leave you to do this dangerous shit on your own."

Of course he wouldn't. I should've known, should've sensed him nearby, but I hadn't. Hell, he'd slipped past all my surveillance and safeguards.

"How long?" I asked, the pit of agitation growing in my gut.

"How long, what?"

"Don't play innocent with me," I snapped, my

patience with him and this whole fucked up scene hitting its limit. "How long have you been tailing me?"

He laughed. It was a low, easy chuckle that let me know, despite his underhanded spying and my undying frustration, we were still on the same page.

"I've been here from the beginning." The trace of humor in his tone turned to a hard line of conviction. "From the moment we first entered this messed up line of work, I've had your back."

"That doesn't really answer my question." Yet, it did, didn't it? Because somewhere in the back of my mind, or maybe deep inside that cage where I'd locked up all those impossible-to-deal-with emotions, I'd known my twin wouldn't abandon me. He'd never be happy to sit back, managing the money and our network, while I was out risking my life.

Or maybe, more importantly, I should've known he'd never let me take down the man responsible for killing his wife—the love of his life—all on my own.

"Do you know where they're taking her?" Finn asked, breaking through my muddled thoughts.

Kira. Fuck, I couldn't let myself lose sight of the only thing that mattered. "I can't be sure, but I'm guessing Rykov's eight-acre, waterside, gold-door estate."

I skirted around a group of women pushing baby strollers, trying not to think about how I might've been jeopardizing their safety. Everyone on the street could be used as a target against me. But that didn't seem to be Shasha's agenda.

No. The longer I trailed after them, the more I was convinced he wanted me to follow.

"You figured it out?" Finn asked, referring to the location of Rykov's compound, not sounding at all surprised.

"She told me."

"Ah." His voice dropped to a contemplative rumble. "So, she's a mark? I've wondered—thought maybe you'd lost sight of the objective for a moment."

The instinct to protect her was something close to goddamn insanity. The compulsion rushed through me, tearing my stomach to shreds and making my pulse roar in my ears. "No, she's not a mark," I said, doing my best to keep my voice low and even as I darted across the street. "I mean, she was at first, but not anymore. She's important to me. She fucking means something."

"Congratulations, Casanova," Finn muttered.

Fuck, I was fed up with his sarcasm and feeling out of control. "All right, smart ass. What the fuck are we going to do?"

"Let them go."

My hand clenched around my phone so hard, I thought I might've heard it crack. "What the hell are you talking about?"

"They obviously want you to follow them. My guess is, they won't just lead you to Rykov, but to your fucking demise." He paused, but I could sense there was something more he wanted to say. Something important he had to tell me.

After a drawn-out silence, he continued. "Rykov's

been after you from the start of this mission. He figured out you were responsible for killing off his crew and put out the call for your head weeks ago. But I don't think he knows about me, which gives us the advantage."

The band of pain around my chest squeezed. "How do you know all of this?"

"I'm a fucking genius, brother. You might've got the brawn, but I got the brains. Trust me."

"I do. Always." And it was true. At least, it had been. But fuck, what else had he been hiding from me? Where the hell was our twin bond? Our goddamn ride or die connection?

Or had I been the one to bankrupt it all when I fell in love with his wife?

"Same, you muscle-bound idiot," he said with true affection in his tone. "Now, listen up. I've got a plan."

CHAPTER
TWENTY-TWO
KIRA

The one man I'd successfully avoided for the past year, and had hoped to keep away from for the rest of my life, was in my face. And he was seething.

"Where did he go, Kira?"

Sasha stared at me with a drop of spittle stuck to his scarred upper lip and hatred in his eyes. Never in all the time I'd known him had I seen him so out of his mind with anger. Not that he was a pragmatic or measured man by any means, but he'd always been exceptional at hiding his rage behind the thick guise of not giving a fuck.

This version of him was beyond unnerving. He was downright terrifying.

His features that I'd once thought boyishly handsome were now a mask of fury. The horrific scowl that I'd never witnessed before seemed permanently etched to his face. Color had risen against the fair skin of his neck and cheeks, and the red splotches that showcased his anger also made the wicked tattoo across his neck look oddly reminiscent of an open wound.

It was ghastly.

I'm so incredibly fucked.

In this worked up state, I didn't know what to expect from him. I didn't know what he was capable of.

Still, I was prepared for the worst. Although he'd never laid a hand on me, I'd seen evidence of his brutality with others, and I was ready for him to strike at any minute. Ready to absorb his fury, no matter how much it hurt.

"Why the fuck did he stop following us?" His hands clenched into hard fists at his sides as he stalked back and forth across the marble floor in front of me.

But I didn't know what to say. What would be acceptable? More importantly, how the hell would I know why Dex chose to do any of the things he did? Every time I thought I had the man figured out, he went and did something unpredictable. Or made me do something unfathomable, like fall for him, right before he left me to fend for myself.

"I have no idea," I whispered, afraid of raising my voice too much, in case it further provoked him.

"He should've followed. Isn't it in his fucking DNA or something to be your savior? We should've been able to take him." It seemed like maybe he was talking to himself instead of looking for an answer, and maybe paying more attention to his predicament than he was to me.

I tested this theory by inching a step backward

toward the door. My heart beat an erratic staccato, making my limbs feel jittery, but I forced myself to move with as much stealth as I could muster.

Just one slow step. Then, one more.

We weren't at Nikolai's estate but at the house next door, which seemed to be set up as some kind of security outpost. There was a wall full of monitors in this room, which I thought must've once been for dining, with a bank of computers in a row underneath. And we weren't alone. I'd seen other men, including the two who helped bring me here, patrolling the grounds.

But I could see the tell-tale golden door of Nikolai's main house through the treeline that separated the properties, giving me my bearings. At some point in time, he must've bought this place, or acquired it through other means.

God, I didn't want to think about that, or what would happen to me if I didn't get the fuck out of here immediately.

"Nik warned me. He warned me and I should've listened. Why the hell didn't I listen?" He was ranting now and not making a lot of sense, but it was clear there was more going on than I was privy to.

Nikolai had warned him about what, exactly?

The temptation to ask—to find out what was going on behind the scenes of my grandfather's beloved Bratva—rose to the point it almost overpowered my need for self-preservation. The question was on the tip of my tongue.

But his attention was stolen when a woman with

huge boobs and bottled blonde hair sauntered into the room.

The same woman who'd been on Dex's arm the night of Bowen Alexander's party. The one who's obvious pride in her own minor celebrity must've overtaken her sense of self-preservation.

Either that, or she was clueless about who she was dealing with.

"I thought you'd be done with her by now," she whined. "You said this business with her and Dex wouldn't take long. You promised me we'd have dinner together."

Tess, the fucking traitor, spoke as though she were safe. As though her body and her connections gave her the upper hand. Like forming an alliance with Sasha guaranteed her security in this fucked-up scheme.

Not that I had any real understanding of what their scheme entailed, but still, she was an idiot if she believed her beauty or fame gave her any power here.

Sasha flashed her a smile that was so disturbingly polite, so ridiculously charming, if I hadn't known any better, I might've swooned. "Yes, you're right," he agreed. "I shouldn't get carried away. We will have that dinner. But first, there's work to be done."

He was completely out of character around her. Or, at least, putting on his usual good show. It made me sick. He'd always been good at faking his way out of trouble, but over the years, I'd come to realize it was more than boyish pranks or childish fibs. He was the dirtiest and deadliest kind of criminal. One without a conscience.

Or perhaps, he really did believe his own lies.

But that would make him psychotic, and that was too simple an excuse.

Still, if the batting of Tess's false lashes was any indication, his answer had appeased her. She'd bought into his pretense, lock, stock, and barrel. "Is there anything else I can do to help, babe?"

Her overly sweet tone and use of the endearing term made me wish I had earplugs, yet I was thankful for her distraction. Maybe if he was preoccupied with her, there was a chance I could get the hell out of this situation alive.

"Call him. I don't care what you say, just get him here." Sasha's smooth tone was clipped, his earlier animosity peeking through his thin cloak of respectability.

Tess, however, didn't seem to notice. "No problem, babe," she said with a smile.

She produced a phone from her back pocket and seemed to scroll through the contents for a minute before the sound of Dex's gruff voice filled the air. "Now's not a good time, Tess."

I was frozen in place, my plan to sneak away forgotten as I waited with the breath stalled in my lungs and my heart in my throat. I was enraptured by the sound of his voice. Or maybe it was just the hope he represented.

"Oh, Dex, thank God," Tess screeched. "He's got

me. Me and this other girl. Kira, her name is Kira…and he says if you don't come now, he's going to kill me. Please, Dex. I don't want to die!"

There was a pause on the other end of the line, and for a moment I wondered if the call had dropped, but then his rough voice was back, and my hope tagged along with it. "Relax. No one's going to die. Yet."

My stomach dropped. Why did he sound so nonchalant?

"Dex, please!" Tess tried again, her dramatics starting to sound as over the top as her appearance. "He has a gun. He's serious."

"If he was going to shoot you, he'd have already done it, kitten," he said with an air of indifference.

Kitten. Was he calling her the same endearment he'd given me? Or did he know I could hear him?

"I'll be there soon."

There was a click and a moment of silence, then the line went dead.

Sasha's face was still blotched with red, and once again filled with fury. "You're lucky that worked out," he said to Tess before turning his stormy gaze my way. "Both of you."

Her plumped-up lips fell open on a sound of distress, like she was offended and fearful all in one go.

But what the hell had the two-faced, treasonous idiot done?

Dex was on his way, and there was no doubt he was walking into a trap. Although, it hadn't escaped my attention that Tess didn't tell him where we were, which made me question a hell of a lot more than just his apathetic behavior.

"Why do you care so much about Dex, anyway?" Tess dared to ask. She was either extremely gutsy or downright oblivious to the level of malice this man was willing to cause.

Sasha crooked his finger at her, a wide smile gracing his lips.

As though she were under a spell, Tess obeyed his unspoken order. When she was close enough to reach, he seized her by the wrist and yanked her to his side.

"Did I say it was okay to ask questions?" His words were menacing, but his tone was almost tender, a jarring contrast that made my head spin.

"N-n-no…" Tess began to visibly quake in his hold.

"No, I didn't." He leaned forward and kissed her softly on the lips. "I care about him because he's a thorn in my boss's side. And he fucked me over. Now, he's going to pay for that."

Her already huge eyes grew wider.

"Now, that's the last time you get to be a nosy bitch with me. Understand?"

God, he was a monster. How had I not seen it before?

"Yes." Her head bobbed on her neck like a faulty puppet. "Yes, Sasha. I understand."

My foot had slid another small step backward when movement on one of the security monitors caught my eye. My stomach sank further when I recognized the yellow Lamborghini. The image of the sleek car rolled from one monitor to the next before coming to a stop at one of the gates to Nikolai's estate.

Damn, even with the Lambo, he'd gotten here fast. Which meant he'd already been on his way when he answered Tess's call. But how the hell had he known where to find me?

Unless, maybe he wasn't here for me, but for Nikolai.

Shit. Looking closer at the feed from the security camera, I recognized the red clay tennis court in the background. It was on the other side of Nikolai's property. It was far enough away, Dex wouldn't hear me yell for help, but close enough to put him in terrible danger.

The action on the monitors had caught Sasha's attention as well, and I looked around the room, calculating if it would be possible to make a run for it.

"Your boyfriend is here," he said, turning to me with a wicked sneer. "And would you look at the toy he brought with him. It's a shame, really."

"Thank God," Tess sighed. Then, maybe realizing he wasn't talking to her, shot me a contemptuous look behind his back as Sasha began to bark orders into a two-way radio.

Unfortunately, he was speaking Russian at a pace I couldn't dream of keeping up with, so I was still very much in the dark when it came to his plan.

When Dex unfolded his powerful body from the sportscar with ease, every cell of my being rejoiced. He was here, and regardless of his reason, I'd never been happier to see a man in all my life. Even on the small monitor, he looked larger than life. Like a man on a mission. A killer out for blood.

My fucking hero—if that's why he'd come. Although, part of me was seriously starting to doubt the likelihood of it.

I watched with my heart flip-flopping in my chest as he flicked the car door closed with ease, then purposefully began to stride away.

The picture suddenly flashed bright, followed by the echo of a booming explosion that rattled the windows, knocked out the cameras, and shook me to my very core.

Tess let out a blood-curdling scream and ran from the room for cover, but I simply stared in disbelief at the static on the screens, hoping—no, fucking praying—they'd come back online and show me an image of Dex, still alive and in one piece.

I needed to see if he was all right. Surely, what sounded like a fucking atom bomb was something simple like a stray firework or some other innocent and easily survivable thing that went boom.

There had to be a happy ending to the soul-crushing pain that was suddenly consuming me.

But the monitors only flickered, mocking me with their black and white snow and the reflection of Sasha's smug smile.

"What did you do?" I choked, my throat clogged with the threat of tears.

"What did I do?" he taunted, turning to me with virulent eyes and ready fists. "What about you, Kira?

After everything I've done for you—making deals with Nik to keep you and your sister alive, keeping your niece and grandmother out of harm's way, and letting you live your life…without me. I've loved you, Kira. Loved you my whole life, even though you've run away. Even though you've destroyed me, time and time again. This," he seethed, his breath heavy as he waved his hand toward the blinking bank of screens, "This is what happens when you fuck with my head. The question isn't what I've done. The question is, what did *you* do?"

God, he truly was a madman. A death wielder.

And in another life…my husband.

"I don't know what you're talking about." My voice cracked with the weight of the words. "You're the one who divulged my entire plan to Nikolai. You're the one who's lack of loyalty got my grandfather killed. And it's because of you I've had to live this treacherous life. Your disgusting betrayal was the reason I ran."

"No, Kira. I'm not stupid enough to believe that. You agreed to the deal I made for you with Nik, but then you chose to leave, anyway. You chose to leave me. And then, you fucked Dex."

My quick comeback caught in my throat because my heart was already lodged there. So many lies. Lies upon lies upon lies. And it was all so messed up, I wasn't even sure I knew which parts were true anymore.

Only one thing was clear—Nikolai was responsible for it all. He'd brought down my family so he could take over, and in the process, he'd screwed over his most loyal man.

Fuck, I almost felt sorry for Sasha.

But then, I remembered the role he'd played in his own demise. I looked at the evil glint of joy in his gaze at the thought of hurting me, and all empathy toward him was lost.

He laughed at the look of shocked distress that was surely on my face, and God, it was a hateful sound.

If I'd had any remaining doubts about him or his intentions, they'd all been wiped clean. There was nothing good left in this man. The decent, caring boy I'd known and once loved was long gone. The man that stood before me now was savage, his concept of love and compassion corrupted beyond recognition. All because he'd put his blind faith in Nikolai.

"That's what I thought," he quipped when I remained silent. "But that's okay, Kira. I already suspected you were a lying whore. That's why I had one of my guys plant a remote detonation bomb on Dex's car. And now, you see, I've fucked him, too. Fucked him straight to hell, where he belongs."

"You killed him?" I gasped, my heart cracking into a thousand pieces.

"No, Kira, you did."

CHAPTER
TWENTY-THREE
KIRA

WITH A STRANGLED ROAR, I CHARGED AT SASHA, TEETH gnashed, claws out, and mind completely lost.

He side-stepped me easily, swatting at me as I rushed past him like I was nothing but a minor inconvenience. Still, I turned and rushed him again, unbothered by the sting of his hand on my ass and the growing look of salacious fervor on his too-pretty face.

When he avoided my assault for a third time, whacking my ass again as I stumbled around him, something inside me cracked and disintegrated. I crumpled to the floor in a useless heap, my shoulders sagging with what felt like the weight of a thousand years. My chest collapsed in on itself, making it next to impossible to breathe. The tears I'd been holding back let loose in a violent crashing wave of despair.

Dex was gone. He'd been killed by a criminal I'd once thought of as family, just like his sweet, precious Emily.

And now, I'd never know if he'd come to save me or to have his revenge. I'd never know how he felt. Worse, I'd never have the chance to tell him the truth or to let him know how much he meant to me.

"I wonder if you would shed these same tears for me, lyubov moya. Or would you dance on my grave?"

I forced my watery gaze up to study Sasha's familiar face—the fine lines around his hazel eyes, the sharp curve of his cheekbones, and the scar I used to trace that cut across his lip. And I laughed. The giddy, high-pitched sound was so bizarrely out of place, so fucking *wild*, I almost didn't recognize it as my own.

It didn't seem to sit well with Sasha, either. His face contorted to an awful grimace, making him look like a cartoon villain. Which only made me laugh harder, the hysterics growing beyond my control.

"Why the fuck are you laughing?" he seethed.

Wiping at my running eyes, I wheezed. "You…you killed him. Just wait until Nikolai finds out."

His brow furrowed and his jaw hardened, but there was something in his gaze that reminded me of fear. "What are you talking about? Nik's been after this guy for weeks, and now he'll know it was me who took him out."

"I'm working for Nikolai, you idiot. Dex was my target." The unnatural smile on my face stretched wider, matching the growing chasm of my soul. "Nikolai wanted him alive. The only person you've fucked is yourself."

His expression was a mix of skepticism, confusion,

and extreme trepidation—a look that would've made me smile for real if there was any space in my heart for happiness, or even simple satisfaction.

But the only thing I had room for was pain.

This was it, wasn't it? This was what Dex had meant when he'd told me killing was sometimes necessary. This was what he'd felt when he'd learned of Emily's death—the gnawing pit of agonizing misery that could only be filled by bloodshed.

No wonder the man had gone on a killing spree.

And no fucking wonder my hand was inching toward my knife, hidden at my back.

Another man strode into the room, his eyes bouncing back and forth between me and Sasha. Although I couldn't remember his name, I recognized him. He'd been absent the night my grandfather was murdered. Not that it meant much, but if there was a scrap of the old Bratva loyalty left in him, maybe he'd take pity on me.

I did my best to look weak and hapless—not that it was a far stretch in my current state.

But he diligently ignored me, his spine ram-rod straight and his jaw ticking. "We have a problem."

Sasha finally acknowledged him, turning his hateful gaze away from me. "Why aren't you taking care of it?"

The man leaned a little closer and whispered something in his ear.

"For fuck's sake," Sasha's voice boomed. "I don't have time for this shit." Yet, he turned to me with a finger pointed at my face. "Don't you fucking move an inch," he ordered, before stalking into the next room.

He stayed in view, but his back was turned to me, and the other men in the room were mostly hidden behind a wall. None of them had a clear line of sight to me.

With my nerves shot to hell and my soul splintered into fragments too small to recognize, I pulled my knife from its sheath and crawled backwards toward the door. The minute I was out of the room, I stood and silently bolted the rest of the way to the exit.

There was no one around to stop me, which seemed too convenient to be true, but I didn't question it. With a quick look out the sidelight, I silently turned the knob and walked out the door.

How had that been so easy?

Fuck, why was I still standing around to analyze it?

This was it—my chance to run. The best opportunity I was going to get to save my own life.

But then what?

Was I supposed to go back to working for a gangster who had no moral code, no sense of duty or honor, and no concern for anyone but himself?

Maybe returning to my meager apartment in one piece should've been enough. But what about my sister? Was I supposed to feel okay about leaving her behind again?

Because I didn't. Everything inside me rebelled against the idea.

So, instead of choosing to run away and protect

myself, I ran headfirst into chaos. I sprinted toward the mansion on the other side of the trees, toward that gold fucking door and the monster who lived behind it.

Straight toward Nikolai.

My freedom and security, even my fucking life— none of it was worth a damn if the despicable bastard responsible for this terror was still breathing. I'd never have peace as long as he walked this fucking earth. Especially not if he had Yelena.

And if I couldn't have Bodhi, the least I could do was avenge him. I could finish the job he'd started as Dex...

I could strike Nikolai Rykov off his list.

After making it to the trees without incident, I stopped momentarily to scout ahead. Despite being less than an hour out of the city, it was almost peaceful without the sounds of people, traffic, and industry. Briefly closing my eyes, I inhaled a steadying breath and nearly choked on the faint smell of burning oil and rubber.

A sense of madness overtook me as I searched for signs of the fire. It was there, on the other side of the estate grounds—a black column of smoke rising and dissipating over the trees that surrounded the property. From this distance, it was impossible to see the details, but whatever remained of my beaten heart shattered a tiny bit more.

God, he'd really done it. Sasha had blown up the fucking car. With the best man I'd ever met beside it.

The tears returned, silently streaming down my face

like a running faucet. The sorrow would debilitate me if
I let it. And fuck, maybe I would.

But first, I'd get a taste of revenge.

There wasn't much shelter here, the trees were old
and huge, but they were only a row deep, and the
surrounding shrubs were shorter than I was. I'd probably already been standing in one spot for too damn
long. Still, I did my best to blend in while I looked
across at the home that should've been mine.

Fuck, if I do kill Nikolai, maybe I'll take it back.

There wasn't time for that thought to settle before I
was spotted. A man, who looked like he was out for a
casual stroll with an assault rifle slung over his back and
a cigarette dangling from his lips, nearly walked right
into me.

He came around the trunk of the tree in front of me,
and both of us had a moment of staring in silent alarm.
The cigarette fell to the ground as we both took action—
him reaching for his weapon, and me lunging with my
knife, already in hand.

By sheer force of will, I managed to get him pinned
to the tree, but he was bigger, stronger, and adept at
keeping himself alive. He blocked my attempt to slit his
throat, with his arm braced against mine. His other
hand, which had been trapped behind his back, pulled
free. With brute strength, he turned my weapon
against me.

The point of the knife was now angled in my direction, and despite all my time spent training and all the
animosity coursing through my veins, the asshole

succeeded in jamming my prized weapon straight into my arm.

My first instinct was to howl from the searing pain. But I didn't. I shifted backward, dropping both arms to my sides, and allowed him to move away from the tree. "That was a stupid move, motherfucker," I snarled, and swept his legs out from under him.

He went down like a hammer, but only to his knees. Which was fine by me because it made it all the easier to deliver a solid roundhouse kick to his head.

The vibration of the hit traveled up my leg, momentarily distracting me from the shooting pain in my arm. And when the back of his head ricocheted off the trunk of the tree…fuck, I almost smiled.

Except, now wasn't the time for celebrations, and I didn't have it in me to even try.

Dropping to a crouch, I peered through the bushes to see how many of Rykov's crew had witnessed the showdown. But the grounds were completely empty, not a single person in sight. No one in front of me, and no one behind.

Which meant Sasha hadn't noticed me missing yet, and the rest of the men were either slacking on their duties, busy on other business, or laying in fucking wait inside the mansion.

Fuck it.

With a final look around, I darted across the open lawn, over the cobblestone walkway, and straight up the driveway to the five-car garage.

The shadow of the behemoth house fell over me as I

advanced with caution. No matter how abandoned the place seemed, I knew better than to trust in it. Overconfidence would get me killed, and at this stage of the game, I didn't trust anything or anyone.

One of the garage bay doors was open. With my breath held, I peeked inside, finding nothing but a row of sleek, black cars. God, the man had all of this—money, power, possessions, loyalty—yet, he wasn't even creative enough to choose another color?

There were three doors on the other side of the garage from where I stood. One of them was open. The soft soles of my runners carried me soundlessly over the concrete. I moved swiftly, but still took precautions to stay out of sight.

I slipped into the house unnoticed and followed the short hallway into the butler's pantry.

Even here, the opulence was excessive, but I ignored the ridiculousness of my surroundings and pushed past the pain, creeping around the sliding door into the main kitchen.

And came face to face with Yelena.

I'd spent the last year of my life doing everything in my power to get her out of here. To help her escape what I'd imagined to be a dungeon or a cell, only to find her sauntering through a luxury kitchen, wearing a full face of makeup, a fabulous dress, and giant diamonds in her ears.

Fighting, flirting, scheming, risking my life—Bodhi's fucking life—whatever it took to set her free, I'd done it. And so much more. I'd given up any semblance of a normal life, all in the hopes of seeing her again. Now, my sister was here, in front of me, but she looked like a stranger, with dead eyes and a thousand-dollar haircut.

She startled as we stepped in front of each other, her manicured hand flying to cover her mouth and her eyes growing impossibly wide. Her head began to shake violently, and I wasn't sure if it meant she was scared for our lives or wanted me to leave.

It didn't matter. There was no time to waste on a reunion. Not when we were in danger and there was a man to kill.

"Where is he?" I hissed, moving to grab hold of her arm.

She flinched backward, out of my grasp, her hand falling away from her mouth and her features smoothing into an unconcerned look of boredom. "Who?"

What the fuck was wrong with her?

"Nikolai." My voice was a ragged whisper.

She shrugged. The gesture was so common, so unbelievably careless, it took everything in me not to scream.

"Well, let's go fucking find him," I snarled, and stalked away.

There was no point hanging around here and listening to more of her bullshit. Whether she was brain-washed, trying to send me a covert message, or simply content to live this life, it was disturbing, and it wouldn't get me anywhere.

I moved through the enormous kitchen into a solarium, hoping like hell she'd follow. Because no matter the reason for her behavior, I was going to save her—right after I killed her captor.

She was still my sister, after all.

The glassed-in room was long and narrow, filled with potted ferns, marble statues, and a floor-to-ceiling waterfall built into the center of the back wall.

My eyes scanned the area outside, searching for signs of a patrol or a trap. But there was nothing. No armed men, no cameras that I could see, and no evidence of anything amiss. Was there anyone else even here?

When I turned my gaze back to the lush solarium, my question was answered.

He came into view at the other end of the room—tall, broad, powerful, and with a gun pointed in my direction.

No, the weapon was not just turned in my general vicinity, he had me targeted.

Shock and confusion flashed through my system. It was a debilitating mix of disbelief, longing, and fear that sent my body into uncontrolled tremors.

Bodhi's alive.

But he didn't look happy to see me.

In fact, he didn't quite seem like himself. Colder and crueler, he looked not only downright murderous, but a little unhinged. And all that simmering rage and animosity was aimed directly at me—along with his gun.

Fuck. I'm so fucked.

I never thought this would be easy, never believed myself invincible, but I'd hoped things might go a bit smoother. And after everything we'd shared, I'd hoped he wouldn't turn on me—wouldn't fucking betray me.

I sure hadn't planned on dying.

Fuck, I still didn't.

But as I stared into the enraged eyes of the killer whose gun was pointed at my chest—the darkest side of the man I'd fallen head over heels for—I wondered if fate had finally given up on me. Maybe the universe had saved my ass one too many times and it'd grown tired of bailing me out. God only knew, I'd grown tired of the fight. Tired of failure.

Fall down seven times, stand up eight.

Babka's favorite proverb came back to me, urging me never to give up. Still, I had to wonder if maybe this was the eighth fall, and I wasn't meant to stand a ninth.

My eyes strayed to Yelena, frozen in fear only a few steps away. Silently, I implored her to do something, anything, to help me. To help herself. But she watched with a void sort of detachment as the gun was raised higher and aimed at my head.

It was like she'd expected this to happen. Like she'd already given up and none of the suffering had ever mattered—not hers, mine, or even Anya's. It had all been for nothing.

Her impassiveness cut me deep, deeper even than the knife, and finally I allowed the sorrow that had become my constant companion to swallow me whole. It hurt too much to continue pushing through it, so I gave into the grief. I allowed the searing ache of my chest, the tearing twist of my stomach, and the brutal crush of my heart to take over.

Still, as much as it hurt, as defeating as it was to believe I was going to die, somewhere deep at the center of my being a small flame of anger flickered, refusing to be doused. Not even my utter devastation could smother it. That tiny light glowed hot and true.

Movement caught my attention from the corner of my eye, and I craned my neck to see Sasha. He'd not only found me, but had somehow managed to sneak up from behind.

He still looked angry. No, furious. But there was also something in his gaze that hinted at distress. Like he was analyzing the situation and not liking the options he had available.

Fuck, he could join the club.

Blood dripped from the tips of my useless fingers. My entire arm had started to go numb, and I worried the damage might be permanent. The numbness probably was a good thing, though—I was sure it would've still hurt like a son of a bitch if I could've felt it.

At least I still had my knife. Sure, it was lodged in my arm at an odd angle, but it was stuck in there good, so I wasn't likely to lose it, and the blood that flowed around the blade was a trickle, not a stream. I didn't think I had to worry too much about passing out.

I only wished I had the strength and mobility to use my damn hand, since I had the urge to wrap it around someone's neck.

I looked back to the soulful blue eyes of the man with the gun. I barely recognized him with his lips drawn, teeth bared, and slow, even breathing rumbling through his chest like a growl.

The fire inside me burned brighter.

He was spattered in blood—his or someone else's—and was limping badly, but it didn't lessen his threat. I'd seen him beaten and ragged before. Wounded and worn down. Now, I'd also seen him cheat death. No matter the injury, I knew Bodhi would never quit. He wouldn't stop until he had what he wanted.

"What the fuck?" I dared through the pain.

He didn't answer, but his expression intensified. A look of barely constrained, seething rage. A look that told me what he wanted most in this world was me…

Dead.

"Better shoot me, then, and make it count," I warned. "Otherwise, I'm starting a list of my own and your name's going straight to the top, *Bodhi Decker*.

CHAPTER
TWENTY-FOUR
DEX

It was a trap. I'd known it was, and yet, I'd walked right into it, anyway.

The car fire was a raging inferno behind me—a bright, shining ball of fiery death. Without fuel, it would eventually burn out. But probably not before the cops and the fire department showed up.

I forced myself to my feet, staggering when the movement splintered my skull with a pain so bright it made the fire seem like nothing more than a glowing ember. My stomach rolled, but I held back the urge to vomit, not willing to give into the effects of what was probably a concussion.

Everything was burning—my clothes, my face and hair. Fuck, even the air in my lungs. My whole goddamn world was on fire, and I didn't know where I was going. Didn't know up from down. Didn't know how I was still alive.

It didn't matter.

The only thing that mattered now was Kira. Despite how reckless, foolish, or chaotically out of whack, I still needed to uphold my promises. I needed to show her I could be a hero. Fuck, I needed to prove it to myself, too. But more than the urge to be the good guy for a change was the need to get her back.

To keep her where she belonged—safe with me, forever and always. I just hoped it wasn't too late.

"Bodhi!" Finn's voice was clear and urgent. It cut past the roar of the flames, the ringing in my ears, and straight through the pained haze clouding my head.

"Bodhi, watch out!" He swayed in front of me. No, wait…that was my eyes.

He was maybe ten, twenty, or fucking three hundred feet away—it was impossible to know without depth perception—and he was dragging an armed man backward, on the other side of the busted, open gate.

Two other men were headed my way, both with guns in hand.

I staggered again before dropping to one knee, pulling my weapon and taking aim. My vision was still doubled and my head was still swimming, but my hands were steady and my finger fast on the trigger. I let out a slow breath as I took both gunmen out of commission, each with a single shot.

They hollered in pain. One was shot in the shoulder, the other straight through his hand.

"Fuck you, Dex!" one of them cursed, his Russian accent thick and slurred. I recognized the voice. It was the same one from the night I'd killed Moore—the man who'd gotten away. The one who'd sworn me dead.

He reached for his gun with his non-injured hand.

Without a word, I shot him in the chest.

He clutched at the hole in his sternum, his face a mask of disbelief as he crumpled to the ground.

The other man raised his shaking hands in surrender as a bloodstain bloomed across his shirt.

Back on my feet, I fought for balance, taking a deep breath to steady myself and focus on the sound of Finn's voice, leading me toward the towering mansion ahead. I forced myself forward, holding my aim on the surrendered man.

He flinched as I kicked the guns out of his reach.

"He's not dead," I huffed, motioning to the man who was slowly bleeding out on the ground beside him. "And neither are you. If you're smart, you'll want to keep it that way."

I didn't wait for his response. My objective was set, and my will was unstoppable. With my weapon firmly in grasp, I stormed past him into the fucking lion's den.

The plan had been clear—enter the house from opposite ends until we'd cleared it or ran into Rykov. Regardless of which of us found the son of a bitch, we'd promised each other not to kill him until everyone else was safe. Kira, her sister, and any other woman who was being held here against her will would be set free.

And I'd deal with Sasha.

Oh, I'm going to deal that fucker something wicked.

Except, now that half of Long Island knew we were

here, thanks to the exploding goddamn car, most of our plan was fucked. We couldn't exactly be stealthy when they knew we were coming.

But we could be fast.

And we still had the added advantage of an unknown and unexpected man. Because if Finn was right, they didn't know he existed.

As planned, I'd dropped him at the opposite end of the compound before driving around to the side gate. The lucky bastard had narrowly avoided getting blown to smithereens. And no, I still didn't believe in shit like luck, but if we lived through this, I'd reconsider my stance.

It had been Finn's idea to come in hot and heavy, and it looked like he was getting what he'd wanted. Although, we'd only planned to take out their surveillance, not to blow up my poor rented Lambo.

Finn had disappeared ahead of me, and another of my plans had literally gone up in flames. I was barely standing, had no clue what I was up against or even where the hell I was going, but I continued to stumble forward, anyway. Who needed a plan when shit kept going sideways?

Hell, maybe if I started winging it, I might actually find some semblance of control.

Still in a fog, I managed to slip inside the house. The place was a fucking maze, though, and as I wandered through it, I thought I might be going in circles. I was already dizzy from the explosion, but this shit was out of hand.

With caution, I came around a corner and raised my weapon at the man in front of me, only to realize it was my own banged up reflection.

Shit. I looked beyond rough—like someone had blown up a car beside me. Shards of glass still glinted in my hair, blood caked to the side of my face and neck, and one of my eyes was nearly swollen shut. And those were just the parts I could see. I didn't want to guess the state of the rest of me. It didn't fucking matter, anyhow.

"Better shoot me, then, and make it count." A voice filled with fury sliced the silence, shooting sparks along my spine and assuring me I wasn't simply functioning but fully fucking alive.

Kira's voice was still the most deliciously enigmatic, magnetic thing I'd ever heard. And like the first time, it was a siren's song, calling to me from somewhere in the distance.

"Otherwise, I'm starting a list of my own and your name's going straight to the top, *Bodhi Decker*."

She really was magnificent—a wildcat out for blood —but either my brain was more damaged than I'd realized, or something truly fucked up was happening. Why was she threatening to kill me?

I followed her intoxicating sound to a room of glass and greenery. The sudden jarring light from outside temporarily blinded me, and the sound of trickling water turned to an aggravating roar, further fragmenting my already splintered head.

Fuck, I was in bad shape.

But when my vision cleared and the rest of my

senses came back online, I was faced with something far, far worse than my own physical condition.

My twin brother—the one person I should've been able to trust most in this world—had his weapon targeted at Kira.

"Finn, you're pointing that thing at the wrong person," I said through the burning sensation at the back of my throat.

"Am I, brother?" He didn't shift his aim. Fuck, he didn't even twitch.

My heart, which had once been a void of darkness, thundered recklessly out of control, and I had no idea how to tame it. How could I keep it under my command when it belonged to the woman at the other end of his trigger?

Finally, I allowed my gaze to drift to Kira—to the smudges of dirt on her pale face, her tangled platinum hair, and the familiar handle of the knife embedded in her arm. Fuck, seeing her blood flow out around the wound, and realizing it might not be the last of it that I saw, was enough to send me into a rampage.

Only, what good would it do? My outrage would only result in more carnage and put her life in further jeopardy.

My eyes traveled up to meet her shocked amber gaze, and I did everything in my power to keep myself in check—to find whatever was left of my illustrious control and brandish it like a goddamn weapon.

"Yes," I said, my tone exacting but my outward

presence calm. "You want to be pointing that thing at the asshole standing behind her."

I didn't miss the bitter glare Sasha threw my way, but it was irrelevant. That's what he was to me: fucking irrelevant.

At least, he would be after I was done with him.

But Kira? I didn't care how little sense it made, she was irreplaceable. The most precious thing in the world to me.

"I don't think so." Finn's voice, normally so full of sarcastic wit, was eerily composed. And still, he didn't take his aim off her. "I hate to be the bearer of bad news, but you've been sleeping with the enemy."

My unrestrained heart faltered. "If you mean she's been working for Rykov, I already know."

Everyone's gaze seemed to zero in on me, except for Yelena, who'd been studying Finn with an odd degree of fascination this whole time.

"I'm sorry," Kira gasped as tears formed in her eyes. "I wanted to tell you, I just didn't know how."

"I know, kitten. It's okay."

"Okay? How is that okay?" The barrel of Finn's gun shook with his outburst, and my gut cramped from the thought of how many ways this could go wrong. "You think you know, brother, but you don't. You know nothing!"

Was this it—the moment my twin finally snapped?

His eyes held a mix of sorrow and rage, so potent I could feel it. But despite his anguish, and regardless of his madness, he was my brother. I would do anything for him.

Anything, except sacrifice Kira.

Gun still in hand, I raised my arms in surrender and edged closer to him.

"You don't understand," he rasped, the sound of his breaking voice almost breaking my heart. "She's not who you think she is."

"And just who do *you* think she is?" I eased a fraction closer. My hands were still held high, but my confidence was running thin.

His eyes narrowed on me as though cursing the bond between us, but he answered, "Kira Markova, orphaned granddaughter of Ilya Markov—the man Rykov killed and replaced. She was next in line to run their pathetic gang, but I'm guessing Rykov didn't like the idea of a woman taking over. On paper, she's the owner of this monstrosity of a house, and four other properties in various locations around the state."

As his voice wavered and lost steam, the aim of his gun began trailing downward. "Everything Rykov has belongs to her. Even her sister. What do you think someone in her position would be willing to do to get it all back?"

My cramping stomach seized.

"She's been using you, Bodhi. Can't you see that?"

I stepped in front of him and his weapon. "I get why you'd think that, and I love you for looking out for me," I said, wrapping the fingers of my free hand around the barrel until he let the 9mm drop into my hand. "But that's not who she is." I kept my voice low and tucked his gun into my holster. "She didn't need to use me because I volunteered. And I already knew everything you just told me—Robin's good at the job."

Kira gasped from behind me, and I turned to see that Sasha had seized his opportunity. He'd grabbed her, locking her to him with his arm around her throat and a gun to her ribs. With his face buried in her hair, he breathed, "Lyubov moya, I already know all about you, too. But you're not going anywhere."

Sasha might've been a dangerous asshole, but he wasn't a fool. He'd been waiting for Finn to distract me long enough for him to get his lecherous hands on her.

Yelena continued watching, her mouth hanging open and her arms like limp noodles at her sides. She was nothing like her sister, and completely useless to me—fuck, to everyone it seemed, since no one was paying attention to her and didn't seem to consider her a threat.

Kira's eyes were huge, her cheeks stained with tears, and her poor mangled arm still seeped blood.

"It's all right," I assured her, raising my gun to aim it at Sasha's head. "I'm going to keep my promise."

"Which one?" she croaked as Sasha increased the pressure on her neck.

With my gaze locked on hers, I forced my mouth into the cockiest grin I could muster. "All of them."

CHAPTER
TWENTY-FIVE
DEX

WITH HIS FACE TURNING RED AND USING KIRA AS HIS shield, Sasha bellowed, "Enough."

But I ignored him and took an angled step forward, motioning to Finn from behind my back.

"Don't come any closer," he called. "And drop the gun."

"Why?" I continued to tread in a slow, wide semi-circle around them. "You're threatening to kill the wrong woman. Where is Tess, anyway?"

Sasha laughed, turning to keep me in his line of sight. "I know you're not as stupid as you look, Dex."

I shrugged, trying not to give away the fact that Finn was moving toward Yelena behind Sasha's back. "Maybe I am. I mean, I showed up here, even though I knew Tess was full of shit. Even though your plan was ridiculously obvious. And even though I knew you'd try to kill me."

The arrogance he'd been wearing only moments

earlier evaporated. "Oh yeah? You think you know so much, big man?" he taunted like a schoolyard bully. "Well, did you know Kira's my wife?"

Fuck, I should've opened that last message from Robin. Maybe then, my recently repatriated heart wouldn't have felt like it was trying to leave my body, and my mind wouldn't have needed to work so hard to tie it all together.

Were all the puzzle pieces mine now? If so, I didn't know what to do with them. I didn't recognize the picture they were supposed to create.

The fall of water over rocks and the leftover buzzing in my ears took over the silence in the room. My favorite gun felt abnormally heavy, but I kept both it and my focus lasered on Sasha as I worked to maintain my calm.

"You got me there," I admitted. Then, without missing a beat, I shouted to Finn, "Go. Get Yelena out of here."

"What about you?" he yelled back, his arm securing Kira's sister to his side. "And what about Rykov?"

"I'm good, brother. Now, forget about Rykov. Just fucking go."

Sasha laughed under his breath, the motion somewhat loosening his hold on Kira. "Yes, go. Take the simpering little bitch with you. We've all had enough of her, anyway. Just pray you don't run into Nik, 'cause he'll kill you for it."

The ugly fucker was getting cocky now, but it was fine by me since it gave me the advantage.

"Come on, Bodhi," Finn urged, his eyes full of disbelief. "I know you want to help me put the bastard down. Remember why we started this mission. For Emily."

My gaze trailed to Kira's beautiful face and amber eyes that I'd come to know so well. They were filled with tears, torment…

And trust.

"Sometimes, killing might be necessary, but sometimes…it's not." My voice almost broke over the words. "Emily would want you to save the woman. It's what I want, too."

Her luscious lips pulled to a quivering smile, and I allowed myself a moment to drown in the calm she created—to bask in the peace and perfection of the fucking feelings that had bloomed to life inside me.

"I guess I'll see you when I see you, then, brother." Finn gave me a final pained look, hustling away with Yelena in tow.

What might've once felt like failure on my part, now seemed like a victory.

At least, it would have if it weren't for one exceedingly annoying asshole still standing in my way.

"I can't believe you actually fell for her lies and bullshit." Sasha laughed again, and the arrogance of it made my head throb harder. "I guess she forgot to tell you she's mine."

I pretended not to notice Kira's fingers deftly working their way around the hilt of her knife.

"I own her, Dex." His arm moved from around her

neck, his hand running cruelly over her collarbone before shooting up to grasp hold of her jaw. "She's my wife. Bought and fucking paid for." With a nasty sneer, he forced her face to his and kissed her.

And fuck, was she kissing him back? I inhaled sharply, ignoring the way my stomach turned, fighting hard against my unreliable perception.

Shit might have been falling apart—hell, Sasha might have even had the upper hand—but I was still in fucking control. And if Kira could trust me, then I had to believe I could trust her, too.

"You want her? She's yours." I placed my gun on the ground and slid it toward them.

Their lips broke apart and Sasha's triumphant smile widened.

"She's too feisty for me, anyway," I said with conviction, hoping like hell he believed me. "All I really wanted was my brother out of here. I don't want a war with you."

"It's too late for that." He moved his gun from Kira's side to point it at her head. With his hand at the back of her neck, he pushed her forward a step, moving in tandem with her. "You started the war when you and your brother double-crossed me."

I shook my head, and the motion made me dizzy. "I don't know what the hell you're talking about."

"No? You've got a short fucking memory." His expression was crazed, but the look in his eye told me he wasn't bluffing. This wasn't a lie, or something born of delusion. He was telling the truth.

But fuck, I had no idea what the hell was going on.

My gaze flashed to Kira, but the only thing I could interpret on her face was pain.

"You weren't supposed to kill Moore. That's not why I hired you."

"You never hired me." But even as I said it, it dawned on me... "At least, I didn't know it was you. My brother must've left that part out."

Finn had not only lied, he'd manipulated me. But to what fucking end?

"It makes no difference," Sasha said, seemingly unfazed by my admission. "Your job was to stop her from killing Moore—"

"Why the hell would I kill the scientist?" Kira interrupted, whipping her head toward him, his gun now positioned right between her eyes. "Nikolai sent me there for him." She raised her injured arm, pointing it in my direction.

Blood flowed and dripped in a steady stream from the wound where her knife used to be. The knife which was now clutched tightly in her other hand.

"Shut the fuck up," Sasha demanded, pushing her another step forward.

Only this time, she went to the ground. Flailing forward, she landed on her hands and knees with an agonized protest.

My hands clenched into tight fists at my sides as I cracked down on the urge to charge the motherfucker— he still had a gun on her, after all. And there was something about Kira's sudden helplessness that seemed a little…contrived.

"I don't give a shit why she claims she was there," Sasha seethed. "She only knows how to lie. You were supposed to stop her, then bring her to me. Instead, you killed our connection to Alexander's empire. And then, you fucked my wife. Did you think that shit was going to wash?"

Kira gasped, her eyes flashing to the doorway behind me.

"I told you to shut the fuck up," Sasha bellowed, knocking her further to the floor with his booted foot.

On another injured cry, her body pitched forward.

"Oh, what a tangled web we weave when first we choose to lie. Isn't that right, darling Kira?" The faint smell of cigar smoke followed Rykov into the room, the smug expression on his face verging on boredom.

Kira was still on the ground, but her body contracted and tensed as he drew nearer and she regained her crouched position.

"So many lies, it's hard to find any truth," he drawled. "For example, did Sasha believe Kira was going to kill Mr. Moore? Yes, because I told him so. But you see, that was a lie, wasn't it, Kira?"

All of Sasha's bluster had deflated, leaving him staring after his boss in disbelief.

"And, Kira, wasn't it you who told me Sasha's men had prevented you from apprehending Mr. Decker on that night?" Rykov continued, his voice full of condescension. "But that was a lie, too, now, wasn't it?"

Kira silently bristled, and although her eyes were full of tears, they were also full of fire. "Fuck you, Nikolai."

"Fuck me, *and* you call me by name," he said through a patronizing laugh. "No more *boss*? What's the matter, darling Kira, have I lost your respect?"

"You never had it, you piece of shit. You only had my sister." Her ferocity broke on a choked whisper. "And my guilty conscience."

"Guilty?" Rykov mused, his fingers tracing over the outline of the cigar peeking out of his breast pocket.

But I was done. I'd had enough of his derisive show-boating. This man was a coward without value or morals. At least Sasha had a fucking purpose to his rant, and a woman he loved that he was fighting for.

But so did I.

"I've got a question," I interrupted, throwing a cocky smirk in for good measure. "I get that my brother probably gave up my info in a misguided attempt to lure you out to the open. He's another liar, by the way, Sasha —he lied to both of us."

I hesitated a moment, giving the disgruntled-looking man a moment to catch up. Although, the way his head was shaking, it might've taken more time than I was willing to sacrifice, and more time than Kira needed.

Turning my attention back to Rykov, and making as big a spectacle as a grumpy asshole like me could manage, I asked, "But why the fuck do you care about me when you've got all this? I mean, look at this place, it's fucking spectacular. Why am I important? Who the fuck am I to you?"

Rykov's glare went from deadly serious to plain old deadly. "Well, that's an excellent question, Mr. Decker. Who the fuck are you, other than a semi-decent hitman? Why have you been systematically killing off my men for the last year?"

Shit. Even though I'd seen this moment coming, I still wasn't prepared for how the hell to proceed. What had made me think I could do all of this without a proper plan?

"It's my fault," Kira murmured, her fierce, tortured gaze landing on mine.

"No, kitten. This isn't on you. Don't try to cover for me."

"I'm not," she said, her voice gaining strength. "It *is* all my fault—the reason he's after you, the reason you do what you do…the reason Emily is dead."

My body ached, and it wasn't from the explosion. Anger, fear, guilt, and betrayal battled for control as my mind spun in circles. My cage of control cracked wide open. Emily?

Kira was responsible for Emily's death. But how? And why the ever loving fuck?

My heart revolted against the idea, yet some spark of intuition whispered in the back of my head that it was true. Of all the things she'd been withholding, it might've been the only truth that mattered. The one truth that could break me for good.

Or possibly, make me whole.

"The night my grandfather was killed, Emily was there. I tried to stop it all from happening—to put an end to Nikolai's sick business, set his captives free, and have him thrown the fuck out," she said through a sob. "Instead, he killed them all."

Fuck. Now, the picture from those puzzle pieces made sense. Now, I could see it all.

Now, I had a goddamn plan.

Rapidly approaching sirens sounded in the distance, and I almost breathed a sigh of relief. Almost. But this showdown was far from over, and the only direction it could possibly go was from bad to worse.

"All right, I've had enough of this melodrama," Rykov said, with an air of nervous authority. "Sasha, kill them."

Sasha, who looked like he was still trying to figure it all out, muttered, "What?" He redirected his aim from Kira to me.

"Shoot them—your wife and the man who fucked her. Shoot them both. In. The. Head."

My frantic heart pleaded with me to change my mind about the fucked-up scheme I'd devised.

But there wasn't time to come up with a Plan B.

"Better do it, Sasha." I motioned to Finn's gun, still tucked safely in my holster. "Because if you don't shoot her, I will."

CHAPTER
TWENTY-SIX
KIRA

The sirens outside were drawing closer, and Bodhi and I were running out of time.

Or at least, I was.

The pain in my injured arm and all the guilt and sorrow of the last year was nothing compared to the heartbreak on his face.

I was glad the truth was finally out, but fuck, was he really was going to shoot me?

I'd thought the universe had sent me this steadfast man to be my salvation, to help me do right by my sister. But maybe I'd been wrong. Maybe the universe had put me in his violent path to teach me a lesson.

Whatever the reason, I knew I couldn't look him in the eyes and lie to him anymore. I couldn't allow him to go on believing he had somehow failed Emily.

Fuck, I couldn't even let him think Nikolai was all to blame. Not that the monster was innocent, but without me and my interference—my belief that I was untouchable—there was a chance Emily might've still been alive. Bodhi might've found a way to rescue her, the same way he'd come to save me.

His life could've been completely different—murder free and happy. Without me.

That thought hurt more than anything.

Yet, now that I'd spilled my secret, now that Bodhi knew everything, I somehow felt lighter. Like the burden of carrying all those lies, half-truths, and hidden agendas had been holding me down. Holding me back.

Now, Bodhi could see the real me. No matter how horrible that image was.

Nikolai threw his head back with laughter, and my throat closed in terror. The man was more than a monster—he was the fucking devil, taking pleasure from the pain and suffering of others.

"You are entertaining, I'll give you that," he said, pulling a cigar from his pocket. "But it won't change my mind. You've killed too many of my men. But…"

He pointed the cigar at Bodhi before clenching it between his teeth. "I wouldn't mind watching you fight Sasha to see who gets to kill her. That might be fun."

"Boss, please." Sasha's voice was next to pleading, and I could tell from the sneer Nikolai gave him, it wasn't going to work in his favor.

"You've got the advantage, Sasha," Bodhi said with authority. "I've got no gun in my hand. But if you drop yours, I can promise you a fair fight."

God, he really was determined to put me down. Still, as terrifying as the threat was, nothing compared to the ache of my racing heart when I thought of seeing him get hurt. Or worse.

I'd already believed him dead once. I didn't think I could live through it again.

"You were right," he said, his gaze landing on mine. And *God*, that gaze was filled with emotion. But not just any old emotion.

No. It was fear.

Not sorrow, rage, or even regret. Bodhi Decker was afraid—something I'd never seen before—and that could only mean one thing.

He was about to do something stupid. And he was doing it for me.

"I was never going to save the damsel in distress," he said, his expression begging me to understand. "I'm not that type of man, after all. But you're not that kind of woman, either, are you, Wildcat?"

Wildcat. What was it he'd said before when he'd called me by that name? That I was deadly, and my heart was made of steel. But what the fuck did he mean?

Sasha shook his head, the barrel of his gun hovering somewhere around Bodhi's middle. "I was wrong, you might just be as stupid as you look."

Smiling, Bodhi lowered his arms. "True," he said, and the rumble of his voice traveled straight through me, lending me the strength I didn't have. "But she's not."

Hell no, I wasn't.

On a manic cry, I plunged my knife backward into

Sasha's leg. At the same time, Bodhi dropped and pulled the gun he'd taken from Finn.

I twisted as Sasha howled and shots rang out, but I couldn't tell who all was shooting or the trajectory of those bullets.

Sasha ducked and careened toward the waterfall, a trail of blood dripping from his leg where my knife was stuck and a stark red stain spreading across his abdomen where a bullet had torn through. His injured leg caught on the rocky ledge, and he fell backward into the pool of flowing water.

Bodhi and I collided as he landed on the ground beside me, his arms wrapping around my waist in a protective gesture.

But Sasha's weapon was on the floor, and his hands were busy covering his wound as he sputtered under the waterfall.

And Nikolai…

Fuck, he was gone.

"Where did Rykov go?" I asked as my shaking hands lowered Bodhi's gun that I'd retrieved from the floor. It wasn't just my hands that were shaking, it was my whole damn body.

"I don't know." He maneuvered me to face him and relieved me of the weapon, carefully setting it aside.

His arms tightened around me, like I was something precious he was afraid to let go of, and my heart lurched in my chest. He wasn't only comforting me, he was holding me together.

"I promised I wasn't like him," he muttered, burying his face in my neck. "I wanted to prove it."

"You did," I cried brokenly, new tears coursing down my cheeks as I scrambled even closer to him. "But I already believed in you. I knew you'd save me."

"No, Kira, you were never the damsel. You're wild and deadly. You saved your-fucking-self." His fingers ran over me in a gentle caress, moving down my arms until our hands were linked and he was pressing them tightly to his chest. "You saved me, too. In so many fucking ways, you saved me."

The pain in my body seemed more like a distant memory as I turned my face up to meet his intense blue gaze. "Fall down seven times, stand up eight."

"Yeah, kitten. But I might need help getting up. And we need to get the fuck out of here."

"What about him?" I asked, nodding toward Sasha, who'd managed to pull himself back to the edge of the pool.

"I'd leave him for the professionals to deal with." After securing his weapons, he staggered to his feet with a groan and a wince, then pulled me up to join him. "But it's up to you, since you're the one who shot him."

Fuck, I'd shot him. My own damn husband. What did that say about me?

That I was willing to do anything for the man I loved.

"Do you trust me?" I asked, holding his hardened gaze.

"With my life."

I wrapped my non-injured arm around him, trying my best to help hold him up. "Even after all this? After what I told you?"

"Because of what you told me." He hugged me tightly to his side as we scrambled out of the room, back the way I'd come.

The house was still vacant, and I had to wonder if it was because Nikolai was so paranoid, he wouldn't let his own men near him. Or if something else had happened.

Or maybe *someone* had happened. Someone like Finn.

"How'd you know?" Bodhi asked as we made our way to the back of the house and headed toward the water. The speedboat was gone, but the yacht was still bobbing gracefully at the end of the pier.

It would have to do.

"Know what?" I asked, thankful my keys were still tucked in my pocket.

"About Emily. How did you figure out it was her on that night?" Pain speared through his voice, but I knew it wasn't from his faded feelings for Emily.

He was breathing heavily and struggling to stay on his feet. My hero was gravely wounded, and I worried he wouldn't make it to our escape.

"There's a photo in Sunny's spare bedroom. Emily's in it," I explained, helping him up the dock. "How'd you know where to find me?"

"Your phone," he grunted. "I activated a tracking

app when I added myself to your contacts. I knew you'd never notice."

Sneaky, arrogant ass.

"Does this mean you're going to be following me all the time now?"

He stopped and pulled me around to face him, his ardent blue gaze making my heart stutter. "I'm not letting you out of my sight."

And then, his lips were on mine. They were hard and soft all at once, and his tongue swept over mine with an urgency that rivaled every promise he'd ever made me—the best fucking kiss of my life.

Unfortunately, now wasn't the time.

When his mouth tore from mine, it was on an injured protest, and he grunted, "I mean that, you know."

Despite the arrival of the authorities in the distance and the terrible shape we were both in, I smiled as I helped him down the rest of the pier.

Once we were finally aboard the yacht, I unlocked the cabin for him before untethering us, and breathed a sigh of relief as I steered us toward Long Island Sound.

"The fancy-ass boat's yours, too, isn't it?" he asked through a pained laugh.

"Yes, Bodhi, it's all mine. But the only thing I want is you."

CHAPTER
TWENTY-SEVEN
BODHI

THE BED DIPPED BESIDE ME, AND I HELD BACK A GRUNT of pain.

My lungs still felt like they were on fire, and every time I moved the shooting agony in my head reminded me what a lucky son of a bitch I was.

If Sasha had hit the detonator only two minutes sooner, I'd have been blown up inside my car. There were also countless moments throughout our standoff when he could've easily shot me. Hell, my own twin might've done the deed during his meltdown, even if by accident.

The universe, as Kira liked to call it, had been smiling down on me. And *fuck*, I was thankful for it.

Because, apparently, I was now the kind of man who believed in shit like luck, hope, and even divinity. At least, I was learning. Kira was teaching me.

Midday light filtered in through the curtains, but the warmth of the room lulled me back to sleep. Until I was roused again by another dip of the bed, followed by a giggle.

Inquisitive brown eyes peered at me from beneath a halo of fuzzy brunette curls.

"Good morning," I slurred.

Her head tilted to the side, studying me as a shy smile graced her pretty face. The soft glow of light around her made her look deceptively angelic.

I closed my eyes with a tired sigh.

"You seepin'?" Anya chirped, her redundant question making me smile.

"Not anymore." I cracked my eyes again, turning to look at her chubby cheeks. "A little devil woke me up."

She giggled at the nickname I'd given her, crawling closer to me on her hands and knees, her intense scrutiny making me squirm.

"What?" I asked when she continued to stare.

With a mischievous smile plastered on her sweet face, she reached out, her little hand landing squarely on my chin, brushing back and forth over the beard I'd been growing.

"Anya." Kira stood in the doorway with her hands planted on her trim hips. "What are you doing in here, little dove?"

"Him's furry." Her fingers patted my cheek.

When I laughed, a wave of pain seized me, causing the sound to catch in my lungs.

Immediately, Kira moved toward the bed and lifted Anya away. "You need to let Bodhi rest," she scolded. "He needs to get better."

"I'm better," I argued, catching my breath.

Kira raised a skeptical brow at me before placing Anya on her feet and shooing her out of the room. "Go see Babka and Sunshine," she instructed. "They're making us lunch."

Kira turned her attention back to me, closing the door behind her and flipping the lock. "Better?" she purred, stalking toward me, her gorgeous bare legs peeking from under a simple blue dress.

"One hundred percent."

She climbed onto the bed beside me, her hand moving to my face, running her fingers seductively over my jaw. "You sure about that?"

Ignoring the discomfort, I reached for her, winding an arm around her waist and pulling her closer. "Why? Are you anxious to take me for a test drive, kitten?"

Her amber eyes sparkled. "How on earth can you be thinking about sex with a house full of people and a concussion? Not to mention all your other injuries."

"How could I not?" I smirked, my hand dropping to squeeze her ass. "You know you want it, too."

Her sweet breath skated across my lips as she bent closer, her leg rubbing high up over my own. "Flat on your back, and you're still a cocky ass."

She pecked my lips before burrowing her face into the crook of my neck, her silky hair falling over me. We lay in silence, her hand softly running over my jaw and my chest full of more emotion than any one man could surely handle.

Shit was still a mess.

Thanks to Sunny, I'd been able to steer clear of the hospital and the scrutiny that would've gone along with it. My sister had patched me up without questions—either because she knew I wouldn't answer them, or because I wasn't in any condition to.

There'd been tears in her eyes as she'd fussed over me, though, hinting that my brush with death might've been closer than I'd imagined. And every time she looked at me now, it was with a level of worry that was over the top, even for the mother hen.

But she'd forgive me. Eventually.

According to Robin's intel, both Sasha and Rykov had disappeared. The police had warrants out for both of them, but if Robin couldn't find them, I highly doubted the police would.

They were in the wind, and even though it should have probably made me nervous, I wasn't bothered by it a bit.

Sasha was an asshole, but without Rykov to pull his strings, he wasn't much of a threat. And since Rykov had rewarded his loyalty with deceit and violence, I had to believe Sasha wouldn't fall back in line with him.

Also, since Kira shot him, I had a feeling he wouldn't be so intent on getting her back.

Either way, we were prepared. And totally off grid in a cozy four-bedroom cabin, upstate.

My biggest worry was Finn.

Despite his apology and having kept Yelena safe, something was still off with him. He couldn't look me in the eye, and he refused to be alone in the same room with Kira or her sister.

Maybe he was angry because he'd missed his chance to take down Rykov. Or maybe he just didn't know what to do with himself now that we were out of business.

Whatever the problem, it was a big one.

His entire personality had changed overnight. There were no more bad jokes or sarcasm. No more inappropriate laughter or even a smile.

It broke my goddamn heart to know I'd failed my brother. I didn't feel let down by his deception. There was no more room in my soul for vengeance, not when it came to him. I knew Finn wasn't evil. I didn't believe he'd hurt me intentionally. Whatever plot he'd schemed, whatever strange mission he'd been on, I knew he'd believed it was right.

His mental stability had finally given way.

I hadn't protected him when he needed me most. His breakdown was inevitable. My inability to save a life had pushed him there, long ago. I just hoped it wasn't too late to reel him back.

Yes, shit truly was a mess.

But beyond it all, there was Kira.

She hadn't hesitated. Hadn't thought twice. Disgusting bastard or not, Sasha was still her husband, and she'd shot him to save me. She'd trusted me. Kira put her faith in me, even without reason, and she hadn't left my side since.

"Bodhi?" she murmured against my skin as she stretched her leg farther over mine.

"Yes, kitten?"

"How are you always so fucking right?"

"About what?"

"I do want it." She raised her head to look me in the eye, lust pouring from her gaze. "Sex," she clarified. "I want you."

"I'm right here, kitten, and I'm all yours." I smirked.

Despite my cocksure attitude, I meant it. Even though I had no plan. No order. No idea what the hell we were going to do next. I was hers.

And *fuck*, I needed her to be mine.

"Kira," I murmured, my heart banging in my ears. "I'm going to need you to get a divorce."

Light danced in her amber gaze, and she ran her delicate fingers down my chest. "Why? Don't you like sleeping with a married woman?"

"Not unless she's my wife."

The look on her face was pure fire, and fuck, it was a beautiful thing.

"That can be arranged," she murmured, her mouth falling to the shell of my ear. "My first marriage wasn't legal."

I tugged her hair hard, pulling her back so I could capture her teasing gaze again. "Are you fucking kidding me right now?"

She bit down on her bottom lip and shook her head, sending me into a tailspin of emotion.

"You can be mine. For real."

Her cheeks heated to a pretty shade of pink, and her leg grew restless. "Are you asking me to be?"

"Yeah, kitten. I know it's crazy, but after everything, I want us to belong to each other."

"God, you really do know how to get to me." She held my face tenderly, her shallow breath weaving a spell. "Now, kiss me," she begged.

With my fingers tangled in her hair, I pulled her back down to me and let my lips slide delicately over hers, feeling her softness, tasting her sweetness.

Tearing away on a groan, she demanded, "Kiss me like you fucking mean it, Bodhi."

There she is. My feisty, chaotic little kitten. "Is that a yes?"

"Yes," she purred. "I want to be yours, and I want you to be mine."

"If you want me," I murmured, wrapping her hair around my fist, and pulling, just to hear her moan again, "You'll have to take me, Wildcat."

So, she did. She straddled my waist as she kissed me, hot and hard. Her mouth was urgent and demanding, even as her hands moved soft and slow. Gently, she lowered my sweatpants before lining herself up over me, lifting her dress and then sinking back down, bringing our bodies together. Bringing *us* together.

We were chaos and control. Wild and goddamn deadly.

And it was the best fucking thing on Earth.

ABOUT THE AUTHOR

Kimberly is a contemporary romance author, born procrastinator, and lover of morally gray heroes. She enjoys lively conversations, usually with imaginary people, and can often be found daydreaming at work.

She writes gritty, messy, dangerous romances, featuring beautifully flawed characters, pursuing love at all costs. It's romance with rough edges.

When she's not busy writing, you can find her with a coffee in hand, dog at her side, and exploring the wilds of her hometown in Ontario, Canada… Or on her couch, getting lost in a good story.

Subscribe to her newsletter https://kimberlyquinn.
myflodesk.com/newslettersignup, visit her website
https://www.kimberleyquinnbooks.com, and follow her
on Goodreads https://www.goodreads.com/author/show/
27348216.Kimberly_Quinn

instagram.com/kimberlyquinn.books

amazon.com/stores/Kimberly-
Quinn/author/B0BV18S35M

bookbub.com/profile/kimberly-quinn

threads.net/@kimberlyquinn.books

tiktok.com/@kimberlyquinn.books

ABOUT THE PUBLISHER

Harbor Lane Books, LLC is a US-based independent digital publisher of commercial fiction, non-fiction, and poetry.

Connect with Harbor Lane Books on their website (www.harborlanebooks.com) and social media.